The Turnabout Years

JOHN CHAMBERLAIN

The Turnabout Years

America's Cultural Life, 1900–1950

Jameson Books, Inc.
Ottawa, Illinois

THE TURNABOUT YEARS

Jameson books are available at special discounts for bulk purchases for sales promotions, premiums, fundraising or educational use. Special condensed or excerpted editions can also be created to customer specifications.

For information or catalog requests, write:

Jameson Books, Inc.
P.O. Box 738
Ottawa, Ilinois 61350

815-434-7905; FAX 434-7907

5 4 3 2 1 95 94 93 92 91
Printed in the United States of America
ISBN 0-915463-61-X

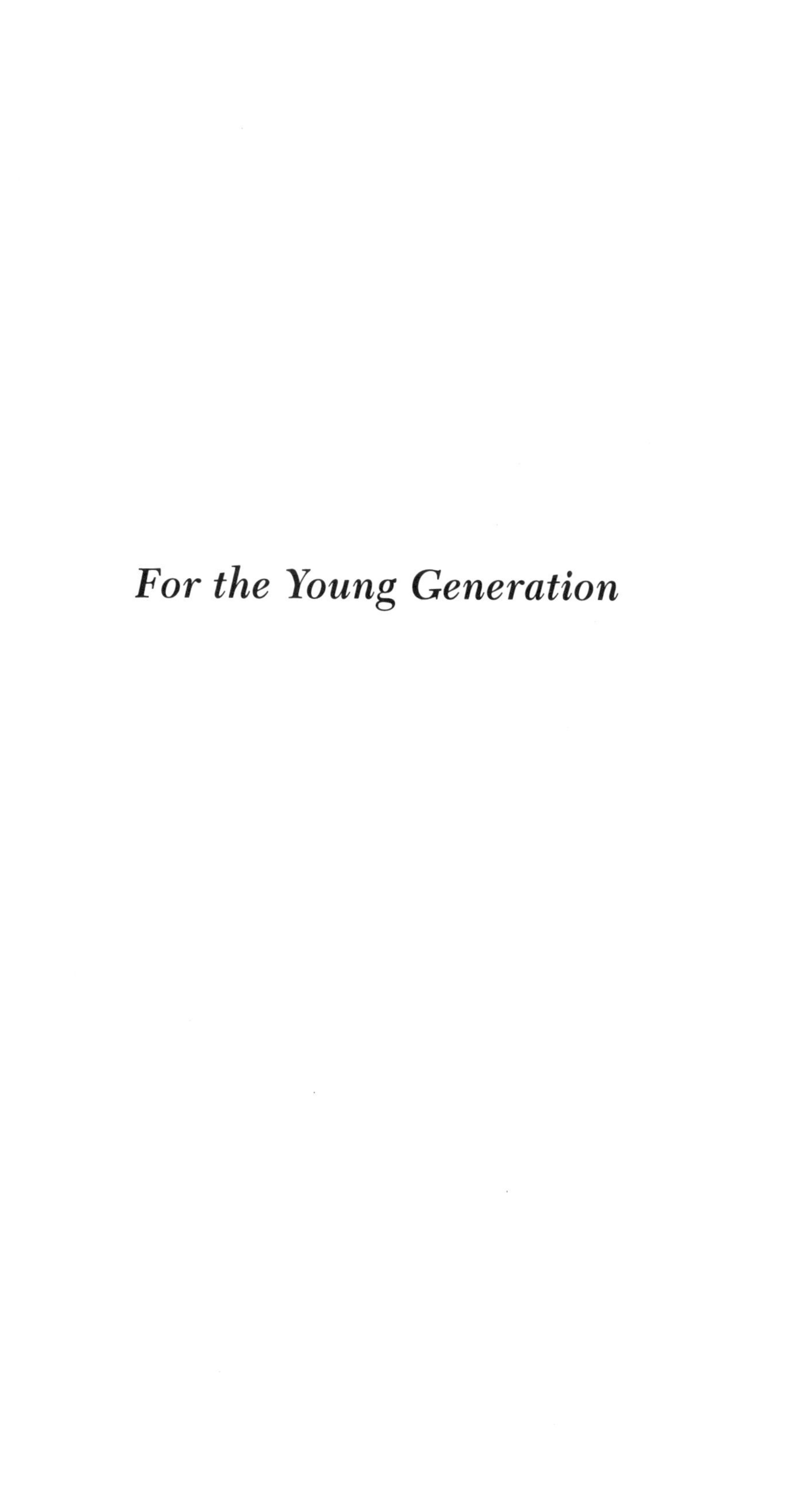

For the Young Generation

CONTENTS

EXCURSIONS AND SAMPLINGS

THE INGENIOUS AMERICAN

WHITTAKER CHAMBERS AND A GENERATION ON TRIAL

FOREWORD

In 1950 a tiny band of embattled conservatives: anti-Communists, antisocialists, free-market economists and libertarians founded a magazine called the *Freeman*. This was at a time when conservatism was on the run. Russell Kirk had yet to write *The Conservative Mind,* Ronald Reagan was still driving Borax's twenty-mule team. Bill Buckley graduated from Yale that June. The driving forces behind the *Freeman* were Henry Hazlitt, the economist, *Plain Talk* editor Isaac Don Levine, and John Chamberlain. (Don Levine would depart the scene almost at once and be replaced by Suzanne LaFollette, whose first job had been on Albert Jay Nock's distinguished original *Freeman,* published 1920–1924. The money was largely Alfred Kohlberg's.) Chamberlain would edit the back of the book and write the fortnightly lead book review. These would be reviews in depth—twelve to fifteen hundred words long—space for a critic of John Chamberlain's resourcefulness to explore not only the book under review but also the climate in which it was written, and the larger questions it raised, or sought to answer.

The *Freeman* would fold as a general-interest magazine two or three years later but in that time John Chamberlain produced over a hundred essays that, taken as a whole, reveal much about what he would later characterize as "the struggle for the soul of the *New York Times,*" by which he meant the determined attempt by the journeymen of the Left—often manipulated by the Communists—to "capture New York, the word capital of the United States." This they accomplished, and for a couple of decades and more, the men and women who ran the book sections of the major newspapers and magazines in America dictated that few conservative authors would be reviewed, and hence published, and that those who were reviewed would be savaged whenever they stepped over a certain line.

John Chamberlain was a bloodied veteran of these wars. His 1982 autobiography is well titled *A Life with the Printed Word*, dealing as it does more with his intellectual pilgrim's progress than with his personal life. To recapitulate his story very briefly: John Chamberlain graduated from Yale in the early twenties at a time when the intellectual elite of the West, demoralized by the wasteful slaughters of World War I and mesmerized by a romanticized view of Bolshevism—I have seen the future, and it works—swung left. Young John Chamberlain swung with it. He was as left as they come, and a pro-Communist to boot. But disillusionment with communism came fast. The persecution and exile of Leon Trotsky, an encounter with Walter Duranty, the *New York Times*'s Stalin-loving Moscow correspondent, and a hands-on experience with Communists in the Guild unit at *Time* magazine, made an anti-Communist of John. He remained a socialist until he went to work for Henry Luce on *Fortune* in the thirties and wrote a notable series of articles on American business, industry, and labor that would later result in his two major books, *The Roots of Capitalism* and *The Enterprising Americans.* That experience, plus a stint for *Life* magazine as its "text man" in Washington in the war years 1941–44, completed John Chamberlain's political education. He became distrustful of government, of statism, and of practitioners of government. All politicians, he found, "even so enlightened a politician as Bob Taft, had varying degrees of the Chanticleer complex: they thought that their crowing had something to do with the sun coming up." And he discovered a greater truth still, as he explained in a *Freeman* review in March 1952:

> The notion that man's future can be planned collectively, with the state serving as the compulsory planning agent, seals the creative and the spontaneous founts that lie deep in human nature. It closes the future to the benefits of inventiveness, of energy, of elegance, of amusing diversions, of adventure, of expression, and of success in any one of the seven arts and the manifold theoretical sciences. It is not only that a Henry Ford

would have no chance under socialism. A Shakespeare, a Josiah Willard Gibbs or a Max Planck would be equally impossible. And a Jesus of Nazareth would be strangled at his first suggestion that Caesar is not God.

Finally John Chamberlain brought to his job at the *Freeman* a unique experience as a book critic. William Lyon Phelps has called him "the best critic of his generation." At thirty, John wrote the daily book review for the *New York Times*, turning a book review in to his editor every weekday afternoon at five o'clock for three long years. He reviewed for Irita Van Doren at the *New York Herald Tribune,* for *Time, Life* and *Fortune,* for the *New Republic,* the *New Leader, Harper's, Barron's,* the *Wall Street Journal*—you name it.

John Chamberlain and I lunch together two or three times a year at Nicola Paone's on Thirty-fourth Street in New York, a block and a half from my office. At eighty-seven John still writes in the space he inherited from George Sokolsky nearly thirty years ago, although the frequency is down. He writes only an occasional piece instead of six a week, as he did for many years. Every Tuesday he comes to town from his Connecticut home to chat with the fellows at The Heritage Foundation or the Syndicate and put the finishing touches on his current work. That's when we lunch.

It was very quiet in Paone's this particular Tuesday about a year ago, and we were, as we often did, lingering over our cappucino. John mentioned that he had just been rereading the reviews he had written for the *Freeman* nearly forty years earlier and had been struck by their relevance to today's problems and dilemmas. He laughed in a self-depreciatory way (John has raised self-depreciation to Olympian heights) and mumbled—John does mumble—something about wondering whether there might just somewhere be some interest in bringing these reviews out again. He had found them, upon rereading, well, humph, pretty interesting. He looked at me inquiringly. "Yes," I said, "John, I'd love to read them." A few weeks later the reviews arrived by mail neatly encased in a three-hole cardboard binder. To read them was an education. I urged John to get them back into print. Material of this quality shouldn't lie moldering in the yellowing pages of the *Freeman.* They are too vibrant, too important to be lost.

Here in a nutshell is the intellectual story of America in the first half of this century. Anyone who was anyone in the cultural life of America in the first half of the century makes an appearance. Novelists, biographers, critics, essayists, poets, economists, journalists—John writes about them all with grace and wit. The literary figures: F. Scott Fitzgerald, Edna St. Vincent Millay, Ernest Hemingway, John Dos Passos, J. P. Marquand, Louis Bromfield, Sinclair Lewis, Edmund Wilson, Alistair Cooke, Joseph Conrad, E. B. White. The China hands: Owen Lattimore, Freda Utley, Irene Kuhn. The economists: Friedrich Hayek, William Graham Sumner, Ludwig von Mises, Henry Hazlitt. The polemicists and journalists: John T. Flynn, Ralph de Toledano, Victor Lasky, Frank Chodorov, H. L. Mencken, Frank Hanighen. The women, those wonderful embattled women: Isabel Paterson, Rose Wilder Lane, Alice-Leone Moats, Taylor Caldwell, Marguerite Higgins, Dorothy Thompson, Ayn Rand. The men at the barricades: Walter Duranty, Herbert L. Matthews, Arthur Koestler, and Whittaker Chambers, John Chamberlain's dear and cherished friend. Chamberlain's three-thousand-word review of *Witness* is stunning. The following passage encapsulates the difference in quality and courage between Chambers and the critics who sought but failed to silence his witness:

> ... most of us who came off the college campuses of America in the twenties and the thirties succumbed to the evil of collectivist thinking in little, comfortable ways. We were the Fabians. We were the lukewarm. Whittaker Chambers, who believed in being a living witness to his faith..., was never lukewarm. Nevertheless, in his journey to the end of the night and back again, Chambers described at high-voltage intensity the arc of experience that has been universal to a generation.

A few weeks back while finishing up this foreword I called John to ask what had been decided on as a title for the book. Silence at the other end of the line, and an embarrassed laugh. "Priscilla, I can't remember." There had, he explained, been a number of tentative working titles. "Just a minute, I'll go look it up." He was back in seconds. "It's either 'The Turnaround Years' or 'The Turnabout Years.'" Which did I like?

Foreword

I liked "The Turnabout Years." The fifties were the turnabout years for an America bemused by the awful fact of the cold war. On June 25, 1950, the conflict would erupt into a bloodbath in Korea and bring about a reevaluation of many deeply ingrained premises of the thirties and forties.

I liked it for another, more personal reason. In 1951 John Chamberlain, in what my brother Bill has characterized as "an act of reckless generosity," wrote the introduction to *God and Man at Yale.* Turnabout is fair play. And so I take great pleasure in my small part in bringing *The Turnabout Years* to the launch pad.

PRISCILLA L. BUCKLEY

Sharon, Connecticut

PREFACE

As I discovered during the writing of a "semi-autobiography" called *A Life with the Printed Word,* it is virtually impossible to pin down the process of intellectual conversion in dates. But the year 1950, when I signed on with Henry Hazlitt and Suzanne LaFollette to bring out a new magazine, the *Freeman,* focused things for me by giving me a platform, the nature of which Priscilla Buckley has explored as I could not have done.

Priscilla hasn't missed much. Her introduction tells the intellectual story of the first half of the twentieth century in America, with the names of the more important novelists, biographers, critics, economists, and poets duly displayed.

In retrospect, it may seem strange that since the 1950s there have been no additional authors of comparable literary skill. But that is another story, beginning, deceptively, with the Flower Children and spinning off in a violent and juvenile radicalism, the baneful influence of which on American letters and thought has yet to be worked out.

It suffices, however, to Priscilla's account that the Scott Fitzgerald of *The Last Tycoon,* the Max Eastman who kidded Hemingway for the "false hair on his chest," the Dos Passos of a number of novels and first-rate patriotic histories, the *Human Events* editors Alan Ryskind and Tom Winter, the Bill Buckley of *National Review,* and the George Orwell of *1984,* were all set in their characters in 1950, giving formal structure to an epoch.

I might add parenthetically that the first important anti-Stalinist intellectual, Sol Levitas, the publisher and editor of the *New*

Leader, seems to have escaped Priscilla's attention. I used to watch Sol catch fish off the Menemsha jetty in Martha's Vineyard. He loved to fish, but couldn't abide eating them. So he passed his catches along to me, along with the latest stories about Stalin's horrible doings in Russia of the 1930s purge trials. It was a real education. Sol had been mayor of Vladivostok before the Bolsheviks moved in.

Priscilla speaks of "those wonderful embattled women: Isabel Paterson, Rose Wilder Lane, Alice-Leone Moats, Taylor Caldwell, Marguerite Higgins, Dorothy Thompson, Ayn Rand." There is an omission here—she neglected to include herself.

The Literary Scene

1
John Dos Passos Takes a Bow

November 13, 1950

Away back in the antediluvian thirties, when young Americans were succumbing in droves to the strange belief that they could cut loose from their eighteenth-century libertarian heritage to follow the authoritarian star of Marx, a gifted novelist sat in a Manhattan restaurant and gibed across the room at a group of his fellow writers. "Intellectuals of the world, unite," he declaimed with good-natured solemnity, "you have nothing to lose but your brains."

The novelist who uttered this parody of the Communist Manifesto was John Dos Passos. The stupidity of attempting to force intellectuals to think "in committee" was only just beginning to dawn on Dos Passos, but he was to learn fast in the later years of the Cock-Eyed Decade. An indefatigable traveler, Dos Passos had been batting about the world almost from childhood. He had been in France during the later stages of World War I; he had watched the rise and fall of the revolutionary surge in Russia; he had let his poet's eye rove over the burnt landscapes of medieval Spain; he had, in Malcolm Cowley's expressive phrase, hitched his ivory tower to the last car of the Orient Express.

As a young man fresh out of Harvard, Dos Passos had welcomed the activity induced by the collectivist heresy—though for paradoxically individual reasons. He sided with the radicals of the day because he disliked injustice, not because he was in love with the illusory order of collectivist organization. His real psychological affinity was with the anarchists of his beloved Spain; he had not yet come to see that some government is necessary to protect the natural rights of the individual.

Unlike the average so-called intellectual, John Dos Passos really had an intellect. Which is to say that he was willing to test his preconceptions, his hypotheses, in the light of consequences. He didn't like the consequences of the Russian Revolution. He didn't like the consequences of Soviet interference in the Spanish Civil War. His keen eye for realities caused him to break intellectually with all of his erstwhile comrades—with Archibald MacLeish, with Ernest Hemingway, with Malcolm Cowley. Often a man who breaks with old friends over ideas and beliefs carries with him into his future life a bitterness that acts as a corrosive on expression. But Dos Passos has never been bitter; he has never written a line out of fundamental ill will.

Dos Passos's book *The Prospect Before Us* is a clear-eyed attempt to present a comparative audit of political systems. Rigged up as a series of illustrated travel lectures, complete with imaginary movies and a polyphonous critical audience, the book darts hither and yon, from England to Buenos Aires, and from the rolling Nebraska prairie to the railroad sidings of East Palestine, Ohio. The intent is to compare such diverse phenomena as Attlee socialism, *peronista* authoritarianism, and life in the new America of Fair Deal bureaucracy, big corporations and big unions. This comparative audit of systems is illuminating for the similarities it turns up on three continents. It is also illuminating for the differences it ultimately stresses. Dangerous though the centralizing and bureaucratizing trends in the United States may be, there is still a far greater measure of social and psychological health in North America than elsewhere. Ever the rational optimist, John Dos Passos thinks we may yet succeed in adapting ourselves to the facts of the big corporation and the big union without losing our individualism, or our genius for local solution of local problems.

Dos Passos aptly says that "the heresies of thirty years ago are the dogmas now." The fads and theories of the Greenwich Village rebels who used to drink in the basement of the Brevoort in 1914 are today the orthodoxies of the college campus, the fashionable lecture circuit, and the anterooms of political Washington. Every fool and his brother believes in administrative law, and in the agonized improvisations that go by the strange name of the "planned economy." Keynes has replaced Adam Smith as the totem.

If only because the young must eventually revolt against the deadening mediocrity of sloganized leftist thinking, the new orthodoxies cannot last forever. Belief in the various allotropes of socialism must crumble before the realities of bureaucratic life. What then? Dos Passos is not sure. He thinks that profit sharing may blow new life into the capitalist economy; he thinks that the device of the voluntary cooperative may be used to solve many individual and regional problems that demand some sort of organized approach. He doesn't try to lay down any blueprints; he merely says that our destinies cannot safely be allowed to settle in the gummy hands of Washington, or of any boardrooms that have lost contact with local feelings and local pride.

Dos Passos writes of Brazil, of Uruguay, of the Argentine Republic and of Chile with warmth and understanding. He is a little haphazard and sketchy about Peru. He brings the flour-milling industry of the North American midwest to life, and he writes sympathetically about Akron and the rubber workers' union. His best pages, however, are about farming in Iowa and about the strangulation of the individual in modern England. It is the point counterpoint provided by Clement Attlee's socialism and the enthusiastic agricultural experimentation of Bob Garst of Iowa that lends vivacity and human meaning to *The Prospect Before Us.*

Theoretically, as Dos Passos willingly concedes, the modern Englishman is not a slave. He can still throw his government out of office by the vote. He can still change the laws of Britain by recourse to parliamentary methods. But can a young Englishman dispose of his own future as he sees fit? Can he move about the world as he wills? Can he start a business for himself?

Dos Passos says no to all such hypothetical questions. In Birmingham he ran into a couple of toolmakers who, twenty-two years ago, had gone into business for themselves. "Suppose you were young fellows coming out of the service now," asked Dos Passos, "could you do the same thing?" "Couldn't be done," said one of the toolmakers. "You'd be licked before you started by the regulations and where would you get the capital when taxes take all your savings? It would cost five times what it did prewar. And 'ow could you get the materials when the quotas are based on what a firm used in 1938?"

So much for freedom to start a new enterprise in Attlee's Britain.

In Iowa it is different. There a man can still buy a farm. If the philosophy of controls continues to be pushed in Washington, he may depend for a profit on support prices that will ultimately be taken from him. But the Iowa farmer is still free as of the moment of writing to experiment with fertilizers, with new plowing and disking methods, with new hybrids.

Freedom to experiment naturally entails risk; an unwise experiment may come to nothing. But does making a fetish of security necessarily abolish the risk? In Chile Dos Passos listened one night to Dr. Cruz Coke, a conservative politician. Said Dr. Coke: "Passing laws . . . proved no cure. They [the politicians] tried to protect wage workers and farmers, in fact everybody's income, by law. The result was that everybody was sinking into poverty together. The result of the law assuring business enterprises a margin of profit was that it wasn't any longer to the businessman's advantage to run his business efficiently because he got his profit anyway." That was the experience in Chile; it will be the experience in the United States if current economic trends are pushed to their logical conclusion.

2
The Basic John Dos Passos

The legend still persists that there were two John Dos Passoses. The legend has been nurtured by a combination of surface manifestations. In the twenties and early thirties we had the Dos Passos of *The 42nd Parallel, 1919,* and *The Big Money,* which together composed the trilogy published as *U.S.A.* In broken rhythms *U.S.A.* satirized capitalism as the leftward-moving intellectuals of the time perceived it to be. The villains of the piece were the public relations counselors who practiced "social engineering," and the womenfolk who gravitated toward any manifestation of power.

Then, in the later thirties, came a shift. Dos Passos, who had gone to Spain with Ernest Hemingway to help make a pro-Spanish Loyalist film called *The Spanish Earth,* chanced upon the evidence that the Stalinists had executed his good friend Jose Robles as a probable Fascist spy. It was a rude jolt to Dos Passos, who suspected Marxism anyway but hadn't thought it capable of such a deed when the "line" called for a United Front.

Recalling that Carlo Tresca, the anarchist, had warned him against going to Spain ("John, they goin' make a monkey outa you, a beeg monkey"), Dos Passos uncovered more instances in which the Communists seemed far more interested in displacing social democrats and anarcho-syndicalists in the Loyalist high command than in winning a war for a pluralist democracy. The double standard was apparent everywhere behind the Loyalist front lines.

Dos Passos had known Jose Robles in Baltimore, where Robles had taught Spanish at Johns Hopkins University. Edmund Wilson had known Robles too, as a vacation visitor to Cape Cod. Both

Wilson and Dos Passos were certain that Robles, a non-Communist leftist, would have been incapable of betraying the Loyalist cause. When Dos Passos protested against the Stalinist double standard to Ernest Hemingway, he elicited a strange response. Hemingway said the "New York critics" would "crucify" Dos if he were to make an issue of the Robles affair in the United States. Hemingway's tone was menacing. Whereupon Katy Dos Passos, a friend of Hemingway's since childhood, interjected, "Why, Ernest, I never heard anything so despicably opportunistic in my life."

That was the end of the Hemingway–Dos Passos friendship. Parenthetically, we jump out of the 1950–53 *Freeman* sequence to say that the full story of the quarrel over Robles is told with remarkably few differences in two biographies of Dos Passos, one by Townsend Ludington and the other by Virginia Spencer Carr. Writing in the eighties, each biographer, turning to the aftermath of the Hemingway–Dos Passos contretemps, puts a dramatic emphasis on Hemingway's continued mean-spiritedness. A "one-eyed Portuguese bastard," said Hemingway of his erstwhile friend.

Dos Passos's prevailing good nature would have permitted a reconciliation if Hemingway had been willing. But Hemingway, a political naif, clung like a limpet to the general leftist line that "he who is not with us is against us." The Hemingway theory that everything should be forgiven the Left to protect the "larger" good of the socialist revolution is still riding high, as anyone who follows the liberal response to such contemporary conflicts as Nicaragua and El Salvador must know.

Hemingway, however, did say one truthful thing: Dos Passos was indeed crucified by the New York critics when he returned home from Spain to write his "Farewell to Europe" for the magazine *Common Sense.* Jim Farrell was one of a few critics to stand by Dos Passos. Dos's post–*U.S.A.* fiction, beginning with the semi-autobiographical *Adventures of a Young Man* and continuing through his *District of Columbia* trilogy, was generally written off as evidence of a tired capitulation to the Right. This was nonsense: *Adventures of a Young Man* concerns an ends-means squabble between two sets of leftists. What Dos Passos had done was violate a taboo that had kept proletarian fiction writers from dramatizing their differences. But there were differences, as Dos Passos, a born dramatist, well knew.

It is true enough that Dos lost some of his zest for technical innovation in the novels he wrote in the forties before he returned to the *U.S.A.* pattern of mixed, though converging, narratives in his labor novel called *Midcentury.* In this book Dos displayed all his old skills, mingling "Camera Eye" interjections and offsetting Whitmanesque prose poems about important contemporaries with various narrative strands. The subject matter of all his post–*U.S.A.* fiction was hardly a concession to anything that General Francisco Franco stood for in Spain or, for that matter, to anything that could be described as monopolistic business in America. Nor was Dos Passos's fictional depiction of Huey Long any recommendation of Democratic politics as it was practiced in the one-party South.

Dos Passos was transparently honest when he said his values hadn't changed at all. He was for the individual versus the big organization no matter what name the bureaucratic oppressor of the moment might take.

Both Virginia Spencer Carr and Townsend Ludington, in their incredibly detailed biographies, select specific instances in which Dos Passos was nettled or frustrated by his personal need to fight the Big Battalions. There was the Sacco-Vanzetti case, of course. Bartolomeo Vanzetti, with his eloquent concern for what Dos Passos described as "free communities of artisans and farmers and fishermen and cattle breeders who would work for their livelihood with pleasure," provided in his halting but fervent words an intellectual self-portrait of Dos Passos himself. Ludington makes more of this personal angle than does Carr, although both authors stress Dos's conviction that Vanzetti and Nicola Sacco had been railroaded to the chair for their anarchistic beliefs. (Later evidence shows that Dos might have been wrong.) Dos Passos himself had escaped the reach of Big Bureaucratic compulsion in World War I by volunteering, as a Harvard pacifist, for service in the Norton–Harjes Ambulance Corps. Like other self-proclaimed Harvard aesthetes, Dos wanted to see what was going on. He didn't object to putting himself in the line of fire, but he wanted to be free to comment on what went on in an army raised by force in a war that many Americans opposed.

Dos put his observations into *Three Soldiers*, forerunner of Erich Maria Remarque's *All Quiet on the Western Front*, and into the autobiographical *One Man's Initiation*. In the end, however, Dos was caught by the draft and sent to a training camp in America before being returned to France.

His worst fears about bureaucracy were confirmed when his final discharge application was lost in the adjutant general's headquarters in Paris. This was after he had actually seen a paper with his discharge stamped upon it. Convinced that he had been reduced to "nonbeing" (life, he said, "under these conditions is absolutely worthless"), Dos took matters into his own hands and went AWOL. Slipping past the military police, he boarded one train, then another, and still another until he had reached army headquarters in Tours. A search through the files finally yielded Dos's entire service jacket, with the missing papers in a pocket. The whole scary episode is presented most graphically by Virginia Spencer Carr. Dos Passos never mustered the objections to World War II that he held against World War I (he described the first conflict sarcastically as "Mr. Wilson's War"), but he kept his eyes and ears alert for what he knew would be Stalin's effort to use our help as a springboard to usurp Hitler's role as a would-be world conqueror once "peace" had come.

Dos Passos was glad to be in the fight against Hitler and the Japanese once it was joined. He particularly savored reporting the war in the Pacific (see his *Tour of Duty*), for it involved a bypass strategy that was economical in the expenditure of men. But he was disgusted by the naiveté that allowed Soviet Russia to pass the captured Japanese arms to Mao Tse-tung while we boycotted the donation or sale of American arms to our ally Chiang Kai-shek. And he was doubly horrified by Stalin's emergence as the conqueror of eastern Europe.

After 1945 the Big Battalions were no longer the capitalists. Communists were calling the shots in most of Europe and Asia, and a new generation of labor leaders in America was busy ignoring productivity in the push for a wage scale that showed little regard for either the consumer or the investor.

Dos Passos was a paradox in many ways, and neither Virginia Spencer Carr nor Townsend Ludington sees fit to deny it. He was ambivalent about his father, a corporation lawyer who felt he had to wait until the death of his first wife before he could legitimatize Dos by marrying his mother. Dos was personally congenial, a most good-natured man, and his own two marriages were happy combinations of love and companionship. Dos knew how to make friends, and he kept those friends by carrying on a voluminous correspondence that makes one wonder how he had the energy left over to write books. He had high hopes for his country, and he spent most of his working time in his later years writing about our Founding Fathers in order to revive what he called the prospects for a golden age. But in his fiction the pessimist in him almost invariably took charge. (His novel *Chosen Country* is one exception.) He was, first and last, a satirist. He believed that good and bad intermingled in all too many people, and he was concerned to depict it as he saw it.

There is little to choose between the Carr and Ludington biographies. Dos Passos made the job easy for both authors by leaving behind a treasure trove of notebooks, correspondence and drafts. Besides being a wide-ranging man of letters he was his own biographer in many ways, as Townsend Ludington has shown in an earlier book, *The Fourteenth Chronicle,* which is a collection of Dos's letters and diaries extending, with narrative connectives, to more than six hundred pages.

The Carr biography presents a picture of Dos Passos's second marriage, to Elizabeth, or Bett, Holdrige, a picture that is slightly more detailed than that found in Ludington's book. Ludington, on the other hand, is a little stronger in his analysis of Dos Passos's individual works. But it is of the same man the two biographers write.

An earlier Dos Passos study, Melvin Landsberg's *Dos Passos' Path to U.S.A.*, spoke eloquently of Dos's provocative moral vision, which portrays "the evil of abusing men for private or political ends." This "moral vision" infuses both the Carr and Ludington works. The books are very much worth reading by a generation that is in danger of forgetting that Dos Passos is just as much a part of modern American literature as Hemingway and Scott Fitzgerald, who get superior billing in the schools.

3
The Merged John Dos Passos

January 14, 1952

As we have noted, there were two stylistic Dos Passoses, the same man at bottom, but with two styles of writing. One Dos Passos was a poet with the eye of a painter; he wrote richly impressionistic travel books, "camera eye" interludes and melodic paeans to his favorite heroes and villains in American history. The other was a novelist who hewed to a rigidly naturalistic, functional line, making his prose as spare and bare as an elm bough in winter. The poet delighted the senses; the novelist did a great deal toward taking his reader to the heart of contemporary life. But somehow this conscious splitting of an artistic personality never made much sense once one had discounted the proposition that modern life is inevitably dull and hence deserving of only the barest prose. One always had the feeling that the two Dos Passoses, good though they were, would function much more effectively if they could but meet and work as one.

Well, they have finally met and merged completely in a new Dos Passos novel, *Chosen Country*. Herein the painter-poet's eye has been welcomed back into the fiction writer's company. This is the story of a happy marriage and the antecedents that went to make it. The distaff side of the narrative focuses on Lulie Harrington, who inherited an indomitable individualism from her professor–father and a lively beauty and quiet sense of fun from a Kentucky mother.

Lulie is unforgettable, Dos Passos's most rounded and engaging woman. She stands out among Dos Passos's Janey Williamses and Margo Dowlings, as a person with character always stands out. But the best thing about Lulie is her shattering impact on the aesthetic theories of her creator. She just will not look at the world with the eye of a cold naturalist. On page 80 of *Chosen Country* Lulie stands gazing out over a northwoods lake. What she sees is not an ordinary evening star, but "a great nasturtium-colored planet" blazing in the west. In a world that finds floral hues flaring in the night sky, the poet that is Dos Passos can work at the top of his bent.

There is a great deal of transmuted autobiography in *Chosen Country*. Jay Pignatelli, the young man who makes a detour across three continents to find Lulie Harrington, does and says most of the things that John Dos Passos was doing and saying while he was growing up. Jay's father was an Italian immigrant; John Dos Passos's father was from Portugal. Like Dos Passos, Jay Pignatelli was dragged from Chicago to Belgium, and from England to Harvard, at a time when other boys were playing sandlot baseball and eating banana splits at the corner drugstore. In Jay Pignatelli Dos Passos has created a character who has to provide his own roots. Jay tries to get sustenance from a score of soils—from the world of cosmopolitan hotels; from the ambulance service in World War I; from the radical movement that went to pieces, ideologically speaking, when the Bolsheviks made opportunism their fetish; from the practice of the law. But no truly vitalizing sap comes up until Jay absorbs the meaning of his immigrant father and finds the right girl in Lulie Harrington.

The search of Jay and Lulie for each other makes for one of the best things that John Dos Passos has written. It is a novel of rich overtones, for Dos Passos has explored the social history of a generation to build up his background. *Chosen Country* moves through the America of the muckrakers, the America of the crusade to make the world safe for democracy, the America of the Palmer raids, the Sacco-Vanzetti case and the speakeasy culture of the twenties. As is usually the case in a Dos Passos novel, there are interludes that do not at first blush seem to have much organic connection with the main story. Through the interludes of *Chosen Country* one gets a sense that Dos Passos is painting disguised portraits of Lincoln Steffens and Clarence Darrow and Jim McNamara, the dynamiter; or of Mary Heaton Vorse and Elizabeth Gurley Flynn; or of John Reed. These portraits are skillfully done, and they suggest that Dos Passos would make a first-rate biographer. They add to the richness and depth of his novelistic picture. And they do have their impact on the ideas that shaped the mind and culture of Jay Pignatelli.

Unfortunately, the Dos Passos habit of interrupting the narrative line of a story, for instance to give the reader a portrait of a Bay State Radford who becomes an archaeologist and marries an Englishwoman, becomes downright annoying when it is Jay Pignatelli and Lulie Harrington that you want to read about. *Chosen Country* is far less of a labyrinth than the earlier *The 42nd Parallel* or *The Big Money.* Nevertheless, it does have its elements of a maze, and the minotaur that one is seeking is not always just around the corner. The Dos Passos interludes make excellent short stories, excellent vignettes. Still, one wishes more and more that Lulie Harrington, who has definitely changed her creator's theory of novelistic prose composition, would also change his theory of dramatic presentation.

No doubt there really are nine-and-ninety ways of constructing tribal lays. Some novelists assemble their stories as the General Motors Company assembles a car; some use the "wheel technique" of first creating the separate spokes and then fitting them into a hub and giving them a whirl until they all blend together. It does not matter what devices the novelist uses to build his story and get perspective, provided he can create a sense of progression within a unity. But the Dos Passos method, although it does add up to unity, plays hob with the reader's sense of progression. *Chosen Country* offers a scenic ride through beautiful country, but a ride that jolts to annoying stops and goes off on more than one side trip up a dead-end lane. The detours are worthwhile in themselves, but one wishes that Dos Passos would find some way of putting all his scenery along the main road.

4
Edna Millay's Friends

November 19, 1951

The destiny of man in our barren epoch seems to be almost inextricably bound up with politics. Yet politics is the least satisfying, the least rewarding, of human preoccupations. The more we intensify our political activities, the less time we have to spend on personal development, or the arts, or creativity in general. It is some such realization, I think, that is at the bottom of all the recent refurbishing and revaluation of the decade of the 1920s. Few of our "intellectuals" loved the American twenties when they were living through them: that was the decade when the superior children of the arts were saying "Goodbye, Wisconsin" (or Kansas, or wherever), when Main Street was considered a hopelessly benighted place, when our "business civilization" was being damned from hell to breakfast by renegade businessmen turned writers. But in the twenties no one had to enlist for self-protection, or for the protection of a way of life, in murderously serious political wars. Life had (or at least it seemed to have) a margin, an area of velvet; the human being had time to love, to create, to play.

He also had time to make a damned fool of himself, which is what hordes of people did. During the thirties all that could be seen in retrospect were the foolishness and the wantonness of the period. In their rush to hail the new bottomside nobility of the proletarian cult, our critics tended to dismiss all the salient figures of the twenties. Two particularly representative luminaries, F. Scott Fitzgerald and Edna St. Vincent Millay, sold off in the literary market just about as disastrously as Radio Corporation sold off on the Big Board. Fitzgerald was remembered, if at all, as the man who tried to make Princeton University into a country club. Edna Millay was typed as the girl who had lost her spontaneity when she turned from flapper defiance of the conventions to more sober and classic themes. What the new critics of the thirties failed to perceive was that both Fitzgerald and Millay loved the more solid and lasting boons of life as well as the froth. Hanging grimly to a pendulum that was gathering momentum in its swing toward Moscow, our critics, who are always more fashionable than free, forgot that their first duty is to grasp and analyze a phenomenon in its balanced entirety.

Now the penitents are coming back. Vincent Sheean, for example, has discovered that Edna Millay had the same rapport with the world of glowing nature that one finds in Shakespeare. His memoir of Miss Millay, *The Indigo Bunting,* is an odd little book, for it betrays a naiveté that seems strange in a person as well traveled as Sheean. Edna Millay loved birds. She fed them, and observed them as they were feeding, at her bosky home at Steepletop, near Austerlitz, New York. She even had gulls flying around her head at her summer refuge on Ragged Island in Maine's Penobscot Bay.

Now there is nothing occult about such human relationships with the animal world; beasts and birds respond to friendliness even as human beings. I get along with three black cats, a Dalmatian hound, a horse, a dozen bantam chickens and a turtle, the accumulated menagerie of my children, and no one would ever mistake me for a person of occult powers. Yet Vincent Sheean thinks Edna Millay had some secret and extraordinary relationship with gulls, sparrows, finches, rose-breasted grosbeaks and the indigo bunting. Millay hooted at this particular display of Sheean mysticism; she met his persistent attempts to pursue the mystery to its bottom with a downright statement, "They come here because I feed them." This Maine Yankee earthiness should have satisfied Sheean, who should be humble enough to realize that all things, whether "material" or not, are part of the great encompassing mystery of creation. The very cobbles in the street are touched with a wonder that no scientist can finally fathom; origins always dissolve into origins further back. But Sheean cannot be content with the commonsensical order that exists within the grain of the universe; he persists in his feeling that Edna Millay was a witch (a very nice witch) who had somehow chosen the indigo bunting in preference to a black cat and a self-propelling broom.

It's all very touching and a little foolish, of course. But it is lucky for his readers that Sheean can go overboard. For his preoccupation with Miss Millay's adventures with the birds has led him back to the lyrics of her *Second April,* to the pantheistic feeling of *Renascence,* to the poems in which the sea and the sky and the equinoxes and the solstices are the pervading influences. Edna Millay was born a woman and distressed by all the needs and notions of her kind, but she was also born with the faculty of feeling the earth-forces that moved the Elizabethans three centuries before her time. Her lyrics and sonnets are, as Vincent Sheean indicates, almost Shakespearean in their feeling. But they are not derivative. They are not the old clipped coin of the Romantic tradition in English poetry. Millay's vocabulary, her turn of phrase, her informing spirit, all derive from the Maine Penobscot country, where New England takes on amplitude as it faces toward the tides of Fundy and the open Atlantic.

Vincent Sheean saw Edna Millay only a few times. He is such a sensitive observer of human moods, however, that his spasmodic contact with his subject has resulted in a subtly revealing book. *The Indigo Bunting* makes it clear that Sheean's true love is not politics (a subject on which he has wasted half his life), but the whole human range of creativity, from which the state should be banished utterly. Now that Sheean has found his vein I hope that he goes on exploiting it.

I hope, too, that Malcolm Cowley and Alfred Kazin, two critics who spent a good deal of their time in the 1930s cultivating the illusion that the way to free man was to put his energies under the control of socialist politicians, have turned for good to other themes. Cowley has just finished rearranging F. Scott Fitzgerald's *Tender Is the Night* in accordance with an outline left by Fitzgerald himself in his notebook. The rearrangement of the components into more strictly chronological order does improve the novel. Edward Dahlberg, who thinks Fitzgerald is overrated, sent me to reading the new Cowley–Fitzgerald version of *Tender Is the Night* with trepidation: I was afraid that I would discover Fitzgerald had become a diminished figure. But I found that the writing is just as good as I thought it was in 1934, when I first read it. There is a shoddy strain in some of Fitzgerald's work, and Dahlberg is quite right to feel angry at the general American habit of periodically overpraising what has been neglected and underpraised before. But Fitzgerald had purified both his style and his attitude for the writing of *Tender Is the Night*.

Alfred Kazin's *F. Scott Fitzgerald: The Man and His Work* is a collection of criticisms and appreciations of Fitzgerald that span a full thirty years. The collection makes for some interesting reading. One thing it proves inadvertently is that our off-the-cuff reviewing has been considerably better than our more pretentious criticism. When a single critic feels he has to drag in the names of Racine, André Gide, Goethe, Milton, Proust, Yeats, Shakespeare, Dickens, Voltaire, Balzac, Henry James, George Moore, A.E. (George William Russell), Stendhal, St. John of the Cross, Wordsworth, Keats, Shelley, Dostoevski, Byron, Shaw, and Samuel Butler to explain Fitzgerald, the traffic becomes a trifle overburdened, to say the least.

5
The Girl from Maine Is Dead

November 1950

Edna St. Vincent Millay, the girl from Maine whose *Renascence* was the first full-throated harbinger of the American poetic revival of the teens and the twenties, is dead. Rather callously and sloppily, I thought, the newspaper obituary writers fastened upon those aspects of her life that had the least poetic significance. The flaming-youth, burning-the-candle-at-both-ends verse was quoted almost universally; then the obit writers skipped rapidly over many years to emphasize the didactic stuff (bad poetry, even though written with noble ends in view) that Miss Millay produced in the early forties to wake the world to the crimes of the Nazis.

Annoyed and disheartened by the obituaries, I got down from dusty shelves the slim, chastely printed black-and-gold volumes of *Second April, The Harp-Weaver* and *A Few Figs from Thistles*, and the more opulently designed *Wine from These Grapes* and *The Buck in the Snow.* The very heft of the slender books brought long-dormant emotions to life. As I have long suspected, the best of Edna Millay has the least to do with the social history of her epoch. The Younger Generation verses, which the whole youthful tribe once seemed to wear on its sleeves in lieu of hearts, date badly. But the sonnets and lyrics that grew out of Edna Millay's experience of loss and bereavement are still wonderful:

> That April should be shattered by a gust,
> That August should be levelled by a rain,
> I can endure, and that the lifted dust
> Of man should settle to the earth again;
> But that a dream can die, will be a thrust
> Between my ribs forever of hot pain.

And:

Oh, there will pass with your great passing
Little of beauty not your own, —
Only the light from common water,
Only the grace from simple stone.

The elegies and dirges that Edna Millay wrote for her dead Vassar friend, "D. C.," are similarly moving. And just as authentic, if slightly less beautiful, are the Maine coast poems, lyrical evocations of a lost childhood:

Always before about my dooryard,
Marking the reach of the winter sea,
Rooted in sand and dragging drift-wood,
Straggled the purple wild sweet-pea;
Always I climbed the wave at morning,
Shook the sand from my shoes at night,
That now am caught beneath great buildings,
Stricken with noise, confused with light.

Edmund Wilson has spoken of Edna Millay's reminting of the old, worn coinage of the Romantic poets. Actually, her best poetry remints nothing; it is personal to the experience of the little girl from the Penobscot country. It could never be mistaken for Keats or Shelley or anybody who ever wrote a quatrain or a sonnet about a lark, a nightingale or a Grecian urn.

6
The Fitzgerald Revival

November 27, 1950

The twenties are haunting the imagination of 1950. To prove it, there is the F. Scott Fitzgerald revival. *The Great Gatsby,* Fitzgerald's one perfect book, is part of most of the standard new college seminars in Eng. Lit. 36, a classic to be read along with *The Scarlet Letter* and *Ethan Frome.* A biography of Fitzgerald is scheduled for January. And within the month Budd Schulberg, the talented refugee from Hollywood, has published his *The Disenchanted,* a tumultuous novel about a writer who, like Fitzgerald, cracked up and died before he could finish a manuscript that gave every promise of being first rate.

Schulberg, a Dartmouth graduate of the mid-thirties, never knew the twenties from personal experience. But, as the son of the head of Paramount Studios, he did know the Fitzgerald legend. During his last years Fitzgerald worked on motion-picture scripts and made notes for a novel about movie land (a truncated version of which exists as *The Last Tycoon*). As the seeming shell of a once famous writer, Fitzgerald must have been taken as an awful warning by aspiring young scenarists as he walked about Hollywood in the late thirties. There was no gainsaying the fact, however, that he had written some enchanting prose in his time. To Schulberg, both the Fitzgerald books and the guttering end to a great career needed explanation. Hence *The Disenchanted,* which draws liberally for its many flashbacks upon Fitzgerald's own autobiographical writings. Indeed, it is hard to see how *The Disenchanted* could have existed had it not been for Fitzgerald's own superior version of the story that has been printed in *Tender Is the Night* and in the notes and essays that Edmund Wilson edited into the fascinating volume called *The Crack-Up*.

To get at the essence of the Fitzgerald story, Budd Schulberg has himself tried to stand outside of time. He has taken a character, Manley Halliday, who, like the Gloria Swanson of *Sunset Boulevard*, lives almost solely on memories of the twenties. Halliday, a bright novelist of a departed epoch, is trying to recoup himself financially by taking a ten-week job (at $2,000 a week) at the studios of Victor Milgrim. Milgrim, a snob and a sadist, carries Halliday off to the New Hampshire Ivy League college of Webster to collaborate with young Shep Stearns on a script depicting young love at the midwinter Ice Carnival. (Out of the script, and the filming of Webster ski jumpers as appropriate background, Milgrim hopes to conjure an honorary degree for himself.) Webster happens to be Stearn's own college, where he was graduated in the mid-thirties into the Era of Social Consciousness, which also is the era of glib pigeonholing. In the personages of Halliday and Stearns, the collegiate twenties and the collegiate thirties face each other across a psychological gulf. They criticize each other, they seek to understand each other—but, as Schulberg has written the story, they tend to cancel each other out. The twenties failed because when man puts all his energies into being an island he wears himself into a frazzle and can't complete his work. The thirties failed because concentrating on being "part of the main" involves a disastrous neglect of the self. The Schulberg moral would seem to be that neither island nor main can win.

Standing outside of time, Schulberg tends thus to dismiss both decades. Yet the margin of victory, however faint, lies with the twenties, and Schulberg admits as much. At least Halliday–Fitzgerald created works that live according to laws of their own. None of the Fitzgerald characters, from Amory Blaine to Dick Diver and Monroe Stahr of *The Last Tycoon*, is a type to be pigeonholed, or to be wholly explained by background or social movement.

In giving the verdict to the twenties by a shade, Schulberg obviously is right. No decade that produced Willa Cather's *A Lost Lady* or Sinclair Lewis's *Arrowsmith* or Elizabeth Roberts's *The Time of Man* or Glenway Wescott's *The Grandmothers* or Ring

Lardner's stories can be written off as a failure. Nevertheless, *The Disenchanted* is not really Scott Fitzgerald's life. The man is not to be understood in terms of contrasting decades.

Schulberg lets us look at his Halliday–Fitzgerald during a week in which the doomed novelist is on a monumental binge. Tumbling off the wagon on his way to Webster with Stearns and Milgrim, Halliday ultimately freezes his feet in the snows of New Hampshire, gets gangrene, and dies of an embolism after an operation. The drunken Halliday babbles endlessly about his talent—and the twenties. Nothing that he says or does makes any connection with the Fitzgerald who actually finished his career writing an understanding and entirely objective book not about the golden twenties of the Paris expatriates but about the movie colony of Hollywood itself. Unfinished though it is, *The Last Tycoon* is the work of a mature artist; it could only have been done by a disciplined, forward-looking man.

Only superficially did the tragedy of Scott Fitzgerald lie in the passage of time. It has been said that he tried to make a career, and not a preparation for a career, out of his youth. He and his wife Zelda (the fascinating Jere of Schulberg's novel) supposedly roistered their days away. The champagne, the white nights on the Mediterranean, the house parties, the debts, finally caught up with them. But other men, women and couples have survived all these hazards, whether of drink, debt or wasted time. The truth is that Fitzgerald himself survived the wasted years at least long enough to write *Tender Is the Night* and *The Last Tycoon.* (The fact that his heart ultimately failed him in his forties is an accident of the genes as much as anything else; for example, Grover Cleveland Alexander, a great pitcher and a classic drunk, having a different combination of genes, lived some twenty years longer than Fitzgerald.)

No, the tragedy of Fitzgerald was not the passage of time; it was something else that Schulberg misses entirely. In the light of *Tender Is the Night,* that story of a doctor's attempt to make a go of a marriage with a girl who has been ruined by her father, it might be said that Fitzgerald's trouble was a response to Zelda's psychopathology. But no one can be ruined in adult years by another's psychopathology; people stand for better or worse on their own feet. No, the Fitzgerald troubles must have gone back to his early formative years—to things that are barely hinted at in *This Side of Paradise.* If the heroine of *Tender Is the Night* is to be explained by a faulty daughter-father relationship, the hero of *This Side of Paradise* is to be explained by a hothouse son-mother relationship. The two psychopathologies, if we may rely on the evidence of the Fitzgerald novels, crossed paths in later life—with interesting and sometimes horrifying results.

Artistically, however, Fitzgerald's frequently harrowing experiences and relationships constituted no tragedy at all; they presented him with self-knowledge and the knowledge of others, and gave him the substance of his art. To quote from his own introduction to the Modern Library edition of *The Great Gatsby*: "It was my material, and it was all I had to deal with." But it was material good enough to sustain a writing career that was far from negligible even in the last sad years of personal loss and lowered physical vitality.

If Schulberg misses the point about Fitzgerald, he still poses an interesting question in confronting the twenties with the thirties. Why is it that the novelists of the twenties produced fiction that will live, while the novelists of the thirties, with a very few exceptions, are already being forgotten? The answer would seem to be that a novel cannot be made of time—or a social system—pressing in on a person if the person has nothing apart from either that time or the social system to throw back at it. The novelists of the twenties knew as much. Willa Cather's "lost lady" had a hunger that would have tried for expression in any age or society. Fitzgerald's Gatsby, the eternal romantic, would have gone his way to rebellious doom no matter whether Coolidge or Stalin were his ruler. Almost by definition the novel is the form for dramatizing the individual's pressure against the limitations of space, time and other people. The novelist must start from the individual's end, or his emphases will be wrong. If a novelist goes at his business from the outside in (as the novelist who deals in social categories must do) he will wind up writing a bastard form of history, not fiction. Fitzgerald's books are often good social history, but the fiction is the main thing. The history is merely the by-product of a man who observed all things accurately and well.

7
Freedom at the Source

February 12, 1951

Sterling North, writing in the *New York World-Telegram and Sun* the other day about the F. Scott Fitzgerald revival, was moved to wonder about the current nostalgia for the 1920s. Is it merely a belated adolescent hankering for the days when we felt that we could be carefree and irresponsible? That may account for some of the nostalgic impulse. But there are deeper reasons why the twenties are now looming up as a period of particular importance. One reason is that Americans, in the twenties, believed that man could be a creative agent by his own free decision. The man of the twenties believed that "anyone could do anything"—provided he really wanted to do it. He did not have to wait upon permission from a government, an institution, or a set of social conventions. The man of the twenties believed in freedom at the source, working outward from the dedicated individual.

Unlike Budd Schulberg, who tended to miss the point of the twenties in his recent novel about F. Scott Fitzgerald, *The Disenchanted*, Arthur Mizener has caught the inner spirit of the decade in his vivid and sympathetic *The Far Side of Paradise: A Biography of F. Scott Fitzgerald. The Far Side of Paradise* is both a re-creation of a life and a work of creative scholarship, related in its own way to *The Road to Xanadu*. Where Budd Schulberg was fascinated by the spectacle of Fitzgerald's supposed collapse and disintegration, Mizener is primarily interested in the way a talented artist digested and reworked the material presented to him by experience into the living drama of great fiction. This is a refreshing departure from the Schulberg negativism.

That Fitzgerald pursued many a false god and did many an idiotic thing nobody in his right mind would deny. His remarkable book titles—*Tales of the Jazz Age, Flappers and Philosophers, The Beautiful and Damned, All the Sad Young Men, Taps at Reveille*—stressed the fizzy side of his nature that fitted so patly into the *Era of Wonderful Nonsense.* But there was always the voice of conscience to call Scott Fitzgerald back from his dissipations, his revels and his eternally adolescent pranks. The "spoiled priest" in him knew when he was sinning. In his most mature works he sat in judgment over all his lapses, big and little. He may have been disorganized in his personal relationships and his finances, but he was seldom disorganized in the practice of his craft. An artificer of great integrity, he would cut and rework and rephrase, achieving near-miracles in the subtle modulations of his evocative prose. Two of his books, *The Great Gatsby* and *Tender Is the Night,* will be read as long as English literature is read anywhere.

Fitzgerald had an ambivalent attitude toward wealth, toward the American worship of success, toward the values of undergraduate life, toward the world of the commercial short story. As the spoiled son of an indulgent mother and an ineffectual, beaten-down father, he was self-centered without ever achieving any real measure of self-confidence. His feeling of being "black Irish," of coming from the wrong side of the tracks in a St. Paul, Minnesota, that made much of its Summit Avenue "best people," gave him an inferiority feeling that often tricked him into outrageous behavior. But the data of psychiatry are, in Fitzgerald's case, the materials of art. And he used these materials honestly and well, which is his justification both as an artist and as a man. After all, one grows up by making use of one's mistakes.

In all of his most fully realized characters—Amory Blaine of *This Side of Paradise;* the romantic bootlegger, Jay Gatsby, of *The Great Gatsby;* Dr. Dick Diver of *Tender Is the Night;* and Monroe Stahr, the movie executive-producer of *The Last Tycoon*—Fitzgerald has projected his own story, with all of its grandeurs and miseries. If Fitzgerald had not been the dreaming undergraduate cub, the immature worshipper of the distant and incomprehensible rich, the baffled husband of a beautiful woman who succumbed to schizophrenia because of something that had happened to her in childhood, and the hopeful artisan who worked overtime to write a perfect movie scenario in his last Hollywood days, he would never have possessed a world to transform into fiction. He may have been highly uncritical, a veritable patsy, at the moment of experiencing any given phase of his life, but the warmness, the sensuous wonder, of his prose derive from the very intensity of his abandonment to immersion in his "own material." Fortunately for the more symmetrical aspects of his art, the immersion was—in time—followed by sober second thoughts, by an act of spiritual self-levitation; Fitzgerald could finally achieve a belated perspective, the "exterior view" which assesses the worth of experience. Fitzgerald's best work is wholly in accordance with Wordsworth's definition of poetry—"emotion recollected in tranquillity."

Fitzgerald's hero, the "man of the twenties" who insisted on his individualism, inevitably became a cropper. But was it because individualism must be accounted a deficient philosophy? I do not think so. The man who must wait for a signal outside himself to act, whether from "society" or from a social category or from the state or from a convention, will never bring anything new into being. The fault of Fitzgerald's characters resided not in their individualism but in their failure to cultivate the self-discipline that pushes freedom into truly creative channels. The sports heroes of the twenties—Babe Ruth, Bobby Jones, Jack Dempsey, Bill Tilden, Helen Wills—had an almost formidable faculty of self-discipline. But on the higher levels of life, the American of the twenties did not emulate his sports heroes; he let his individualism flow haphazardly over the landscape, completely out of channel.

At that, the American of the twenties was betrayed primarily by a *political* act that had happened before he himself came onto the scene. The American businessman of the twenties, for example, has been blamed for the depression of 1929. But the depression came from government cheap-money policy in the immediate instance and, beyond that, from the activities of the peacemakers of Versailles, who saddled the German capitalist system with a vast and uneconomic debt that could not be paid out of production. The tariffs, the exchange controls, the repudiations, the devaluations and the quotas that were invoked after the political time-bomb of Versailles exploded were the secondary effects of a political coercion that antedated the twenties by at least a year.

Fitzgerald's "man of the twenties," then, was caught in the meshes of statism even during the period when statism had seemingly receded into the past. Being a novelist, not a social philosopher, Fitzgerald never quite understood what had happened to his world after 1929. He was fascinated, for a while, by the young Communists who came to visit him in Baltimore, but he soon came to see that there was no health in their attitude toward art. Since his intellectual mentor was Edmund Wilson, his old Princeton college friend, he respected the idea of the "socialism" that Wilson espoused. But he was never caught up in it—and it is significant that his last vital act on earth was to write admiringly of a "last tycoon," not of a newly fledged adherent of the leftist cult of the state.

8
The Faddish Critics

July 2, 1951

American criticism, within my lifetime, has been a series of fads. In the mid-twenties the imitators of H. L. Mencken rode high. In the late twenties the New Humanists took up most of the space in the literary magazines. Then came the proletarian cult, the Marxists, the pluggers for social significance. And these, in turn, were followed by the logic choppers, the "grammar boys" (Edward Dahlberg's phrase), and the *partisan reviewer* specialists in Kafka and Henry James.

Because the fads have bloomed and died with extreme rapidity, the literary landscape is littered with critics out of jobs, with comparatively young men without vocation. Only a pertinacious few have lived through the fads; these go on writing criticism because they never made the mistake of trying to merge themselves with the fashions of the moment. An Edmund Wilson, for example, has persisted because he could never give his heart wholly to the demands of any cult. He has always remained Edmund Wilson, a master of expository clarification, even in the midst of his dalliance with aestheticism and Marxism. But the Edmund Wilsons among us are few.

One of the handful of critics who have saved their souls by ignoring the claims of the cultists is J. Donald Adams, whose column, "Speaking of Books," appears every Sunday in the *New York Times Book Review.* Because most of his life Adams has functioned as an editor, his critical output is comparatively slim. But he is a man of learning and of taste, and his deeply abiding convictions go back a long way. His *Literary Frontiers,* while it lacks the heft and body it might have had if the author were not so immersed in the demands of weekly journalism, gives one the measure of a full man who is well worth the knowing.

I worked for Mr. Adams on the staff of the *New York Times Book Review* some twenty years ago. I remember his complaining then that American novelists seemed bent upon evading the manifold challenges of American life. A great Emersonian, Adams always believed, with Emerson, that "all life remains unwritten still." In *Literary Frontiers* this modern Emersonian documents his case against the American novelist. Where, for example, is our big novel about Washington politics? Or about American industry? How many of the women in our fiction are true women? Where is the good novel about the westward movement? Where is our good war novel? Where is our good comprehensive novel about New York City?

To ask these questions is almost to answer them, but Adams spells out in detail the lacks in our most important writers. He is willing to grant that William Howells, Theodore Dreiser and Sinclair Lewis have hit off certain aspects of certain types of businessmen in their novels, but their portraits of the movers and shakers of our industrial culture are extremely limited. Worst of all, these portraits have been taken as stereotypes for imitation by a hundred lesser novelists. A couple of generations ago, back in the muckrake days, there was an outpouring of political novels. Since that time only Elliot Paul (see his *The Governor of Massachusetts*) and John Dos Passos have seriously concerned themselves with public figures.

As for the novel of New York City, Adams notes that many writers have assayed the magazine and publishing worlds. We have had our "Big Wheels," our "Hucksters." But only an occasional Thomas Wolfe or Dos Passos has tried to get around the town from the quiet back streets of Brooklyn to what Adams refers to as the crush and loneliness of the subway at Times Square.

Without ever quite saying it in so many words, Adams puts his finger on the weakness of the American novelist. The weakness stems from a preoccupation with autobiography. If the novelist is in the Hemingway tradition, he tends to be the personal lyricist, not the dramatic observer. Hemingway is magnificent when he is creating from personal mood. But his women, for example, are mainly projections of a very masculine desire. In *A Farewell to Arms* the Hemingway dream girl is called Catherine Barclay. The same dream girl turns up in *For Whom the Bell Tolls* with a Spanish accent and cropped hair. In *Across the River and into the Trees* she is a young *contessa*. In each case she is docile, passionate—and completely imaginary. As Adams points out, Hemingway's most successful women characters are Lady Brett Ashley, the bitch-type female of *The Sun Also Rises*, and Pilar, the earthy old Wife of Bath in *For Whom the Bell Tolls*. But for the rest, Hemingway has specialized in making his women "a mirror for narcissism."

Curiously, the inability to create convincing women characters goes back a long way with the American male writer. Adams points out that Melville did not write of women, that Hawthorne's Hester Prynne was a wraith, that Mark Twain's universe was one of boys and of boys grown older, that Dreiser's women were "little more than objects of male desire," that Dos Passos's are two-dimensional, that Sinclair Lewis has succeeded only with Fran Dodsworth, that Fitzgerld's girls are "iridescent bubbles." Our women novelists—Willa Cather, Ellen Glasgow, Edith Wharton, Elizabeth Madox Roberts—have done better by their own sex, and by the masculine-feminine relationship in general.

Occasionally I would quarrel with the detail which Adams uses to support his generalizations. For example, Dos Passos has been very successful with one type of feminine character, that of the dedicated social-worker gal who has enlisted for the duration in the "class struggle." (He doesn't make the breed very appetizing, but that is something else again.) As for Fitzgerald, he once spoke of his girls as being "warm and promising"—and they are all of that. But they are also on occasion considerably more. Nicole Diver, in *Tender Is the Night*, is a very modern psychotic—and fully as much of a symbol as Hester Prynne. But if Adams tends to miss the importance of *Tender Is the Night*, it is one of his very rare errors. In general, his choice of illustrative detail is wholly relevant to the point he is endeavoring to make.

The most rewarding sections of *Literary Frontiers* are devoted to the American novel. But there are good things in the closely linked essays on *The Wonder of the World* and *Words*. Adams has a predilection for the short and lovely words of English speech, words such as "dawn" and "dusk." He doesn't like Latinity; "how few indeed," he says, "are the Latin words woven into the texture of English which have fiber and life." (How about "fortitude," "imperious," or "suave," Mr. Adams?) As for certain words that have lost their luster in recent years—words like "liberty," "honor," "freedom," "faith," and "glory"—Adams aptly marks that the fault is not in the words themselves. They have lost their luster because we have betrayed them and cannot look them in the face.

Sinclair Lewis's posthumously published novel, *World So Wide*, is mildly interesting, but it is a far cry from the big Lewis stories of the twenties. When Lewis lost his taste—or was it his nerve?—for big social themes, he lost the one thing that made him an important writer. The canvases of *Main Street*, *Babbitt*, *Arrowsmith*, and *Dodsworth* were wide and inclusive; the canvas of *World So Wide* is as narrow as an alleyway in the Italian city of Florence where Lewis spent his last days.

The story of *World So Wide* is about an American's rather self-conscious search for the spirit of medieval and Renaissance culture. Hayden Chart, an architect from Newlife, Colorado, is looking for wider horizons after the death of his shrewish wife, but what he discovers is that a nice, sympathetic hometown girl whom he had casually known for years is worth a lot more than a suit of chain mail or an illuminated manuscript, or even a female professor who is good at library research. This is a good sentimental theme, but Sinclair Lewis's attitude toward it fluctuates so aberrantly from page to page that one is at a complete loss to know what is being satirized, and when. In *Main Street*, Carol Milford's yearning for culture seemed both poignant and pathetic. But Hayden Chart's attempt to become a latter-day Henry Adams is hardly motivated at all. The writing in *World So Wide* is firm enough, and the description of a wild and wintry drive from Venice to Florence through the Apennines is good. But there just doesn't seem to be much purpose or conviction behind the whole thing.

Write this off as one of Lewis's lesser efforts. But don't forget that, in his day, Lewis cast a mighty shadow. Although he was a stern critic of American manners, he never sold short on American fundamentals.

9
Can Writers Think?

January 8, 1951

Most critics will trim occasionally, whether out of considerations of tact, or of deference to the whims of an editor, or of respect for a reigning shibboleth or point of view. Most critics will adapt their approach to the medium, writing one sort of review for a quarterly, another sort for the *New York Herald Tribune* or the *New Yorker*. But not Edmund Wilson, as his *Classics and Commercials* demonstrates anew. Wilson always sounds like the same stubborn, quietly embattled Wilson no matter where he appears. To paraphrase the legend below the post-office pediment, neither enemy nor friend nor trend nor fashion of the day can stay Edmund Wilson from the swift completion of his appointed critique.

In an age when all things are in flux, it might be accounted a good thing that Edmund Wilson definitely knows his own mind. For myself, I always read him with profit and enjoyment. I like many of his quirks and share many of his prejudices. He is bored by mystery stories and so am I. He hates bureaucratic man and so do I. He responds to every last fragment of F. Scott Fitzgerald, and so do I. He doesn't give a damn what the boys are saying about him either in the office of the *New Republic* or in the circles that make a god out of Franz Kafka. I would like to think that I am equally oblivious to the snipers who try to enforce the orthodoxies of the standardized literary avant-garde and the equally standardized Left. But in the final analysis of Edmund Wilson's work, one is forced to echo Isabel Paterson's immortal query: "Can writers think?"

Wilson, as Mrs. Paterson has pointed out, has a wonderful gift of narrative. He can make a moving romance out of Karl Marx's tenderness for his wife Jenny, or Lenin's loyalty to his brother. In *Classics and Commercials* he does a wonderful job with such things as Alexander Woollcott's youth in a socialist phalanstery at Red Bank, New Jersey, or Max Eastman's early career as an editor, or the history of Oscar Wilde's losing struggle with the spirochaeta pallida. Wilson can suggest an intellectual atmosphere or parody a style or explode a fakery or reduce a complicated subject to a few clear lines as no other critic in America can. His virtues as a writer are so positive and so manifold that they almost serve to hide his one glaring deficiency. But after one has read a few score pages in *Classics and Commercials,* which consists of a selection of Wilson's work over a decade in the *New Republic,* the *Nation,* the *New Yorker* and elsewhere, it becomes more and more apparent that Wilson has no immediate intention of trying to make his basic assumptions add up. He is a man who seems doomed to be perpetually at war with himself, and he manages to give the outward impression of solidity and composure only by an adamant refusal to question the intellectual loyalties he picked out of the air in his youth.

Mr. Wilson has long been disillusioned with Soviet Russia and the American writers of the Stalinoid persuasion, and his remarks on Joseph E. Davies as a stylist and on Dorothy Parker's collapse into the "expiatory mania" of the Hollywood swimming-pool proletariat are calculated to make one chortle. Nevertheless, Edmund Wilson still insists, in the face of all the mounting evidence, that socialism and human freedom can be made to fit into an equation that actually equates. He writes twelve pages about Max Eastman without ever grappling with the really essential point of his subject, which is Eastman's utter rejection of the idea that socialism can be had without coercing people's tastes, compelling their economic services, and maiming or killing their bodies. Wilson respects Eastman's courage, but he doesn't know wherein Max's courage actually exists. Eastman's supremely courageous act was to change his mind not only about Marx but about all the Fabian dilutions of the socialist gospel as well.

Wilson hates the bourgeois. It is a standing obsession with him, and it blinds him to reality. He cannot see that the middle class is the only class in history that has ever sought to make legal "rights" the universal possession of all men. The "bourgeois" may despise the Bohemian, but he is willing to leave him alone. The bourgeois is even willing on occasion to pay the Bohemian's bills. But in spite of the dependence of Bohemian upon bourgeois, Wilson speaks of the "boring diligence of commercial activity." He commends a Kafka story because it reads "like a Marxist–Flaubertian satire on the parasites of the bourgeoisie." He tosses off the cliché about the United States of "the trust-ridden eighties and nineties." And he reserves his praise for the America of the early nineteenth century, when "the country was still uncommercialized." To listen to Wilson's strictures on a business culture, one might think him an anchorite, or a hermit on the order of Thoreau, or a rather Spartan poet who actually prefers a hard cot in a cold winter attic.

The internal evidence offered by some of Wilson's verbal byplay, however, is not that of a man who really hates and rejects the products of an advanced business system. He speaks on one occasion of the good "steel penknives, good erasers and real canned sardines" that one could buy before World War II. The steel in a good penknife depends, of course, on a hardening alloy brought, let us say, from the Congo or the Caucasus by very commercial-minded businessmen. Good erasers depend on the organization of rubber plantations in the East Indies, and who organizes a plantation better than a member of the bourgeoisie? As for good canned sardines, they require the interacting commerce of the fisherman, the maker of machinery for Bolivian tin mines, the producer of olive oil, and the retail grocer on the corner of a bourgeois city street. Wilson might hope to eat good canned sardines under a socialist system, but wouldn't he rather gag at the idea of swallowing the product of slave labor?

Edmund Wilson has never faced up to the mechanics involved in socialist production of goods and services. If a government is to plan production, it must have control of all the factors of production. But the factors of production come down in the last analysis to human energy. So it is the human being who must be controlled. How can a government establish control and force a plan except by persuading (that is, propagandizing) or coercing people to do what it wants? And what if large numbers of the people object? Wilson thinks he has disposed of the menace of compulsion when he attacks the idea of "state socialism." But is there any other type of socialism? True, there have been voluntary socialist colonies in the United States, but they have been kept from coercing or bulldozing people solely because there has been a route of escape from their walls into the free world outside. Similarly the "socialism" of the Scandinavian world has been kept palatable by the presence of a large free market outside of the socialist preserves of the state. In other words, socialism is only good when there is a going capitalist concern outside of it to keep it humane. The more capitalism there is, the more the check on the coercive aspects of socialism.

Mr. Wilson is not an economist. Economics is a "dismal science" to his completely literary way of thinking. Actually, Wilson's socialism is a pure verbal fetish. He really belongs to a tradition that either predates Marxism by a matter of decades or grew up alongside Marxism without much reference to it. His real animus against the modern world is Carlylean and Ruskinean—which is to say, he looks back to an aristocratic order of society. Wilson is, *au fond,* an aesthetic critic of capitalism. But capitalism doesn't have to be nonaesthetic any more than it has to be vegetarian. To the extent that people develop aesthetic tastes, capitalism is perfectly willing to cater to such tastes. The willingness to give people what they want, to satisfy the consumer, is what justifies capitalism. Witness the case of Wilson's "real canned sardines," which were made and sold in the marketplace because people wanted to buy and eat them.

There may be something to Wilson's hunger for an aristocratic pre-capitalist world. Certainly the old aristocratic order knew the virtues of craftsmanship. But, as Ludwig von Mises is fond of pointing out, only six million people could make their living by the practice of their various crafts in an aristocratic, pre-capitalist England. By going over to capitalism, England was able to increase her population to forty-two million. Wilson is entitled to his preferences for the good old days, but is he willing to ordain the liquidation of thirty-six million Englishmen to get back to them? The answer is no; yet in spite of his no, Wilson is unwilling to question the ultimate reference points of his own snarled-up philosophy.

10
Whangdoodle Mencken

January 22, 1951

On a hot August day in 1906, old Colonel Henry Watterson, the ebullient editor of the *Louisville Courier-Journal*, came across a gaily impertinent reference to himself on the editorial page of the ordinarily stodgy *Baltimore Sun*. Amazed by the unexpected discovery, Marse Henry replied in kind. "Think of it!" he said. "The staid old *Baltimore Sun* has got itself a Whangdoodle. Nor is it one of those bogus Whangdoodles . . . but a genuine, guaranteed, imported [article] direct from the mountains of Hepsidam."

The Whangdoodle which so delighted Marse Henry was, of course, H. L. Mencken, and the incident is worth setting down here for the simple reason that an even newer Whangdoodle has been fledged out of contact with the old. The newest Whangdoodle is William Manchester, whose biography of Mencken, *Disturber of the Peace*, is worthy in every way of its engrossing subject. Mr. Manchester is all of twenty-eight years old and this is his first published book. With a background of graduate school work at the University of Missouri and police reporting in Oklahoma City, Manchester is eminently qualified to deal with the combination of opposites that is H. L. Mencken. Manchester writes with the verve of a Sonja Henie doing a pirouette on her skate points; he has the true Mencken delight in burlesque and in outrageous overstatement delivered as if it were understatement of the severest kind. Yet for all his Menckenian qualities, Manchester manages to maintain a distinct style of his own—a miraculous performance for one who has had such a prolonged immersion in that most contagious of all contagions, the prose style of Henry Louis Mencken.

When a young Whangdoodle comes to grips with a gaffer of the species, one is tempted to call out a brass band and go parading through the streets. But let us not go completely overboard in eulogy of the subject of Manchester's biography. Let us eulogize where eulogy is due and then turn to the reservations. H. L. Mencken was undoubtedly the chief liberator of my own college generation in the early twenties. We had read Van Wyck Brooks's *America's Coming of Age;* we had pondered Randolph Bourne's *Adventures of a Literary Radical;* we had listened to William Lyon Phelps's praise of Dostoevski, Tolstoy, Shaw, and Ibsen; we had harkened to the strident clamor of the Chicago Renascence; we had skittered down to Greenwich Village seeking a glimpse of the red tresses of Edna Millay; we had followed the peregrinations of Floyd Dell's callow Felix Fays and "emancipated" Janet Marches. But it was H. L. Mencken who waved his maestro's wand over the whole engaging spectacle, holding the symphonic voices of the goofy but incredibly vital epoch to concert pitch. The intellectual Toscanini of the twenties, he made the music of other men express a magic all his own. His *American Mercury* was the Bible of the campuses, and even the anti-Menckenites of the average college faculty had an occasional grudging good word to say for Mencken's great exploratory study, *The American Language.*

Mencken laughed at politics, of course, and we all laughed with him. But our laughter was subtly different from Mencken's own. What we failed to realize was that the Mencken guffaw had Voltairean undertones. It stemmed in good part from an outraged appreciation of true libertarian political principles, not from mere love of watching the clowns behave idiotically in the anterooms of Capitol Hill. Mencken had read his Jefferson, his John Stuart Mill, and we had not. All we did was to laugh, distrusting any and all principles, whether libertarian or other. The upshot of it was that we had nothing substantial in our backgrounds to save us in 1929 and 1933. Bare and shivering in the economic blizzard, we rushed for any shelter available. Some of us ducked for a tent called Technocracy, lured by the barking voice of the shaman-engineer Howard Scott. Others fell for any one of thirty varieties of neo-Marxian flapdoodle; the then *New Republican* Edmund Wilson, for example, proposed in all seriousness that we "take communism away from the Communists." (As if that would improve the flavor.)

Now, Mencken was not responsible for our more obscene political divagations; he never made any pretense of being his brother's keeper. Whether responsible or not, however, he did hurt us by diverting our attention from the literature of political and economic freedom. As Manchester points out, Mencken was actually a very civilized Tory; but the college generations of the twenties mistook him for a nihilistic anarchist. We thought he was merely kidding when he extolled the "Maryland Free State" and spoke of solacing himself with the state papers of Thomas Jefferson; actually, he meant every word of his praise of the Free State's Jeffersonian past. He had his Platonic notion of the Good Society, his image of the "great good place," shining securely in the back of his mind all along.

Because he had firmly grounded political principles he could not possibly fall for the intellectual zigzagging of the Rooseveltian witch doctors. And if he failed to keep the specifically Menckenian generations of the twenties on the right track by any positive preaching of civilized Tory (or John Stuart Mill liberal) political principles, he at least had imparted a sufficient skepticism to enable them to climb out from the Rooseveltian morass by themselves. It took time for many of the boys and girls of the twenties to extricate themselves from the Marxian and Keynesian heresies of the thirties, but no one who had taken Mencken's laughter to heart in his youth could possibly remain the devoted servant of a New Deal that could leap nimbly from NRA collectivism to Brandeisean trustbusting to price fixing and OPA-ism without ever perceiving the philosophical stultification and dishonesty involved in such chaotic behavior. If Mencken helped by an oversight to mislead a whole host of Menckenians in the twenties, his staunch individualism, which is at last reappearing above ground in a hundred places, may yet save the Republic—and with it, the world.

Manchester draws the moral of Mencken's life only in terms of image; the reader must get the preachment by inference. But no one with a particle of wit can possibly mistake Manchester's implied recommendations. *Disturber of the Peace* is a book to be pondered; one hopes in particular that the young men and women of the forties, the boys and girls who know Mencken only as a philologist and a writer of *gemütlich* reminiscences for the *New Yorker*, will take William Manchester's exhumations to their hearts.

Manchester's portrait of *le maître* is a deftly shaded one; the whole man emerges in all his wonderfully intricate contradictions. Mencken scoffed at the cow colleges, yet he himself first practiced writing by enrolling at a correspondence school. He denounced cultists of all sorts, yet he was a secret fresh-air fiend who slept religiously for years on a cold and draughty porch that would have frightened the most hardened member of the Byrd Antarctic expedition. He laughed at all schools of organized faith, but when he visited Rome he kissed the ring of the pope. He denounced the ancestor worshipers of the DAR, yet he spent a comparative fortune to have his own Saxon ancestry traced by a firm that specialized in such research. A man who had won renown as America's most defiant bachelor, he married late in life and proved the most devoted of husbands. He shocked the bourgeois deliberately and without end, yet all his habits were bourgeois in the extreme. He loved order, he loved sedentary comforts, and he rated the American bathroom more highly than he rated the Acropolis.

For one who spent the twenties in crib and highchair, William Manchester has a most remarkable grasp of Mencken's whole background. I detect only one wrong emphasis in *Disturber of the Peace*, and that is in his treatment of the late Stuart Sherman. Manchester seems to think that Sherman remained more or less an anti-Menckenite until the end. The fact of the matter is, Sherman deserted the More–Babbitt New Humanist group some time before assuming editorial direction of the *New York Herald Tribune Books* in the mid-twenties. Sherman spent the later years of his life praising the very authors whom Mencken and George Jean Nathan had first brought out in the *Smart Set* in the decade of World War I. In fact, Sherman became more Menckenian than Mencken in his latter-day tastes; he continued to praise Theodore Dreiser, Sherwood Anderson, D. H. Lawrence, Floyd Dell, and other fully certified incendiaries long after Mencken had lost interest in the fiction of the New Day.

This review has not touched on Mencken's virtues as an editor (for example, he mailed contributions back within twenty-four hours); it has not dealt with him as Baltimore's greatest journalist; it has not gone into details of the great Mencken–Nathan collaboration; and it has had nothing to say about Mencken's quarrel with the Boston censor and innumerable related Pecksniffs. All I can say in defense of my own narrow selectivity is that one can no more stuff Mencken into a few columns of type than one could stuff Bushman, the great ape of Chicago, into a match box. The man is protean; even in the "prime of senility" (to use his own phrase from a letter to A. G. Keller), he casts an immense shadow. One hopes that Manchester's biography of Baltimore's most eminent citizen will have at least one reader for every original phrase that Mencken coined in fifty years of his hell-for-leather journalistic life.

11
Mark Twain's Fancy Language

October 1950

A perennial reader of *Huckleberry Finn*, I have always reveled in the limpid colloquialism of the author who beyond anyone else set the syntax and rhythm of the modern American literary language. It was with a shock, therefore, that I encountered some pretty highfalutin language a while ago when I was reading *Tom Sawyer* to my two daughters. The highfalutin stuff—such as Mark Twain's ponderous announcement that Tom and Huck and Joe Harper "hovered upon the imminent verge of sleep"—occurred not in Tom's own conversations, but in the purely narrative passages. It seemed ironical, however, to catch Twain using elegant diction in a kid's book.

The children, surprisingly enough, were not aware of the irony. In fact, they lapped up the verbal elegance without a single question. The next night, listening to the ornate prose of *Sinbad the Sailor*, they absorbed some really fancy language. It was at this point that I jumped to the conclusion that maybe the modern pedagogues don't know what they are doing when they stress age graduations of appropriate vocabulary going from the simple to the complex. Probably Rudyard Kipling knew far more about childish tastes when he invented the magnificently resplendent highfalutinisms that stud the *Just-So Stories*. And presumably there is a good psychological reason why *Tom Sawyer* is a kid's book whereas *Huckleberry Finn*, the pure stuff of colloquialism, is for grownups—say, for Sherwood Anderson and Ernest Hemingway. Twain's instinct is a guide to sound pedagogy: titillate the nine-year-olds with talk about the "unimaginable splendor" of Tom

Sawyer's daydreams, but give the adults Huck Finn's complaints about having his hair combed all to thunder.

12
God in a Compost Heap

December 25, 1950

Some years ago I wrote a rhymed review of the seed catalogues and subscribed myself the Squire of Soursoil Farm. Whereupon Mr. E. B. White of the *New Yorker,* who loves a good compost heap only slightly less than he loves the pavement of West Forty-fifth Street, complained that anyone whose soil was sour had only himself to blame. I could only say, "Touché."

Well, the years have passed, and I can now report to White that the Chamberlain garden is all he could desire. Practically everything has gone into it, from horse-hoof parings to the ash content of a decade of subscriptions to the *New Yorker.* I wish I could say that I had done everything according to that Hoyle of gardeners, Sir Albert Howard, whose *The Soil and Health: A Study of Organic Agriculture* is perhaps the classic exposition of how to utilize vegetable and animal wastes in restoring land to good heart. Sir Albert, who learned the secrets of composting old vegetable matter from the Chinese and from the Hunza tribesmen of northwestern India, counsels a most scientific blending of elements in the manufacture of humus for the garden. But Sir Albert is a professional, which means that he has time to spare for his specialty. The amateur who has only weekends to devote to gardening must hit upon a rule-of-thumb (preferably a rule-of-green-thumb) adaptation of Sir Albert's micrometer precision if he is to save both his vegetables and his sanity and still have time for swimming and tennis and reading and a thousand other things for which the proper weekend should be reserved.

When I first began to garden I listened to grandpa's "practical" advice. I pursued weeds relentlessly, ripping even the tiniest patch of purslane from between the rows. My back ached from bending over, and I got blisters from the hoe. Then one summer I went away for three weeks in late July and early August. The latter part of the three-week period happened to be a time of bad drought. I came home from vacation expecting to see the garden burned to a crisp. Strangely enough, however, I had wonderful tomatoes. They nestled down among some high weeds which had gotten a good start before the drought had come. The weeds had kept the tomatoes cool in the hot afternoons. On the other hand, my neighbors who had stripped their gardens of weeds had very poor tomatoes. I concluded then and there that it was a mistake to weed fastidiously. But I never had any scientific answer to gardeners who insisted that weeds rob the contiguous vegetables of both the food supply and the proper moisture. All I had was some empirical observation, to which I added in subsequent years.

It was not until this past fortnight that I learned that science in the matter of weeds is on my side, not on the side of some of my neighbors. Joseph A. Cocannouer, who teaches botany at the University of Oklahoma, has just published a book called *Weeds: Guardians of the Soil,* which actually advocates allowing a certain number of "mother" weeds to flourish in the vegetable patch. Weed roots, says Dr. Cocannouer, are deep divers; they penetrate deep into the subsoil and bring minerals up to the surface, where tomato and cabbage roots can make use of them. They also make channels into the deeper earth where corn roots, for example, can follow their probings. A pigweed growing in a potato hill will not rob the potato plant of nourishment. It will, on the contrary, loosen the soil around the potato plant and thus enable the potato roots to spread into crevices which they could not normally reach.

Naturally, Professor Cocannouer does not advocate drowning one's vegetables in weeds; he merely advocates cultivating the science of "weed control." My own method of weed control probably derived from laziness as much as from anything else. Like other amateur gardeners, I read Edward Faulkner's *Plowman's Folly* when it came out a decade back. The Faulkner recipe for garden success, as the reader will remember, is to leave all the trash—dead weeds, old sunflower stalks, last year's raked-up leaves, any old thing of an organic nature—around the plants and between the rows. Trash isn't pretty, but it keeps moisture in the soil and provides a continual decomposing supply of fertilizing elements. This business of trash farming is the logical extension of E. B. White's perennial effort to discover God in the compost heap. It completes the so-called nitrogen cycle right where it begins: in the garden itself.

In his zeal to keep the trash on the garden surface, Faulkner is against plowing, which turns up bare soil to blow and wash away. This makes admirable sense from the point of view of abstract theory. But as anyone who has tried to work an unplowed field can tell Faulkner, plowing is a necessary evil. You simply cannot get anywhere in spring with a field that has been merely combed by a harrow; the weeds and last year's stubble still remain a refractory element that is enough to break down the strength of a Tarzan.

Nevertheless, the basic Faulkner idea can be preserved even with plowing. The trick is to plow, then get a new cover of trash on the garden as soon as plowing and planting are done. My own method has been to plow, then plant, then throw a blanket of hay, straw, dead leaves or whatever between the rows. The hay keeps the weeds from growing during the early part of the summer. Rain, of course, will slip through a porous trash blanket, so there is no worry on that score.

A fair proportion of weeds will eventually push through a surface clutter of trash, but the weeds will not be thick—and one can control them easily by thinning out the weed growth that threatens to suffocate any given plant. Long before the Joe-Pye is up in August, the corn and tomatoes will be big enough to go it on their own no matter what the weeds may do. By use of a trash blanket I have gotten by with little weed-pulling and a minimum of labor with the hoe. As a rule-of-thumb proposition, I should say that it is a mistake to touch a weed after July 25 or August 1. If you are afraid that you won't get enough tomatoes under this system, just put in a few extra plants. As for lettuce, it will last well into the summer if it is permitted to hide a bit in the shade of a thin forest of ragweed.

When it comes to composting, which is the standard way of developing humus for the garden surface, I am afraid that I would never have the patience to follow the advice offered by Sir Albert

Howard in *The Soil and Health* or by Leonard Wickenden in his fascinating *Make Friends with Your Land.* The so-called Indore process of making compost which is advocated by Sir Albert and Mr. Wickenden involves piling dead leaves, garbage, grass cuttings, weeds and animal manures in a pit. The pit must be wet down from time to time, and its contents must be turned at intervals to help speed the mysterious magic of decay. To build a good compost heap takes two years of piling and turning; then it must be lugged in a wheelbarrow (a deplorably clumsy conveyance) to the garden. The labor involved in all this may be commendable, but where is the garden-loving commuter who has time for it?

My own lazy-man's method of saving vegetable waste is to dump it directly onto the garden throughout most of the year. True, it is unsightly, but in a vegetable garden, as distinct from a flower border along a driveway, it is the produce alone that counts. Anyway, once the corn is tall it hides old beet tops and orange peels that are dumped on the inside rows. During the long winter months the snow covers ugly grapefruit rinds, and by the time the snow is off the ground in March the rinds have bleached to an inoffensive, neutral brownish white. In April they can be plowed under, thus infiltrating decaying vegetable matter into the ground directly without putting it through the laborious composting process. By the time a second April has rolled around the orange and grapefruit skins have become dark humus. The plow that Faulkner scorns then turns this humus up to the surface, where it becomes available plant food. Some value may have been lost by burying the trash with the plow, for undersurface leaching undoubtedly carries good minerals down into the subsoil; and a buried grapefruit rind may stop moisture from rising by capillary action to plant roots near the surface of the garden. But in gardening you must balance loss against gain and settle for the best compromise that is available. At any rate, it is comforting to learn from Dr. Cocannouer's book on weeds that the deep roots of the ragweed will pull the leached minerals to the surface again.

No doubt my own approach to weeds and humus will be set down as shiftless by E. B. White, who is never happy unless his own compost pile is as tall as a young Maine pine. Nevertheless, my garden patch grows richer with the years. We eat well all summer, and enjoy fresh kale and brussels sprouts direct from the garden even into mid-December. We also have good frozen stuff for the winter. A pleasant and nourishing dinner table, not a comely garden surface or a completely scientific approach to composting, strikes me as the main reason for raising food. (Incidentally, for E. B. White's benefit, I do compost my maple leaves directly alongside my garden, but not in a pit.)

A final bit on weeds: there are weeds which the Japanese beetle prefers even to soybean plants and tender corn silk. A few of these weeds left standing in your garden will play the part of the lightning rod in deflecting the bolt from the thing you want to preserve. Dr. Cocannouer has not gone into the subject of offering weed hostages to save one's corn and soybeans. But he does have a few fascinating pages on the kinds of weeds that may be picked and used for human foods. Purslane—or "pusley"—grows so well in my garden that I am glad to know that it can be considered as a food crop in itself. As Indian John, Dr. Cocannouer's Pawnee friend, says, "All wild plants good. Indian eat 'em and live long time!"

13
Throwing Away a Victory

December 11, 1950

The last war was fought by the Western democracies to rid the world of a tyrant. It was fought to save Poland from extinction. It was fought to keep Manchuria from being engulfed by a totalitarian power. It was fought to preserve the Open Door in the Far East. It was fought because of Cordell Hull's sense of obligation toward Chiang Kai-shek. It was fought to stop genocide. It was fought to save the world from statism. It was fought to put an end to the economic policies of autarchy. It was fought to relieve the democracies of the burden of militarism.

Every one of these aims was a noble aim. But the raw, rude facts of 1950 are an ironic reminder that it takes more than zeal, more than military power, more than the recital of winged phrases, to win a war. It also takes brains applied to the proper understanding of man and his history.

For lack of brains, for lack of a proper understanding of man and his history, World War II has become a lost crusade. The world is still threatened by a tyrant. Poland has been extinguished. Manchuria has been engulfed by a totalitarian power. The Open Door in the Far East has been slammed shut. Chiang Kai-shek has been kicked around like a dog. Genocide is a policy, somewhat disguised to be sure, of the Soviet Union, which kills Jews for being "stateless cosmopolitans." The world is lurching steadily toward the final rigor mortis of extreme statism. Economic autarchy reigns practically everywhere, despite the incantations of those who still hope to check it by "most-favored-nation" clauses negotiated in marginal fields that have little effect on the main issues of foreign trade. As for militarism, the costs of armament are rising every day.

How did the United States and Great Britain manage to throw away a great victory in such an incredibly short span of time? The story is told in two recent books, William Henry Chamberlin's *America's Second Crusade,* and Hanson W. Baldwin's *Great Mistakes of the War.* And the cream of the bitter jest is that neither Chamberlin nor Baldwin has written out of hindsight. They both knew what was to be expected from the policy of "unconditional surrender." They both knew that coalitions seldom outlast the disappearance of the common enemy. Mr. Baldwin ran up his warning signals about the fallacy of total war periodically in the *New York Times.* Mr. Chamberlin, though he could command no regular daily pulpit, fought a brilliant guerrilla battle for the truth in publications as diverse as the socialist *New Leader,* the "isolationist" *Chicago Tribune,* the capitalist *Wall Street Journal,* and the humanely traditionalist *Human Events.*

If Messrs. Chamberlin and Baldwin had been the only sources of enlightenment during the days when official Washington presumed to be the keeper of every intellectual's conscience, there might have been some excuse for muffing the victory of 1945. After all, Chamberlin and Baldwin were merely journalists—and journalists, as we are told in season and out, are catch-as-catch-can fellows who fail to meet the stern requirements of scholarship in depth. Franklin D. Roosevelt, on the other hand, enjoyed a widespread reputation among the idolatrous for being a profound student of history. No doubt he did know a lot about the party battles of the Jackson period and the life stories of Commodore Perry and John Paul Jones. But as for the fundamental dynamics of history, which are compounded of ideas and morals acting on force and vice versa, Mr. Roosevelt knew little or nothing. It so happens that in the early forties the great trilogy of Guglielmo Ferrero on war and peace was available to American readers in translation. Ferrero's searching and canny study of the Napoleonic cycle of wars and the subsequent peace of Vienna was a brilliant refutation of the whole theory of unconditional surrender and total war. Did Harry Hopkins ever expose himself to

Ferrero's ideas? Did Roosevelt ever ask a braintruster to digest them for him? If there is any record to such effect it is a record of a vaccination that didn't take.

Ferrero was, indeed, pondered seriously by Walter Lippmann in the late thirties and early forties. But Lippmann, for some unaccountable reason, forgot his own principles as World War II drew to a close. The author of *The Good Society*, a book which conclusively proved that a stable peace is a function of limited government, private-property economics and limited warfare fought to a conditional conclusion, turned his back on Ferrero just as history was about to endorse the soundness of the great Italian's ideas. With no publicist of importance taking up for Ferrero, it is scarcely to be wondered at that our peacemakers were cut off from a wisdom that might have saved them.

The peacemakers of 1945 were more rootless than even the most superficial of journalists. Victims of modernist education, they knew no rules of human action. Nor did they bother to read the Leninist tracts that govern the policies of Soviet Russia and the Comintern. Our Hopkinses and Winants and Stettiniuses were not even aware that Stalin was a Marxist. When Stalin acted as such after Yalta it came as the rudest sort of jolt to official Washington. Dean Acheson can't believe it yet.

William Henry Chamberlin knew about communism, which is the parent of fascism, from long experience in Moscow as a *Christian Science Monitor* correspondent. But he was an irreverent man in the presence of panjandrumry and guff. When he warned the United States to be wary of the hidden aims of its Muscovite ally, he was looked upon as a saboteur of Grand Alliance spirit, a "hang-back boy," to use the lingo of the period. His chapter "Wartime Illusions and Delusions," however, is a vigorous refutation of the theory that you must believe in the organization policies of hell when you are staking one devil to fight another.

Both Mr. Chamberlin and Mr. Baldwin knew from their reading of history that the doctrine of unconditional surrender leads to the creation of a power vacuum and a consequent serious disturbance of the balance of power. They also knew that the vacuums created in central Europe and East Asia by the complete atomization of German and Japanese society would invite a swift expansion by the Soviet Union, which, since it is on a permanent war footing, must live by expansion or die. It was fashionable in 1945 to argue that we could not afford to allow Hitler or the Japanese warlords to set the conditions of surrender. But it was not a question of dealing with either Hitler or the Japanese warlords. As Chamberlin shows, there was a well-organized anti-Hitler underground in Germany ready to rise and deal with us the moment we gave the proper signal. We could have gotten rid of Hitler, Goebbels and Co., by a mere nod of the head. In the case of Japan, we did offer conditional surrender at the twenty-fifth hour, the "condition" being that the Japanese be allowed to keep their symbol of governmental legitimacy and continuity, Emperor Hirohito.

Both Chamberlin and Baldwin think we should have eschewed the landing in southern France and the later stages of the Italian campaign in favor of a landing in force in the Balkans. They also think we should have made peace with a thoroughly defeated Japan before Soviet Russia had a chance to move in force into Manchuria. If we had done these two things we might have limited the Soviet Union to a purely defensive victory—which is certainly all it deserved after signing the Nazi–Soviet Pact of 1939. But we were not thinking of postwar realities in 1944 and 1945; we were thinking of the moment—and of myth. Because we forgot that war is a political as well as a military act, we lost the war politically. A witty man quoted by William Henry Chamberlin has said that Hitler won his war—in the person of Stalin. Only the most obdurate and lunkheaded of fools could doubt either the truth or the wit of this remark after digesting the full import of what Mr. Chamberlin and Mr. Baldwin have to say.

14
A New Beginning?

March 12, 1951

Arthur Koestler is a representative symbol of a tortured age. An ex-revolutionary, he now knows that the Russian "experiment" has become a ghastly error. But he can't quite bring himself to see that the cause of the error is to be found, not in Stalin's personality or the peculiar circumstances of Russian history, but in the basic idea of socialism itself.

Driven by an understandable urge to justify his own revolutionary past, Koestler tends to glorify the ex-Communist. In Koestler's eyes only those who have been through hell with an about-to-backslide Intourist guide are properly equipped to understand the manifold wiles of the devil. But the ex-Communists whom Koestler trusts invariably turn out to be those who hang in a contemporary philosophical void. They are the ones who seem to cherish the myth of the New Beginning, not the ones who have found their way back to the principles of Jefferson, or of John Locke, or of the early John Stuart Mill, or of the expounders of the Christian gospel. The idea that an old credo might very possibly be a true one is a Chestertonian notion which Koestler cannot consciously admit. He is still a believer in the Great Change, still a socialist millennialist. The only faith he could wholeheartedly accept is the one that will be born the day after tomorrow and tricked out in a whole new set of words.

The myth of the New Beginning hangs over Koestler's latest novel, *The Age of Longing*, robbing it of whatever cutting edge it might have had. Like Orwell, Koestler has chosen to write of the future. But the future of *The Age of Longing* is the near mid-fifties and the scene is a Paris that is all too forlornly contemporary in its flavor. Koestler has no love for the gruesome emissaries of the Commonwealth of Freedom-Loving People (that is, the Soviet government) who are busy softening up his beloved Paris for the kill. But the west Europeans of Koestler's tale are too sunk in defeatism, apathy, sloth and spiritual nullity to rally for a last-ditch fight. As for the Americans, they are portrayed by Koestler as innocent and shallow creatures who scarcely understand the magnitude of the crisis that confronts them. Symbolically, the rather appealing American heroine of Koestler's story, Hydie Anderson, misses her aim when she sets out to kill Fedya Nikitin, the New Barbarian from the Black Town of Baku. Hydie means well, but she doesn't have what it takes to play in the same league with Joan of Arc, Rosa Luxemburg and Charlotte Corday. Because she is not a true anti-Stalinist hepcat of the ex-Communist breed, Hydie cannot even carry through a good symbolic gesture of world-saving. If the world is to be saved at all, so Koestler seems to be saying in effect, it will not be by the Americans, but by some new monastic order of a still unfledged twenty-first-century religion. This New Beginning must wait, of course, upon the decaying phase of the Dark Age which Stalin began circa 1927.

What distresses me about Koestler's novel is not its pessimism about the contemporary French effort to survive—after all, the man may be right in his theories about Europe's decadence, which correspond to William S. Schlamm's as set forth in an early issue of the *Freeman.* Koestler may even be right about America's "little and late" psychosis, which is a reflex of its congenital optimism. To justify the case for Koestler's pessimism, it is obvious that Western Europe doesn't at the moment seem to have any sense of urgency about rearming. As for the Americans, they seem to misconceive the whole crisis as a problem of advertising the future disposition of their troops, not of creating a compact power to be thrown against Stalin wherever the battle may be joined. (The decisive field may very well be in Iran, where there is oil; not in a Western Europe which can supply little fuel for the planes that Stalin must use to overpower his abiding enemy, the U.S.A.)

The root trouble with Koestler's novel is not the author's pessimism about French rearmament and American brains, but his inability to see that the old faiths of the West are plenty good enough to throw back the Mechanical Men from the East. Whatever the verbal symbolisms for its affirmations (and they are as many and as richly diverse as might be expected from an individualistic people), the West has always believed that man is something more than the sum of his conditioned reflexes. Even those Westerners who are superficially enamored of the idea of "social engineering" do not really believe that the human personality is to be placed at the mercy of political shamans who would experiment with it in the interests of that consuming Moloch which goes by the deceptively innocent name of "society." When Koestler's Hydie Anderson refuses to let her Russian lover, Fedya Nikitin, reduce her to the level of one of Pavlov's dogs, she is acting as any self-respecting Western girl would act. Her rejection of Nikitin is far more prophetic of the American ability to survive and win than Koestler himself sees.

Because of his contempt for some of the surface manifestations of American life (our preoccupation with gadgetry, our mania for decrying both harmless eccentricity and original thought in the interests of a streamlined conception of good "public relations"), Koestler misses the deeper currents that move the American Republic. One of his characters argues flatly that America has produced no Maid of Orleans, no Madame Curie, no Krupskaya, no Brontë sisters, no Florence Nightingale. So? Well, what about Emily Dickinson, Clara Barton, Mrs. Whittaker Chambers (a *decent* Krupskaya), Mrs. Marcus Whitman, and the thousands of unsung American women who followed their men into Pawnee and Blackfoot country with the full knowledge that a single slip in vigilance might mean their scalps and the lives of their children? Even the Helen Hokinson woman, if cornered, is likely to be a tougher cougar than Koestler might believe.

If Koestler's novel leaves much to be desired so far as its fundamentals are concerned, it remains a most brilliant virtuoso performance on its coruscating surface. Who else has caught the flavor of the tragicomedy of contemporary French "intellectual" life in a way that compares with *The Age of Longing*? Koestler's satirical flaying of a milieu is absolutely dazzling. There is his Monsieur Anatole, the last representative of the culture that once skipped so blithely from republic to empire and back again without losing trust in the ultimate resilience of Gallic man. Monsieur Anatole suffers from paralysis, a collapsed prostate and cirrhosis of the liver, but even though his animal appetites have long since been dulled to a mere echo inside the skull, his intellectual skepticism is made palatable by continuing animal faith.

Not so with the people who come to Monsieur Anatole's parties. There is Dupremont, the fashionable pornographer, who tries to lure people to religion by baiting his books with lechery. There are Touraine, the opportunist publisher, and Professor Pontieux, the apostle of "neo-nihilism" (Koestler's parody of existentialism). Other *dans cette galère* include Navarin, the poet; Father Millet, the priest who rather enjoys having naughty things whispered about him; Georges de St. Hilaire, the Malraux-type novelist; and Lord Edwards, the British physicist who obligingly alters his mathematical equations to prove the case for an expanding or a contracting universe depending on whatever Soviet cosmology happens to be in favor with Stalin at the moment. These characters, and others like them, are either attracted or repelled by the Soviet magnet, but, since they are all utterly blah, it doesn't matter which way they point.

The ex-revolutionaries of Koestler's novel are a more respectable breed. The limping Julien Delattre, who lost his faith and his ability to write revolutionary poems when the Popular Front gave way to the Ribbentrop–Molotov pact, retains a few shreds of human dignity; at least he knows that Soviet communism is evil and wants to do something positive to combat its spread. Boris, the walking cadaver who has survived the forced-labor camp and the liquidation of his wife and child, may be mad, but he is nonetheless an heroic figure. As for Professor Vardi, who decides to take a chance on going home to Eastern Europe after the death of Number One (Koestler's euphemism for good old Joe), he is pitiful in this delusion that a new life may possibly await him as a teacher at the University of Viennograd. (Of course it doesn't; Vardi ends up by "confessing" participation in a "treason" plot, like any other victim of "darkness at noon.")

With the Stalinist barbarians Koestler is also brilliant. Nikitin is fully explained by his childhood in the black oil town of Baku and his subsequent adolescence as a priggish Komsomol. Nikitin's faith in a sort of cyberneticist's view of Marxism is made all too horribly palpable as Koestler really hits his writing stride. Like others of his tribe, Nikitin believes in liquidation as ordained by the selection of, say, the top ten percent of "socially unreliable elements" by the mechanical decree of an IBM punch card winnower. In Nikitin's perverse pharmacopoeia there is no psychic illness that a good reconditioning of the reflexes cannot cure.

In the last analysis, the excellence of Koestler's characterization in *The Age of Longing* varies inversely with the intensity of his hatred. He is first-rate with Nikitin and with the backslid Hero of Culture Leontiev, and he is good with his various French types. But he maligns his American girl, Hydie Anderson, by making her a twentieth-century version of Henry James's Daisy Miller. Just because Hydie proved a deficient marksman when she hit Nikitin in the groin, not the heart, is no reflection on the quality of the determination that could very well have been hers in the light of her tangled inheritance and background. Koestler seems to think it a reflection on her will simply because she hadn't been trained to shoot by Annie Oakley. After all, Koestler might have stopped to reflect that a dedicated Russian intransigent, Dora Kaplan, botched the job when she shot at Lenin.

Thousands will enjoy *The Age of Longing* for its sheer brilliance. Thousands more will be put off by the curious fact that virtually everybody in the book spouts dazzling dialectics with the glib agility of Koestler himself. And thousands more, I predict, will discover that reading the book is comparable to peeling an onion: at the very core of the firm, pearly layers one opens up on—nothing. Mr. Koestler has parodied the "neo-nihilists," but in his refusal to bottom himself on the enduring truths of Western faith he is in danger of becoming the neo-nihilist *malgré lui,* and hence a more pitiful creature than his own Professor Pontieux.

15
Icarian America

March 26, 1951

A little more than a hundred years ago, in the Paris that was then working itself into the emotional frenzy that led to the 1848 revolution, a Frenchman named Etienne Cabet wrote a utopian novel called *Voyage en Icarie.* I remember reading the work in the New York Public Library in the midst of the 1929 depression. Outside the library seedy-looking men were selling apples on the street corners and newsboys were hawking the latest edition of the latest story about Wall Street bankers jumping out of windows. The reason I was reading Cabet had a direct connection with the mood of the times. I was then busy writing *Farewell to Reform,* a book that owed its impetus to my feeling (fortunately transient) that the human race was not up to practicing the rather exacting self-discipline that is demanded of free men in a free system. I needed to know about *Voyage en Icarie* because it was the forerunner of our own Edward Bellamy's *Looking Backward,* the novel that moved so many public figures of the 1880s (including novelist William Dean Howells) to embrace a Yankee version of the communist idea.

To me, *Voyage en Icarie* was a horrifying literary experience. What it did was to present the barrack state as the Kingdom of God on earth. Cabet's Icaria was the logical extension into peacetime of Napoleon Bonaparte's idea of the conscripted nation-in-arms. The industries of Icaria were all nationalized and run by a committee of bureaucrats and engineers. Everyone in Icaria was forced to work; people wore uniforms; the state was the sole employer, the sole arbiter of education and morals. What passed for "public opinion" was dispensed by government publications in the guise of news.

The sobering thing about *Voyage en Icarie* is that it became an actuality for one-sixth of the earth's land surface some time in the third decade of the twentieth century. For what is Soviet Russia but the actual projection of Cabet's Napoleonic fantasy? Far more accurately than Marx, who didn't have the brains or the imagination to draw logical deductions from his own benighted economic notions, Cabet had called the ultimate turn of the radical movements that grew out of the turmoil of his own time. If the realization of *Voyage en Icarie* had been limited to Soviet Russia, the allegedly freedom-loving people of the West might have protected themselves by manning the eastern marches of Europe with a force devoted to quarantining the Icarian plague. Unfortunately for the idea of quarantine, however, the Icarian ideas began sprouting all over the West in the 1920s and the 1930s. Mussolini produced his own Icaria in Italy; Hitler founded an Icaria on the rubble of the Weimar Republic in Germany. In England the Fabians worked assiduously to create a Fabian Icaria, with Sidney Webb as its improbable Cabet; in the United States Franklin D. Roosevelt experimented with his own Yankee Doodling Icarian devices ranging from the NRA to that adolescent "work army" known as the CCC. (Incidentally, when Eleanor Roosevelt advocates "national service" for the young, she is trumpeting an Icarian idea.)

The terrifying ubiquity of the Icarian dream (parade-ground order everywhere, and everyone sacrificed to the goose-step) has inspired a George Orwell to write his blood-chilling *1984*, a projection of Icarian principles on a grandly universalized scale. All of us, says Orwell in effect, are foredoomed to become citizens of Icaria, eating strawberries and liking them even though they give us the hives. If this indeed be true (and what statesmen, what nations, have the fortitude or the principles to stop it?), the great problem of the future will be how to overthrow an absolute tyranny over the human mind and heart. (The bees and the ants haven't been able to do it; will men fare any better?)

My colleague in the next room, Henry Hazlitt, is the first brave soul to hazard an answer to this problem. (Comes the Icarian revolution in America and Hazlitt will be the first to be marched to the guillotine.) Mr. Hazlitt's answer is embodied in a witty and challenging work of fiction called *The Great Idea*. This novel, which combines the titillation of an Edward Bellamy romance with the solid educational virtues of a good Socratic dialogue on economics, might be taken as the utopian novel to end all utopian novels.

But let us have done for the moment with this talk of Utopia. Since it is the real world of the ages of Victoria and Grover Cleveland that has become the utopian dream of 1951, Hazlitt's opening chapters read like straight realism embellished with a grisly Hogarthian humor. The year, as Hazlitt's story commences, is 282 A.M. (after Marx), or 2100 by the old, forgotten bourgeois calendar. The world has long since been won by the Muscovite Communists (hence its new name, Wonworld), and all of the continents and the islands of the sea are run by a Politburo that is predominantly Russian. The Biggest Shot of All in the Politburo is a man known as Stalenin; his Number 2 is Bolshekov. Life in Wonworld is a regimented barrack life; the population is divided into "functional" groups like the society of a hive of bees. Everybody, or course, has a number; names are mere survivals of bourgeois individualism.

Since the histories, the novels, the economic treatises, the plays, and even the languages of ancient bourgeois life have all been destroyed in a series of great public bonfires, nobody remembers what free capitalism and representative government were like. Rebellion is an idea that occurs to nobody in the lesser "functional" groups of proletarians, for they have been conditioned by solemnly proclaimed "axioms" that have been drilled into them from birth. (The new universal language is Marxanto, which is so peculiarly constructed that logical precision leading to doubt is virtually impossible.)

This dreary state of affairs would have gone on until the planet froze if it had not been for a single mistake of dictator Stalenin. This monster had banished his wife and son to the Bermudas because of the strange delusion in Madame Stalenin's mind that Wonworld had betrayed the original faith of Marx. (Being of an upper "functional" group, Madame Stalenin had a glimmering idea that Marx could be interpreted in more than one way.) The son, Peter Uldanov, alone of all the youth of Wonworld, has escaped the conditioning process of Soviet "education"; strangely and unaccountably, he has been brought up on music, chemistry, physics and mathematics. (He even plays the old scores of a bourgeois composer named Mozart, one of the classical composers who escaped destruction in the cultural bonfires for the simple reason that certain musicians had memorized him and were in a position to pass the knowledge on to others. This was impossible in the case of Shakespeare, Goethe and other great literary artists: musical notation in Wonworld remained the same, but knowledge of languages such as English and German disappeared with the first generation that knew only Marxanto.)

Being an unconditioned youth when brought back to Moscow by an aging Stalenin, Peter Uldanov sees things with a preternaturally fresh eye. Accustomed to the bright colors of the Bermudas and the precise accents of music and mathematics, Peter knows that the continental orbits of Wonworld are drab, sad, ghoulish and idiotic. Since his father is bent on making him his successor as dictator, Peter resolves to do something about the situation when he gets the chance. Peter alone in Wonworld wants people to have freedom from fear. He alone wants them to think and decide for themselves.

Knowing nothing of the principles of freedom, Peter is forced to work by guess and by God—and by the logical precision of a mind trained in mathematics. He is opposed by Bolshekov, the malevolent Number 2 of the Politburo, but he has on his side a shrewd Yankee commissar named Adams. How Peter and Adams rediscover the principles of freedom, of private ownership, of the free market and of representative government is the burden of Mr. Hazlitt's tale. Progressively Peter and Adams hit upon all the "great ideas" that underlie the Western philosophy of the free individual in the free society. They rediscover the idea of money as a medium of exchange (and, later, as a store of value). They work their way back to the idea of value as a derivative of desire, as the expression of choice by individuals who have free will. They come to see that economic calculation is impossible in a socialist state. They learn why there has been no invention, no progress, in Wonworld since the last free capitalist government was wiped out. They learn why central planning and tyranny inevitably go together.

It is impossible in the short space of a review to give an adequate idea of the closeness of Henry Hazlitt's reasoning. All that I can say here is that in a series of remarkable colloquies between Peter and Adams, he proves the case for his "great idea" that the nearest we can come to Utopia on earth is to leave the individual free to exercise choice, the sole condition being that the individual will not use force or fraud to hurt others. Freedom of choice naturally implies the freedom to buy and sell in the open market, freedom to own tools of production, freedom to publish one's own newspaper or periodical, freedom to choose one's governmental representatives. The moment that we begin to trifle with controls (that is, with penalties for the exercise of freedom of choice) we are on the path that leads from Freeworld to Wonworld.

While the Socratic dialogues between Peter and Adams are the heart of *The Great Idea,* the economic matter is made easily digestible by the novelistic nature of the book. It may suffice here to say that Peter and Adams had to flee Moscow for America before they could put their "great idea" across. In America they were beyond the reach of Bolshekov's assassins. Even though they had been subjected and conditioned to Wonworld rule for decades, the Americans retained a queer creative bias that came to the surface the moment that Peter and Adams promulgated the idea of freedom to own and control land and productive equipment. They began quickly to outproduce Russia and Europe. With planes and guns pouring from their free factories, the Americans were soon in a position to take the offensive against Bolshekov's glum minions. And in the end, Freeworld became a worldwide state.

I have said that Mr. Hazlitt's book might be taken as the utopian novel to end utopian novels. But Hazlitt is a utopian only in a Pickwickian sense. An individualist can believe in competition between a million utopians, but never in the success of one. That way lies tyranny. It is high time we knew the utopian for the tyrant he is. What *The Great Idea* proves is that the utopian generally starts at the wrong end of things. He begins by trying to set up a universal framework into which all people must be fitted. Naturally the fitting process entails compulsions of a Procrustean nature. Mavericks must be disciplined; dissenters must be suppressed. As the late Benjamin Stolberg once said, "The devil always offers a closed system." And a closed system becomes a prison.

16
New York Publishing Circles

April 9, 1951

Sure, sure, Helen MacInnes's *Neither Five nor Three* is just a thriller. Sure, it has all the stigmata of the breed: the characterization that doesn't allow for hesitancies and contradiction, the tightly contrived plot, the spurts of melodrama, the black-and-white confrontation of good and evil, the presence of a cosmopolitan equivalent of the Lone Ranger, the final satisfying delivery of Right Girl into the arms of Right Boy. Still and all, I got a huge kick out of Miss MacInnes's story. Its plot may be just as preposterous as anything in Conan Doyle or Dorothy Sayers, yet it is a highly intelligent book—and considerably more "real," in its essence, than many a far more naturalistic novel about New York publishing circles.

What makes *Neither Five nor Three* a supremely relevant job for this particular moment is that it recognizes the Communist conspiracy for what it is: a consciously directed attempt to infiltrate every "commanding height" of our civilization, from the government bureaus of Washington to the last little corner of the "opinion industry" that has its center on Manhattan Island. Everyone who has worked in publishing circles in New York during the past two decades must know something of the essential story, yet most people who have run across the spoor of the comrades hesitate to talk about their experiences. For one thing, most Americans don't like to be bothered by the necessity of fighting a conspiracy. (That involves the boredom of creating counter-organizations, it means going to meetings and wasting time on something that cannot, by any remote possibility, be called a part of the happy life.) Second, the job of fighting Communists means that your character will be periodically assassinated, your reputation smeared. The comrades work by instilling fear; they achieve their greatest successes by the tacit cooperation of rabbits who are afraid to fight them.

In Miss MacInnes's story the threads are tied up and snipped off with a neatness that hardly corresponds with anything that has ever happened in actual life. Her heroic personages—Paul Haydn, the feature editor of *Trend;* Brownlee, the self-elected cooperator with the FBI; Jon Tyson, the honest college professor—click with the precision of Pinkerton agents. Her villains—Scott Ettley, the journalist who hates his father; Nicholas Orpen, the Communist watchdog assigned to the Manhattan "opinion industry" beat—go through their paces like Stakhanovites in a tractor factory. As for Rona Metford, the bright and pretty girl who gets involved in the social and ideological warfare between Paul Haydn and Ettley, she is just sufficiently opaque to the difference between hawk and handsaw to spin the tale out to required novel length.

It never happened in quite this mathematically balanced way in the places where I worked and encountered Communists in the thirties and the forties. When the Time, Inc., unit of the Newspaper Guild was penetrated and controlled by skilled manipulators of fellow-traveling mind, it took years of hesitant, half-committed jockeying to clean up the situation. Since nobody can "prove" anything about a Communist who is exempted from taking a party card, the struggle surged back and forth in an indecisive area. The victory was finally won, not by getting any Communists nailed for what they are, but by persuading unit rank-and-file members to stick around long enough at night to vote down the Communist Party line. No Orpens or Ettleys were ever, to my knowledge, disclosed at Time, Inc.—but it is noteworthy that certain people departed when their activities and ideological preferences became so obvious that even blind men could see what they were doing.

Could I prove that I have ever known a Communist? Since I've never laid eyes on a party card, it would be extremely difficult. (For that matter, I never see the moles that ruin my lawn save when my FBI cat brings one up to the light.) But if there haven't been any Commies around, who was it that tried to pressure me in the thirties to write sympathetically about the League of American

Writers? Who organized those cocktail parties that hooked us into giving money for Loyalist Spain? (Query: Did the money ever reach any anti-Stalinist Spanish Loyalist?) Why did I receive frantic letters urging me to get off the John Dewey Commission to investigate the charges made against Leon Trotsky in the Moscow purge trials? How come Commie sympathizers always seemed to be tipped off in advance when I was busy researching and writing something that went counter to their interests? I have no proof beyond what ex-Communists have told me, but when coincidences pile up year after year into a formation as clearly patterned as a crystal or a snowflake, it is impossible to see accident at work. A group of monkeys hitting at typewriters might accidentally write all the books in the British Museum once, but not twice.

Helen MacInnes has caught the signs and universal signature of the central struggle for the control points of Manhattan's opinion industries. She does some things magnificently—as, for example, her description of the heavily oppressive intellectual and emotional atmosphere of a fellow-traveling shindig in a Park Avenue apartment. What, we may ask parenthetically, would the comrades do without the support of the Park Avenue rich? The description of the fellow-traveling response to the Party girl who sings "Guadalajara" is good, straight dramatic writing of a sort that makes one feel Miss MacInnes could manage fiction of the non-thriller type. But since the thriller canons require that all things move swiftly to a violent denouement, *Neither Five nor Three* must end in absolutely black-and-white certainty. The Communists must be exposed as definitely card-carrying members of the tribe; the conspirators must be driven to suicide by jumping in front of subway trains or off fire escapes; the non-Communists must win as triumphantly and as conclusively as the Lone Ranger wins his nightly struggle against the bandits in the race to the railroad trestle or to the place where the map of the old gold mine is hid.

So be it. Miss MacInnes is an "entertainer," and a mighty good one. She is also a propagandist for her side, which is also my side, "our" side. This side needs a few propaganda victories after years of failure and defeat. I wish for the widest sort of popularity for *Neither Five nor Three.* And in so wishing, I nominate Irene Kuhn, who likes to expose the machinations of Communists at strategically placed bookstore counters, to keep an eye on what happens to *Neither Five nor Three.* If it doesn't outsell Rex Stout, then justice will have miscarried for the nth time since Lenin safely alighted from the train at the Finland Station in 1917.

Excursions and Samplings

17
Growing Up in Mexico

July 16, 1951

Some of our best erstwhile Communists and ex-fellow-travelers are getting exercised about something they choose to call "private censorship" by the Right. On the basis of one or two articles such as Irene Kuhn's *American Legion Monthly* piece titled "Why You Buy Books That Sell Communism," they are alleging unfair "suppression" of "liberal" thought. That's a laugh fit for the gods. Here, for two decades, the Left has exercised its own intense social pressure on authors, magazines and publishing houses, achieving in some instances a virtual monopoly of the printed word. But now that the Commies, the ex-fellow-travelers, and the totalitarian liberals are getting a little competition for the first time in years, they are squealing like a bunch of stuck pigs. Out of fear that the book-buying and magazine-reading customer may be in the process of changing his mind about things, which is his privilege in a free society, the lefties are trying to make it appear that the public owes all of their boys a living in perpetuity. If the National Association of Manufacturers ever tried to get away with anything as blatantly raw as that, the Department of Justice would be after it at once with prosecutions and cease-and-desist orders.

The fact that the lefties are finally facing some competition in the literary marketplace must be pleasing to Alice-Leone Moats, author of *A Violent Innocence.* For Miss Moats has had her own experience with the totalitarian liberals. As a war correspondent back in 1940 and 1941, she insisted upon looking at Soviet Russia with sober eyes. Her *Blind Date with Mars* was forthwith given the business by the lefties—and Moatsie, as she is called by those who know her well, soon found herself to be on a number of tacit blacklists. She was accused of being "too frank," of "rocking the boat," et cetera. A good sport about it, she didn't squeal or try to organize meetings at the Town Hall Club to protest about "private censorship by the Left." Instead, she kept on writing.

Her latest book, *A Violent Innocence,* is about her childhood in revolutionary Mexico. It is a higgledy-piggledy book about a seemingly higgledy-piggledy upbringing. Nevertheless, there is a certain artfulness about it, just as there was logic behind the strange theory of education entertained by Moatsie's extremely positive and capable mother. The idea of Moats *mere* was that her offspring should be taught to speak and read five languages fluently by the time she was ten. One consequence of this was a heterogeneous grounding in many traditions and literatures; another was an education in the curious ways of human nature exhibited by as fantastic a gaggle of private tutors as ever was assembled under one roof. At one point in Alice-Leone's zigzag linguistic progress her French teacher was killed by her German teacher. This didn't help with conjugations but did serve to give young Moatsie a precocious insight into human passions.

Meanwhile, violence swirled about the young language student from 1911 to 1920 in the Mexico that was undergoing its famous revolution. Moatsie remembers wading in blood through the streets of Veracruz when Woodrow Wilson's marines were taking over. She was being escorted to a refugee ship by an American colonel, and she recalls asking him: "Would you mind walking on the other side of the street? My shoes are getting so dirty with this blood." After such experiences, Alice-Leone found a New Hampshire summer camp and two years at the Brearley School in New York City to be rather tame interludes.

There is no particular sequence or "story line" to the rambling anecdotes of *A Violent Innocence.* The Mexican revolution thunders offstage while the young Alice-Leone is dressing up in her mother's clothes, or it spurts with staccato gunfire while a little girl is driving a pony cart through the streets of a battered capital. The child's-eye view of a great historical episode may lack something in clarity, but there is a mocking and insistent realism about it, nonetheless.

At the age of eight, Alice-Leone was already a better judge of character than Woodrow Wilson was as president of the United States. At least she saw through Madero, the posturing ninny who thought it was his own eloquence, and not the vast pressure from *mestizo* and Indian Mexico, that was ridding the country of the aged dictator, Porfirio Diaz. She also saw Pancho Villa for what he was, a cruel and lusty lecher who cared about as much for the common man as for a cockroach. Venustiano Carranza, the bearded money grubber whom Woodrow Wilson backed against the Indian Victoriano Huerta, wasn't much better than Villa. As for Huerta, the man who was toppled by Woodrow Wilson's schoolmasterly interference in behalf of Madero's and Carranza's "idealism," he drank like a fish and his relationships with women were not on a high moral plane. But, as Moats puts it, he had dignity, great personal courage, military ability and a love of his country. Washington had no reason to prefer Carranza to Huerta; indeed, Moats thinks President Wilson got just what was coming to him when Carranza proceeded to turn pro-German after 1915.

Aside from Huerta, the only revolutionist who seems to have had any good qualities at all was Emiliano Zapata, the champion of the agrarians. He was as bloodthirsty as the rest, and his soldiers did as much damage to life and limb during their periodic occupations of Mexico City as did the soldiers of Villa or Carranza or Alvaro Obregón. But at least there was a certain consistency about him. He was murdered by the Carranzistas in as dirty a piece of doubledealing as the Western Hemisphere has ever seen. The trickery went this way: A certain Carranzista, Colonel Guajardo, went to Zapata with a story of being willing to change his colors. When Zapata demanded proof of sincerity, Guajardo and his troops obliged by taking a Carranzista garrison and brutally executing all the prisoners. This convinced Zapata that Guajardo was an honest man. The victory over the Carranzista garrison was to be celebrated at a great dinner. Zapata arrived at the banquet hall with his escort of ten and was greeted by an honor march sounded by Guajardo's bugles. As Zapata passed through the gates, the order to present arms was given. The men raised their rifles, aimed at Zapata, and fired. Zapata fell, riddled with hundreds of bullets.

This was the "idealism" of a great revolution in action. Small wonder that Alice-Leone Moats went to Russia in 1941 with no illusions about revolutionary dictatorships.

Miss Moats seems to have survived the violent surroundings of her Mexico City childhood with few complexes or feelings of insecurity. She may not have had the benefits of an orderly upbringing in an orderly community, but she did have the support and love of a remarkable mother and a wise and friendly father. While not exactly a Clarence Day character, her father is a man among men, one of those natively self-confident Americans of an older generation who acts on the MacArthur principle that the only security in this world is a dynamic pursuit of opportunity. Alice-Leone doesn't tell us much in detail about her father's lumber business but we do get enough of the flavor of his operations to prove a point: anyone can do anything as long as he really has the desire and the will to plunge in and do it.

The overall moral of *A Violent Innocence* is that revolutions conducted in the name of the "masses," or the "common man," or the "people," are fated to miscarry. Indeed, over the past few centuries, there has been only one revolution that didn't go off the rails, and that is the American Revolution of 1776, which was conducted, not in the name of the "masses," but in the cause of the "inalienable rights" of the individual who was seeking to fetter the power of the state. It is the unlimited state that remains the prime enemy of humanity, and it matters little whether this sort of state is run by a Diaz, a Madero, a Carranza—or even a Caspar Milquetoast. The only real good a state can do is to get off the people's backs; the only real good a parliament can do in our age is to repeal the laws of its predecessors. As for a slogan to nail at the individualist masthead these days, let it be Frank Knight's: "Save society from the saviors!"

18
Sherman Finds Grant

July 30, 1951

The United States is a great peace-loving democracy. So we tell the world—and the statement is true, up to a point. But once we are inextricably pledged to war, with all our passions and interests aroused, we love peace far less than we love success.

If you have any question about this, consider the evidence offered by Earl Schenck Miers's *The General Who Marched to Hell.* This is the story of General William Tecumseh Sherman's 1864 march through Georgia to the sea, the feat which cut the Confederacy in two and deprived Lee at Richmond of a supporting hinterland. The evidence is of men engaged on both sides to the limit of their lives, their fortunes, and their sacred honor. Sherman piled blow upon blow; when his opponents refused to surrender on the field of battle, he turned his anger against the civilian economy that supported his foes. The Confederate leaders—Sam Hood, "Old Joe" Johnston—gave as good as they got, but after Sherman had destroyed the machine shops and arsenals of Atlanta and of Columbia, South Carolina, the Confederacy had to quit. It had run out of gas.

Miers's method of writing the history of Sherman's exploit is to draw upon contemporary or near-contemporary documents—diaries, letters, memoirs written close to the moment. The result is an extraordinarily fresh sort of narrative-mosaic; the events come through to the reader in astonishingly vivid paraphrase, with the emotional tension of actual participation hanging over virtually every paragraph. We know what it is like to be ten-year-old Carrie Berry when Yankee shells are falling on Atlanta and Sherman is announcing that little Carrie's hometown will soon be a "used-up community." We feel the choking distress of Dolly Lunt on her Georgia plantation as the Yankee midwestern farmboys in dirty blue shoot down her eighteen fat turkeys as "if they were Rebels themselves." We do a quick burn with Sherman when a Confederate mine, planted under a road, rips the flesh from the leg of a handsome Union officer. We feel the hatred and the rancor of William Gilmore Simms, the poet, over the Yankee sack of the liquor supply in Columbia and the resultant incendiary jag which burns most of the South Carolina capital to the ground. We know the exultation of eighteen-year-old Illinois and Indiana veterans as they pile ripped-up lengths of Confederate railroad track on fires of burning cross-ties, then wrap the red-hot rails around trees and telegraph poles. But most vividly of all we feel the hardening process that goes on inside the mind and character of the red-bearded "Cump" Sherman himself.

A peaceful person who objected to the "blind and crazy" men on both sides of the Mason-Dixon line who were bringing on the war by their politics of intransigent "inevitability," Sherman had no stomach for fighting. He loved the South, loved his job of running a military college in Louisiana. His best friends included Braxton Bragg and P. G. T. Beauregard, who were shortly to be arrayed against him. His days as a young officer had been spent at Fort Moultrie in Georgia, where he developed a liking for the "horse-racing, picnicking, boating, fishing, swimming, and God knows what not" that made up the "highly aristocratic and fashionable" social life of the place. But this love of the South could not compete against his early origins. Like most Ohio-born Americans of his day and generation, Sherman carried the idea of the Federal union, "one and inseparable," close to his heart. Before Sumter he cautioned a Southern friend: "You are bound to fail" because the "North can make a steam-engine locomotive or railway car," whereas the South could hardly manufacture "a pair of shoes." The prophecy proved accurate, but Sherman, as a Union general on the Kentucky front in late 1861, was not yet hardened to the point of being prophecy's unrelenting instrument.

The hardening process was gradual with Sherman. It didn't begin to set in until he had found a leader in whom he could trust.

In Kentucky he lived in an agony of fear lest the Confederates break through to Louisville. Because of his jitters he was actually called insane in Murat Halstead's *Cincinnati Commercial.* But then the "nervous-sanguine" Sherman met Grant.

The two men had what it took to make a team. Each had been a failure in civil life; each had his black moments of fear and indecision. But faced with a crisis that involved something much larger than themselves, the two "failures" found a way of nerving each other to the sticking point. Sherman kept the supplies moving up to the slouching Grant in the operations against Fort Henry and Fort Donelson. He argued Grant into staying with the army after the bloody shambles of Shiloh. When the howling against Grant's "drunkenness" was at its height, Sherman stuck by his friend; they were "crazy birds of a feather flocking together." And then came the fall of Vicksburg, which opened the Mississippi to the Union and vindicated Grant.

The vindication of Grant meant carte blanche for Sherman in the great project that was even then burgeoning in the minds of the two friends. According to the Grant–Sherman plan, the idea was to break the South by swinging a flying column through Georgia and up the Atlantic coast while the Army of the Potomac dealt massive hammer-blows at Lee in Virginia. Sherman began his march to the sea in a mood that grew more and more implacable. He was tired of a conflict which he thought was dragging itself out to unnecessary lengths. In his "iron mood" he insisted that the civil population be removed from Atlanta; then he methodically burned Atlanta's foundries and machine shops. The iron mood grew as his "bummers" swung southward toward Savannah. When the Confederate forces mined the roads, Sherman replied by marching Southern prisoners out in front of his own armies as a safety measure. When Georgia planters listened to Jefferson Davis on the advisability of scorching the earth in the path of Sherman's advance, Sherman redoubled his own depredations. By the time the Union forces had reached Columbia, South Carolina, in January 1865, both Sherman and his army were in a mood for no trifling. The Union soldiers burned Columbia out of sheer anger that South Carolina, the originator of the rebellion, could still be persisting in a war that had long since been lost.

Miers does not draw any moral from his story. But the upshot of it all is plain to see: modern war (and the Civil War was the first modern war) turns upon supply. Sherman and Grant won their war not by superior battle tactics, but by cutting the Confederate armies off from their sources of replenishment. First came the opening of the Mississippi, which separated the two parts of the Confederacy. Then came the destruction of Atlanta, the manufacturing and rail center. Then came the capture of Mobile and Savannah, the ports. After all this the Confederate armies simply "died on the vine."

The modern application of Miers's words, as fitted to the world scene, is a rebuke to the Truman administration's view of the Far Eastern situation. Neither in China nor in Korea can the Communists function at the end of a long, inadequate supply line. The Gobi Desert and the insufficiency of the Trans-Siberian railroad stand between Mao Tse-tung and final success, *provided that the United States makes the decision to supply a countering force in East Asia by sea*. . . . In Europe, on the other hand, the Russians can always win by following a policy of retreat into their own heartland, where it is their enemies who cannot function at the end of an inadequate line of supply.

In our fight with communism we are losing because we haven't the wit to digest the lessons of our own past. We haven't yet found our modern Grant, our modern Sherman. Truman could be a Lincoln if he would, but he is still dallying with his McClellans. When will he wake up?

19
Breaking the Clock's Tyranny

September 10, 1951

Cape Cod, by Henry David Thoreau. Introduction by Henry Beston. Arranged with notes by Dudley C. Lunt. Illustrated by Henry Bugbee Kane

An Island Summer, by Walter Magnes Teller. Illustrated by Donald McKay

The other day, while on a vacation excursion, I chanced to drive by Walden Pond on the outskirts of Concord. It was an oppressively hot afternoon, and there must have been a thousand sprawling, shouting modern Massachusetts folk crowding the shores where Thoreau once meditated alone. Pop bottles and beer cans littered the beach; torn paper was strewn everywhere. The snob's instinct would have been to avert the eye and drive on, and I must confess that the contrast between the rusty beer cans and my memory of Thoreau's delight in his bean rows caused my gorge to rise. But on second thought I decided that Thoreau would look with amusement, and even with approval, upon the Walden of a 1951 August day. What he would *not* approve of would be the lives, citified and routinized, from which the thousand 1951 vacationists had fled to seek out the hot beneficence of a Walden sun. The modern Waldensians were being faithful to nature in their fashion, and Thoreau could hardly censure them for obscurely endorsing his own insights.

Thoreau believed in the goodness of any impulse that broke the tyranny of the clock. Because of his loafing habits my good Emersonian friend, Katherine Murdoch, complains that he was a "bum." (Emerson himself was more polite about it: he called

Thoreau the "captain of a huckleberry party.") But the strictures that set Thoreau down as little better than a tramp miss the true import and vocation of the man. If you think he was nothing more than a cosmic *flaneur,* read the new Norton edition of his *Cape Cod* and be disabused. *Cape Cod* represents Thoreau at his best. There is much good meat in *Walden,* but there is also a stiff self-consciousness in it. In *Walden,* Thoreau was defying the routinized prejudices of his Concord neighbors—and the defiance stiffens the prose. But *Cape Cod* gives us Thoreau at his ease. Here, even more than in *Walden,* one discovers the origins of the modern American prose style; as Henry Beston indicates in a pertinent introduction, Thoreau broke cleanly with the orotund and somewhat mechanical balances of eighteenth-century writing, substituting for them a leaner, swifter, sharper sentence. Moralism there is in *Cape Cod,* but it is not the unctuous moralism of the Victorian evangelistic tradition. A truly religious man, Thoreau had a difficult time in church on a Sunday; he couldn't help thinking of the things the congregation did the six other days of the week. But the week-day sins of the congregation did not weigh too much on Thoreau's mind as he watched the terns on the Backside beach of Cape Cod and made notes on the nocturnal habits of the Provincetown cats.

"It is all here," says the Norton dust-jacket blurb writer—meaning by "all" the beach, the dunes, the cliffs, the volute breakers, the seagulls. But there is far more to *Cape Cod* than mere observation of beach plums and saltwater, which are apt to be boring matters in prose recital. Thoreau was a botanist and a naturalist, but try as he might he could not keep his eye from straying from the vegetable and animal kingdoms to the works of man. The "all" of this book includes the human scene of a century and more ago. We see the corpses of the Irish immigrants strewing the beach after the wreck of the brig *St. John.* We have Thoreau's notes on architecture: walking through the Cape town of Brewster, home of retired sea captains, he contrasted the clean functional austerity of the Yankee ships with the gimcrackery of the new houses which the sea captains were building for themselves in the 1840s. The houses, said Thoreau, might have been built in Cambridgeport out of stuff "little removed from lumber" and floated down the Charles River and across Massachusetts Bay.

The way the Cape Codders made their living was always on Thoreau's mind. He wrote of the saltworks (disappearing in his day), the sheep runs (almost wholly obsolete by the mid-nineteenth century), the stunted Cape apple orchards, the cattail flags that were used for caulking barrels, the pine trees planted for soil conservation purposes, the piscatorial-cum-agrarian know-how of the old Wellfleet oysterman, the curing of fish (it revolted Thoreau to see workers casually spitting on the dried cod), the cranberry bogs and the diseases of cranberries, the workaday movements of the mackerel fleet, the processes of stripping the blubber from the "blackfish" (a small sea mammal that yielded good oil to its pursuers). He speculated on such things as the edibility of seaweed and learned that beach peas are good if cooked (they can also be eaten green). In short, Thoreau confronted the world of the mid-nineteenth-century industry (such as it was) very much as if he were a writer for the *Fortune* magazine of the 1930s; the *processes* of manufacturing and husbandry were eternally fascinating objects of his curiosity.

Other things about man interested him, too. He wrote in *Cape Cod* about the revivalist camp meetings at the Millennium Grove in Nauset. He inspected the "charity houses" (shacks put up for shipwrecked sailors) on the Outer Beach. And, though respectful of their spiritual integrity, he was provoked to crude mirth by the failure of the Plymouth Pilgrims as pioneers and explorers. The Frenchman Champlain, who made marvelously accurate charts of New England coastal waters, was far more to Thoreau's taste than the blundering Pilgrim and Puritan fathers, who refused to climb a hill to learn what was on the other side.

The Cape today is a busy place when compared to the Cape of a century ago. Thoreau might scoff at the thronging summer people of the mid-twentieth century, but you may be certain that he would take a huge delight in writing about the garage mechanics in Chatham, the backgrounds of the summer waitresses, the economics of providing twenty-eight flavors of ice cream in the Howard Johnson restaurants, the palettes of the Provincetown painters, and the squabbles of the Wellfleet intellectuals who have taken over the home of the Wellfleet oysterman. And he would add his blessing to a book like Walter Magnes Teller's *An Island*

Summer (about the nearby island of Martha's Vineyard, which is only five or six miles off the Cape at Woods Hole) insofar as it succeeded in achieving a Thoreauvian flavor.

Mr. Teller tries very hard to live up to the Thoreau standard in his book, and on some pages he succeeds. He too is interested in the works of man along the foreshore as well as in the works of nature. He writes very warmly of his own family of boys. But Teller is less of a realist than Thoreau. He writes a paean to the quahog, or round clam, that some might call Thoreauvian. But Thoreau adds a detail to his own words on the sea clam—a detail about how it once made him sick. No mere Arcadian, Thoreau.

As an old summer goer-to-Menemsha of ten years' standing, I liked Teller's book. But there is one inexcusable mistake in it made by the illustrator, Donald McKay. His picture of Menemsha jetty (page 174) shows young Joey Teller catching an eel from a *wooden* pier. Actually, Menemsha jetty is built of solid, jagged rock. This may be a footling matter, but it shows what has happened to observation since Thoreau's day.

20
Aesopian Doublen Talk

September 24, 1951

The Communists have an "Aesopian" technique of double talk by which they convey one set of meanings to their initiated followers and quite another set to the dupes and innocents who take words at face value. But the Aesopian use and construction of language are not confined to the Communists; they have been applied to the American Constitution by the New Dealers since 1932. The result is that we have no fixed Constitution; we have merely an elastic document that can be stretched to cover any whim of a majority bent on despoiling a minority or robbing an individual of his supposedly inalienable rights.

This thesis is ably argued by Thomas James Norton in his *Undermining the Constitution: A History of Lawless Government.* According to Norton, a Vermonter who has spent forty-six years in the practice of law, the New Deal and the Fair Deal governments have virtually destroyed the force of the Tenth Amendment to the Constitution by an Aesopian, or flagrantly latitudinarian, construction of the general-welfare clause. The Tenth Amendment, as everyone ought to know, says, "The powers not delegated to the United States by the Constitution, nor prohibited by it to the states, are reserved to the states respectively, or to the people." Among the powers *not* delegated to the federal government is the power to engage directly in commerce. The Constitution nowhere delegates to the federal government the power to control rents, to develop electric power, to give money to foreign governments, to build hospitals, to set up a National Science Foundation, to redistribute property, to levy a graduated income tax, to provide capital funds for businessmen, to support agricultural prices, or to exercise other powers of this sort. These were among the powers "reserved to the states respectively, or to the people."

Yet there is undoubtedly a clause in the Constitution which reads (see Article 1, Section 8, Clause 1), "The Congress shall have power to lay and collect taxes, duties, imposts, and excises, to pay the debts and provide for the common defense and general welfare of the United States." Does this clause indicate that Congress has blanket permission to define the "general welfare" as anything that may be thought by a majority to be for the good of anybody? If so, then Congress does truly float "in a boundless field of power, no longer susceptible of any definition." Such blanket construction of the "general welfare" means that 51 percent of the people can vote themselves subsidies or other special advantages almost to infinity, on the ground that the "general welfare" is thereby being provided for.

But this, philosophically speaking, is nonsense. No true general welfare can rest on the tax-and-spend theory of the New Deal and Fair Deal legislators. The general welfare of society can in no wise be considered apart from the security to the individual of the fruits of his labors. If there is no such security, there can be no real incentive to work, to save, or to invest. "General welfare" demands an atmosphere of safety, certainty and continuity. When one group is permitted by law to mulct another, mutual distrust becomes endemic in society. Everybody organizes to get in on the grab. The general welfare is shredded to bits and pieces as the big gangs subject the small gangs to depredations at the gunpoint of the tax collector.

Mr. Norton does not, however, rest his argument on a merely philosophical exploration of the content of the phrase "general welfare." He is strictly the constitutional lawyer in his approach. What he seeks to determine is the precise meaning of the general-welfare clause to the men who framed the Constitution. According to his researches, which are exceedingly well documented, such Founding Father worthies as Madison, Hamilton, Wilson and Jefferson thought of the general-welfare clause as applying to the "enumerated instances" of its own section of the Constitution. The "enumerated instances" permitted the federal government to borrow money, coin money, regulate commerce between the states, establish rules for naturalization, declare war, raise and support armies, establish post offices and post roads, protect inventors and authors, and so on. Not a word about subsidies for farmers, or SEC loans for printing companies, or the promotion of health by federal grants. These and kindred subjects were reserved to the states, and properly fall within the police power of the forty-eight small republics which make up our greater federal Republic.

The Aesopian construction of the general-welfare clause is not the only instance of constitutional infraction by blurred definition of words. By similar Aesopian construction of the phrase "to regulate commerce" the federal government has passed laws that infringe upon the police power of the forty-eight states in regard to local labor matters. And the Aesopian construction of the phrase "soil conservation" has enabled Washington to move in on local agriculture. In short, the strict meaning of the Founding Fathers has been melted away into nothingness by the disingenuous application of modern semantic fallacies. Chief Justice Hughes once said that "we are under a Constitution but the Constitution is what the judges say it is." This might be amended to read "we are under a dictionary, but the words in the dictionary mean what the New Dealers and Fair Dealers say they mean." Noah Webster and common usage have gone the way of the Founding Fathers and the common law. Humpty Dumpty has become our approved lexicographer.

If we were to follow Thomas James Norton and return to the Constitution, would that mean the end of modern "social-welfare" activity? Would such things as soil conservation, or good public health measures, or river control, or social security necessarily go by the board? Not in the least. There is nothing to keep individual states from setting up such things as the Muskingum (Ohio) Watershed Conservancy District. Moreover, the states can compact with each other to create such units as the one which fairly divides the water of the Colorado River and its tributaries. The states can legislate as they please in the field of labor, or of social security, provided they do not despoil the individual of life, liberty, or property. And private individuals do not even have to rely on local legislatures; they have the power to set up their own medical insurance societies, their own cooperative housing projects, their own credit unions, their own voluntary soil conservation districts, if they so choose.

Whether Mr. Norton's book will ever reach the multitudes who ought to read it is doubtful. It ought to be taken out of the realm of "lawyer's language" and simplified for the common reader. Nevertheless, it is an excellent book. Norton thinks our high school and college students should be required to pass an elementary examination in constitutional law as a prerequisite for graduation. The suggestion is a good one. Norton's own book might be made required or at least elective reading in college constitutional law courses. And for younger minds as well as older there exists a remarkably clear book called *Your Rugged Constitution,* by Bruce and Esther Findlay. This book not only prints the Constitution; it also carefully explains just what it is that is denied or guaranteed by each individual provision of the Constitution. The explanatory exposition in the Findlay book is done in non-lawyer language, and there are lines drawn through the original text of the Constitution wherever a subsequent amendment has changed it. The pictorial illustrations, by Richard Dawson, add to the clarity and force of the Findlays' job.

21
The Prophetic Joseph Conrad

October 8, 1951

Joseph Conrad's *Under Western Eyes* was first published in 1911. It fell rather flat at the time, and it has never had the reputation of *Lord Jim, Victory* and *The Nigger of the "Narcissus."* Reading it in this new edition, which comes to us with an instructive introduction by Morton Dauwen Zabel, one can easily see how it came to be neglected. An Anglo-Saxon world that has yet to digest the significance of such things as the Hiss case and the disappearance of the two British foreign-office men could hardly have been expected to become emotionally involved in this story of Russian revolutionists, assassins, spies, informers and double agents on the shores of Lake Geneva in 1904 or 1905. Like the city of Geneva itself, that "respectable and passionless abode of democratic liberty" (Conrad's rather contemptuous words), we have been so much the disinterested routineers in our concern for freedom that, unawares, we have allowed the tides of disintegration to lap close to us. Thus *Under Western Eyes,* which Conrad wrote as a distinctively *Russian* story, threatens to become an English and an American story as well.

The key to *Under Western Eyes* is to be found in an author's note appended to Conrad's autobiographical fragment, "A Personal Record." Disputing the all-too-prevalent Western view that the Polish temperament is akin to the Russian, Conrad, the Pole who became an Englishman, insisted upon Poland's "tradition of self-government, its chivalrous view of moral restraints and an exaggerated respect for individual rights." The Polish mentality, he said, is "Western in complexion," has "received its training from Italy and France and, historically, [has] always remained, even in religious matters, in sympathy with the most liberal currents of European thought." Conrad's own father was a Polish patriot who rebelled against Russian domination in 1863; he was not so much a revolutionist as a counterrevolutionist yearning for the freedoms guaranteed by republican order. The lawlessness of the czar's government in Warsaw and the fate of his father's generation made Conrad into a Russophobe. But it was a very particular Russia that Conrad hated—the Russia that has swung violently from the lawlessness of autocracy to the lawlessness of revolution. Conrad hated the whole formula of "senseless desperation provoked by senseless tyranny," the "ferocity and imbecility of an autocratic rule" basing itself on "complete moral anarchism" and provoking "the no less imbecile and atrocious answer of a purely Utopian revolutionism encompassing destruction by the first means to hand."

No doubt Conrad's linked rebuke to the Romanovs and the Lenins who contested so disastrously for the supremacy of the Russian moral jungle overlooks and slights the Russia of Miliukov, Kerensky, and the Constituent Assembly. However, let that pass for the moment. *Under Western Eyes* may do the Russia of Kerensky an injustice, but it is certainly full of prophetic insight bearing on the mechanics of revolution. The old English teacher of languages who serves as the storytelling Marlowe of *Under Western Eyes* called the turn when he lectured Nathalie Haldin, the trusting sister of the assassin Victor Haldin, in these terms:

> In a real revolution the best characters do not come to the front. A violent revolution falls into the hands of narrow-minded fanatics and of tyrannical hypocrites at first. Afterwards comes the turn of all the pretentious intellectual failures of the time. Such are the chiefs and leaders. You will notice that I have left out the mere rogues. The scrupulous and the just, the noble, humane and devoted natures; the unselfish and the intelligent may begin a movement—but it passes away from them. They are not the leaders of a revolution. They are its victims.

This, written in 1908, is the larger burden of Hayek's *The Road to Serfdom,* written some thirty years later. A public that failed to appreciate Conrad a decade before the Russian Revolution may be forgiven its moral indifference, but what are we to say for a public that has rejected Hayek in the age of Stalin and Hiss?

Until very recently the moral dilemma summed up in the question "To tell or not to tell?" has never had any meaning for Americans. A Whittaker Chambers, a Hede Massing, a Louis Budenz, would have been a meaningless phenomenon in the America of a generation ago. Not so in the Russian life which Conrad so vividly depicts in *Under Western Eyes.* When Haldin, the revolutionary murderer of the minister De P____, who is modeled on the notorious pogromist Plehve, appeals for sanctuary to the young student Razumov, the question is posed in terms that admit of an answer. Razumov tells. But he tells not out of passionate conviction that he is exposing an evil thing. His is a more opportunistic devotion to truth and justice; as Conrad puts it, Razumov is "dazzled by the base glitter of mixed motives." The natural son of a member of the nobility, Razumov fears that Haldin's sudden eruption into his life will spoil his chances for a career. He exposes Haldin to Councillor Mikulin out of mere anger that anybody could presume to endanger his bread and butter.

Thus a good act is rendered evil in the very moment of its consummation—and thus *Under Western Eyes* becomes, like *Lord Jim,* a drama of the attempted resurrection of personal honor. Razumov goes to Geneva to spy on the revolutionists. But he cannot endure the role when he realizes that he is a spy for a cause in which he does not believe. Razumov is no revolutionist; his personal credo is expressed in a set of antitheses:

> History not Theory.
> Patriotism not Internationalism.
> Evolution not Revolution.
> Direction not Destruction.
> Unity not Disruption.

But the czar's government is not concerned with such things as patriotism, evolution, direction and unity. Razumov is engaged in a spy's role in a war that does not involve a single one of his own beliefs. He cannot be a Nathan Hale or a Whittaker Chambers in such a situation. For his own salvation he exposes his role in the hanging of Haldin to the Geneva revolutionists. Even this he does out of the "base glitter of mixed motives," for he is in love with the sister of Haldin. For his truthfulness he reaps a peculiar reward; he is slugged and rendered stone deaf by a thug of the revolution who happens to be a double agent on the order of the notorious Azev.

This is a drama of moral ambiguity that Conrad has written. Since Razumov, unlike Lord Jim, is an equivocal character, *Under Western Eyes* may have no clear meaning for many Westerners in its central characterization. But even in its ambiguity the novel serves as a warning to the West. For if a senseless autocracy provokes senseless revolution, it also confuses the ethical sense of anyone who is out to make a career. When the state itself departs from the rule of law and the guarantee of natural rights, it becomes impossible to teach good morals to the young unless they happen to be gifted with the ability and the will to live monkish lives. If the state is not the conservator of natural rights, then moral man must prepare himself to live outside the state. But that is, for most people, a virtually inhuman task. Only the very strongest natures can resist corruption in a state that does not strive to make natural law (including the Ten Commandments) the basis for the "legal" law passed by legislatures.

Under Western Eyes is a prophetic book: Conrad called the turn on the Russian Revolution before it happened. It is also a warning book, for the Russian Revolution has moved west since Conrad wrote it. We can no longer look down with superior eyes upon the Lasparas, the Sophia Antonovnas, the Nikitas and the Peter Ivanovitches of Conrad's story. We have these characters in our midst in Washington and London, and they bear ancient Anglo-Saxon names. Will they succeed in doing us in? That depends on the passion that we can muster as believers in republican morals, republican legality, and republican order.

22
New York Versus Boston

October 22, 1951

The most interesting thing about John P. Marquand's *Melville Goodwin, USA,* which is a story of a military hero's attempt to cope with the baffling exigencies of a postwar world, is its plentiful evidence that the U.S. possesses at least one novelist who is capable of incorporating new and mature experiences into his work. This hasn't often happened with American novelists in late years: our Hemingways and Faulkners, our Caldwells and Farrells have had very little success with anything outside of their earliest impressions and experiences, their earliest environments, acquaintances and friends. But with Marquand it has been different: he has retained the qualities of plasticity, receptivity and curiosity. He has not subsided into a purely personal lyricism; he has not cut himself off from the nourishing experience that can only come from living in a society that includes somebody besides other writers and artists. In brief, he has continued to grow.

What Marquand knew in his bones at the beginning was the narrow environment of the late George Apley. Like the mind of Cabot Lodge, friend of Theodore Roosevelt and grandfather of the infinitely more flexible present-day Lodges, the Apley terrain was highly cultivated but barren. The Apley world made for good satire; and if Marquand had been a stay-at-home he would have shaped his own small niche as the delightful social recorder of Boston and North Shore foibles. But a wider world beckoned to Marquand when he discovered that the psychological conflict between Boston and New York could produce exquisite tragicomedy. Marquand has exploited the Boston–New York polarization in two contrasting ways. His H. M. Pulham, Esq., made an effort to escape into the freedom and fluidity of Manhattan, where careers are open to talents, where ideas and patterns are shaped and stamped for sale to a nation. But Pulham couldn't stand the strain of freedom and so he fell back into the Apley groove. In *Point of No Return* Marquand played it the other way: his banker character from the North Shore did succeed in making the vital transition. It cost the banker something, but all choices mean a deliberate closing out of certain possibilities. One can hardly go two ways at once.

In exploring the Boston–New York polarization, Marquand naturally met up with characters who have not come out of Apley's world. Proving his emancipation, Marquand did one memorable job in his portrait of the tycoon's daughter who married a New Deal bureaucrat. Now he has done another memorable job with General Melville Goodwin, product of West Point and the regular army. *Melville Goodwin, USA* may not be as interesting as some of the earlier Marquand stories: its protagonist is too specialized and too simple an individual to give Marquand full scope for the social byplay that is his particular forte. But it is a triumph nonetheless that Marquand has managed to wring so much out of such a fundamentally simple theme.

The reason *Melville Goodwin, USA* holds the reader's interest so continually is that it is a satire within a satire, a story of many values even though the main character is a trifle dull. Mel Goodwin grew up in a small town near Nashua, New Hampshire, the youngest son of the local druggist. (This is fairly close to Apley's world in space, but just about as far away from Brahmin territory as Idaho or Arkansas, if it is social likeness that you are seeking.) A "glory boy" from the word go, Mel thrills to the music of a martial band on Memorial Day and spends hours in the local library reading stories about the Civil War and books like *A Plebe at West Point*. He is a "one girl" kid who marries the daughter of a Hallowell, New Hampshire, manufacturer the day he graduates from the Point. Shaped by the routines and the disciplines of Military Academy life and by his sojourns in various army schools and posts between World War I and World War II, Mel becomes a specialist in throwing mechanized armor at an enemy. He knows armor and firepower, he knows how to estimate a situation, and he is able to reach an almost instantaneous decision in a moment of stress. To all of this he adds an instinct for terrain and a good understanding of the GI mind. What he does not know is the world of the civilian, particularly the civilian woman in her more predatory guise. His mixup with the clever, beautiful, dissatisfied Dottie Peale, on which the story turns, leaves him floundering like a fish in the scuppers of a sloop. Fortunately, he is close enough to the water to flop back in with one gigantic leap over the rail.

The history of Melville Goodwin enables Marquand to satirize the world of the twenties and the thirties, when all the patriotic values were being discounted and laughed at. Goodwin may have had a one-track mind and an adolescent's attitude toward glory, but the point made by Marquand is that the sophisticated civilian world must depend on characters like Mel Goodwin when the politicians and the diplomats have made a fatal miscalculation. Marquand doesn't fall for the baloney that there is only one type of military mind: his Mel Goodwin differs from the other military characters who wander in and out of the story. (Some generals are evidently made for combat, some for staff work, some for planning, some for negotiation.) But military men must at least be all alike in their dedication and in their respect for orders if an army is to be saved from degenerating into a mob or a horde in the midst of crisis. Marquand, the satirist, is perfectly willing to kid the military mind for certain things, but he stands in awe of Mel Goodwin's capabilities whenever the Silver Leaf's tanks are swinging into action at Saint-Lô or in the Bulge. Mel knows how to deliver the punch, which is all that counts.

The satire within the satire is revealed when Marquand makes Mel Goodwin almost pathetically dependent on the friendship of Sid Skelton, a radio commentator whose voice drips with synthetic integrity. Sid was in army public relations in World War II, and it was through him that Mel met Dottie Peale. Mel had no personal use or admiration for the world of publicity and radio, but, like the rest of the brass, he had to make his compromises. An army lives by congressional appropriations, and in the modern world it must have a good press to get the funds it needs. In order to achieve a good press the modern army must cultivate the slippery art of public relations. This means cooperation with characters who live by insincerity, by their ability to achieve the fake "buildup," the adroitly arranged payoff line. Marquand has a wonderful time with his broadcasting company fakers such as the oleaginous Gilbert Frary, discoverer of Sid Skelton's voice. He has almost as much fun with a magazine writer and his Girl Friday researcher. Nor does he let Sid Skelton, the radio commentator, off the hook, even though Sid is cynical about the whole business of pretending to "inside information" every night on the air.

Like all of Marquand's novels, *Melville Goodwin, USA* is filled with detail that captures the social atmosphere of time and place. The Marquand eye is fresh, the ear is good, no matter where the Marquand legs choose to stray. The characters are all Very Important Persons, and they racket around from the Pentagon in Virginia to the European Theater of Operations, and from Fairfield County, Connecticut, to the Ritz Hotel in Paris. The reader of *Melville Goodwin, USA* knows that he is in the modern world of planes, of television, of high-pressure publishing, a world of insomnia tempered by Nembutal tablets discreetly used. But through it all Marquand seems to be saying that civilizations depend for their continuity on values as old as the time of the Greek Ulysses, when planes, radio, television, news magazines and Nembutal were unknown.

Since Marquand is virtually our only novelist who can explore new and strange social juxtapositions and contretemps, he is able to achieve a variegated output from book to book. His publisher, Little, Brown & Co., has recently had a lot of unfavorable publicity because of alleged "Communist trouble" in the office. Knowing something of the Little, Brown story, which is tragicomedy of the most ludicrous and at the same time heartbreaking sort, Marquand ought to realize that he has a vein of pure gold to work right close to home. The editors of Little, Brown could achieve greatness of character—and also have a bestseller on their hands—if they would only encourage Marquand to tell the story of what happened to an old Boston publishing company in the age of the fellow-traveler and the infiltrator par excellence. It would take courage for Little, Brown to set Marquand to work on such a theme, and no one seems to have much courage these days. But there is always a chance that courage will come back into its own. We live in hope that Marquand won't muff a story that is made to his hand.

23
No Cultural Hero

November 5, 1951

Louis Bromfield's *Mr. Smith* poses a problem for the reader who knows something of the author. It is a novel of considerable bite, drive and power, written far less slickly than some of Mr. Bromfield's middle-period fiction. The story of a well-meaning upper-middle-class insurance salesman, Wolcott Ferris of Crescent City, U.S.A., it breathes a profound antipathy to Ferris's midwest suburban culture. In fact, *Mr. Smith* might almost be called a novel in the expatriate mood. Yet, as everybody knows, Bromfield himself is no nay-sayer to American life. Indeed, he writes a weekly newspaper column under the general heading "Your Country," which hymns the virtues of the American tradition. Why, then, this novel, with its bleak and bitter excoriation of the culture that envelops practically everyone in America?

The answer is not an easy one. Bromfield is a profound believer in the traditional American political and economic systems. He doesn't believe in British socialism, Keynesian interventionism, or the Marxian state. He is for local action and the inalienable rights of the individual. But if we are to take *Mr. Smith* at face value, what the author seems to be saying is that an excellent political and economic tradition has produced in America one of the world's least satisfying cultures. Can this be true? Or, if it is not true, how do we reconcile the two apparently unreconcilable halves of Mr. Bromfield's work?

Bromfield is on record as believing that our political life has been corrupted by the importation of English Fabian and continental Marxist ideas into the American university world. Yet this would hardly account for the corruption of Wolcott Ferris's midwestern hometown of Crescent City, or the terrible superficiality of his suburban bailiwick called Oakdale. Wolcott Ferris is no New Dealer, no graduate of the Harvard Law School. He is just a simple businessman who is feeling rather tired and let-down in his late thirties. He has a good business, a nice-looking wife, and two normal children. Yet his life is savorless. The twin beds are the symbols of his marital existence. His home—a "lovely home"—is opulent in the Oakdale manner, yet it is completely unoriginal in its decorations and furnishings. He has evidently never tried to reach down into the play world of his children, and they are relative strangers to him.

In brief, here is a man who is ready for a good middle-aged revolt. Yet he lacks the courage to revolt. The most he achieves is a clandestine affair with the visiting granddaughter of one of Crescent City's founding pioneers and tycoons. Mary Raeburn comes back to Crescent City out of a wider world, and for a time she means beauty and release to Wolcott Ferris. But Mary turns out to be a dope addict, and the romance sputters out. Eventually Wolcott "escapes" into World War II. But even here he finds no adventure. Stuck on a back-area island in the South Pacific, he spends his military time guarding some forgotten stores. His companions on the island are a tough extrovert sergeant, a Kansas farm boy, a Jewish kid from Brooklyn, and an ignorant, vindictive, nigger-hating wool-hat from the back country of Georgia. While on the island he writes the dismal chronicle of his Oakdale and Crescent City life. He does this partly to relieve the tedium, partly to find a justification in his existence. But there is no justification for Wolcott Ferris's life, for it has been juiceless, mediocre and lacking in all the ancient qualities of honor, skill, taste, sensitivity, ardor, humor and love.

It would be an easy out to say that Wolcott Ferris is merely one individual. But Bromfield makes him a representative character. That is why the novel is called *Mr. Smith* instead of *Mr. Ferris.* Moreover, the whole Oakdale tribe consists of Mr. and Mrs. Smiths. Nobody reads good books in Oakdale. The only game that is played is golf, which is not a bad game except where it is pursued as a rite. The wives have their garden clubs, but they do singularly little gardening—and when they do raise anything they hire a gardener to do it for them. As for the husbands, they do a little extramarital necking in parked cars down by the country club, and occasionally they go off on a bender at a convention. They all live in houses that have been decorated by the same interior decorator; one mud-toned wall in Oakdale is very like another. Bromfield definitely is out to excoriate the whole milieu of Crescent City and Oakdale, not merely Wolcott Ferris's own part of it.

How could the strivings of the Founding Fathers, the bravery of the early pioneers, and the energy of Crescent City's original tycoons have eventuated in the flat world of Oakdale? Bromfield does not offer any answer. Maybe there is no answer, if we are looking for one in political or economic terms. The fact of the matter is, the same America that produced the gutless, desiccated world of Oakdale has also produced Louis Bromfield, a fellow of infinite variety, humor, honor and gusto. Bromfield is everything that his Wolcott Ferris is not. He has gone and done the things he wanted to do, written the books he wanted to write, earned the money he needed for his family and for the gratification of his tastes—and, where Ferris merely raised backyard roses, Bromfield operates one of the most meaningful farms in all of America.

The point of the contrast between Wolcott Ferris and Louis Bromfield would seem to be this: that no political or economic system can save anyone if the spiritual origins of freedom and morality are forgotten. Wolcott Ferris lives in a comparatively free society; his Oakdale suburb, his business have not yet been taken over by the state. But Ferris has lost contact with the morality that moved his Grandfather Weber, who came to America from the German Palatinate in the 1840s when independence was a cherished thing. Grandfather Weber was an artist in wrought iron and he loved music. He didn't mind being called an eccentric. Neither did Wolcott Ferris's paternal grandfather, a great horseman who had been an Indian fighter, a trapper, a settler and a merchant. These men knew that the desire for freedom, justice and creativeness precedes and *causes* political and economic adjustments. They acted as free men and everything else followed.

Since the American system has produced both the willful Louis Bromfield and the will-less characters of *Mr. Smith*, it follows that neither type is fated by the circumstances of American life. An

American can be what he wills; an act of courage, a dedicated life, a willingness to be called an eccentric are just as possible today in America as they were a century ago. If they seem much more rare today than in former times, that is because the modern American has tended to forget the sources of his spiritual being. The West began by being Christian, and because it was Christian it became individualist, capitalist—and free. Mr. Bromfield, who knows this, has written a powerful novel about a man who has forgotten it and lost his way.

24
Lessons of Plymouth Colony

December 3, 1951

The Virginia colony was founded more than a decade before Plymouth, and there was an evanescent settlement in Maine at the mouth of the Kennebec as early as 1607. Yet America instinctively looks back to the Plymouth colony as its spiritual progenitor. It does so officially each Thanksgiving Day; it does so unofficially every day of the year.

Why should this be so? The answer cannot be found in strict logic, for the Virginia colony established the first representative assembly in America at Jamestown in 1619, a full year before the Pilgrims set out from Leyden in Holland and from Southampton and Plymouth in England to sail for the New World. On the face of it, this would make Virginia the fountainhead of New World democracy. Yet, stubbornly and persistently, the year 1620 tends to take precedence over all other years in the minds of Americans who go looking for their national origins.

The subtler reasons for Plymouth's preeminence are all to be found in Bradford Smith's *Bradford of Plymouth.* A descendant of the great Plymouth governor on his mother's side, Bradford Smith has taken William Bradford's own *Of Plymouth Plantation* (soon to be brought out in a new edition) and built out from it the first full biography of our earliest representative American. Some bits of this biography are necessarily conjectural, the result of the best possible deduction or inference from the available facts. William Bradford was no gossip, no Samuel Pepys, and he kept a Puritan's reserve about his own more intimate feelings. We do not know how his first wife Dorothy came to drown off Provincetown Harbor in 1620, before Plymouth had even been settled. It may have been a suicide, or it may have been an accident. We do not know much of a personal nature about Bradford's years in Leyden, that beautiful city in the Netherlands where the Pilgrims (or the Separatists) sojourned from 1609 to 1620. Smith has had to build up William Bradford's earlier Yorkshire background (Bradford was the orphaned descendant of land-hungry, freedom-loving North Country English yeomen) from a few sparse genealogical facts and dates. But Bradford left his own full record as a public man, and if Smith's book has its bare spots as a personal biography it remains an excellent history of the first colony to take root in New England.

The picture that one carries away from this book might, by magnification and extension, be called a picture of traditional America. Virginia had the first representative assembly, but it was in Plymouth that the American idea of the individual as a person with natural rights antecedent to government was first established. In the seventeenth century this idea, which breathes through the Declaration of Independence and the American Constitution, could only come out of a community which insisted on the direct communion of the individual with his God. The Separatists had quit Yorkshire and Lincolnshire for Holland because they could not abide the identification of the powers of the religious community with the powers of civil government. To establish his right to religious freedom, the Englishman of the seventeenth century had first to insist that there were areas of life which neither king nor politician nor parliamentary majority could touch. It was the Pilgrim attitude, multiplied and extended by later theoreticians such as John Locke, that finally flowered in the Bill of Rights. And, nearly two hundred years before the Rousseauistic "social contract" of the American Constitution was drawn up, there was a Mayflower Compact signed by the Pilgrims aboard ship. The Mayflower Compact was a republican delegation of powers by individuals who retained their individual natural rights. The Pilgrims were not state-worshipers; though they left England before the Cromwellian revolution was well under way, they were still an integral part of a movement that dared eventually to behead a presumptuous king.

Mr. Smith insists upon the superior libertarianism of the Plymouth colony: Bradford, Brewster and the rest were far more tolerant of individual foibles than were the dour founders of neighboring Boston. The political, religious and commercial freedoms of Plymouth undoubtedly owed much to the eleven-year span which the Separatists spent in the free Dutch city of Leyden. When Bradford and Brewster came to Leyden, the Netherlanders had just finished throwing off the oppressive yoke of Spain. Freedom was in the air, and it was a freedom to trade, to enter into contracts, to make the freest possible use of one's individual energy, as well as a freedom to worship, and to choose one's own civil government. Plymouth, after an initial experiment with communism, went over to a distinctly nonfeudal ownership of land and to recognition of the individual's rights to the fruits of his labors—changes that undoubtedly trace to the Pilgrim sojourn in commercial Holland.

We tend to think of the Pilgrim fathers as being elderly men. Actually, they were extremely young men when they sailed for the New World. Of the 104 passengers on the *Mayflower* only four had reached their fifties. Brewster—the famous "Elder" Brewster—was fifty-two. Bradford, Fuller, Miles Standish and Hopkins were all in their thirties. And thirty-three of the Pilgrim band, almost a third of the passenger list, were children under fifteen years of age. The "great sickness" of 1621, which carried off about half the colony, hit young and old alike. When it was over, the young men who lived through it felt themselves steeled and tempered to proceed with full reliance on their own youthful powers. As Smith insists, Bradford, who certainly did not derive from a coat-of-arms noble lineage, was America's first self-made man. And he was the chosen governor of other self-made men.

Smith looks back with nostalgia upon the day when men banded together in a "beloved community" to pursue a "good life" that depended on common brotherly aspirations. He is no anarchist, no devotee of the "dissidence of dissent." But one of the most significant things about Plymouth, as he sees it, is its dramatic demonstration that economic communism does not foster brotherly sentiments. During its first years Plymouth tried to live by the future Marxian formula—"from each according to his abilities, to each according to his needs." What the individual produced went into the common store; what the individual consumed came out of the common store in equal shares. The land was held by the community. The result of all this was apathy—and actual starvation. Bradford, a profound student of natural law, finally took it upon himself to break the agreement with the London Adventurers who had financed the Plymouth colony; he assigned individual acres to each family, and he announced that henceforward every man would raise his own corn. The communal system of production had proved to Bradford "the vanitie of that conceite of Plato's" and of other ancients, applauded by some of later times, that the "taking away of propertie, and bringing in communitie into a comone wealth, would make them happy and flourishing; *as if they were wiser than God*" (the words are Bradford's; the italics are mine).

Plymouth is an instance of a political community that succeeded in throwing off the stunting burden of communism without bloody insurrection. The reason it could do this was that Bradford, Brewster and the other elected officials of the colony were men whose prime ends in life were of a moral and spiritual nature. They were justice-loving men, not mere power lovers. Their example proves that there is a way out of the cul-de-sac of communism in a spiritual community. But in a community that denies the spirit, such as Stalinist Russia, how can "the vanitie of that conceite of Plato's" be overcome? History gives us no easy answer. But the lesson is obvious: trust no man to rule over you whose prime interest is in the act of ruling.

In concentrating on a few central topics, this review has failed to do justice to the richness of Bradford Smith's book. There is a wealth of material in these pages bearing on fascinating minor matters. Incidentally, the author does something to rescue the Pilgrims from the strictures of Henry David Thoreau. In his *Cape Cod* Thoreau laughs at the Pilgrims as pioneers and explorers. But the truth would seem to be that those Pilgrims whose antecedents went back to Yorkshire were fairly expert farmers and stock-raisers. The Pilgrims never could master the arts of fishing; they were not good men of the sea. But Bradford did manage to do a good bit of exploring by sea, and he traded as far up the coast as Monhegan in Maine. He was not an accurate map maker in the tradition of the Frenchman Champlain. But his interest was to found a community, not to chart the bays and shallows of a coast.

25
Paradox Does It

December 17, 1951

Eliot Janeway, who covered the wartime *Battle of Washington* for *Time* and *Fortune*, is a sardonic realist, and a political scientist in the tradition of Machiavelli, Pareto, Mosca and Michels. He is also a worshipful admirer of the late Franklin D. Roosevelt, whom he regards as a latter-day embodiment of Queen Elizabeth, that adept practitioner of the art of solving problems by putting them off. The combination of polar opposites in Mr. Janeway's character (the need to see the true inwardness of a situation and the boyish craving to have a hero) gives a strange tension to his work, but the result, speaking from the standpoint of literature, is happy. For the tension of opposites, of incongruities, provokes Janeway to a constant stream of witty paradox. His book, *The Struggle for Survival: A Chronicle of Economic Mobilization in World War II,* deals with the so-called dismal science of economics, but it is full of things that would have brought Chesterton or any other professional dealer in paradox up sharp.

Paradox, expertly wielded, is a way of riveting the reader's attention. It is also a way of baffling seven out of ten people. Both Roosevelt lovers and Roosevelt haters will be considerably baffled by Janeway's curious ritual of adoration. He calls Roosevelt a great man, invoking the Lincoln comparison on more than one occasion. Yet (and this is Janeway's considered opinion) Roosevelt was as vindictive as John T. Flynn says he was. On Janeway's own showing, carefully documented, our wartime president was untruthful whenever it served his purpose, he was devious, he frequently welshed on political promises, he was a master at kicking men upstairs, he attracted sycophants as a honey jar attracts flies, and he was the world's worst administrator. Now, to call a man a prevaricator, a slippery customer, an Indian giver and an incompetent at organization would seem to be no recommendation for even the most menial of jobs. But politics, says Janeway in effect, is not as other businesses; it is a topsy-turvy world in which all values are turned on their heads. Roosevelt, slippery as a conger eel, was the best politician of his generation, and for this Janeway is willing to forgive him everything.

Janeway believes in Planning with a capital *P*. He thinks a Mixed Economy—or rather, a Mixed-Up Economy—is here to stay. He is attuned (or maybe resigned) to Keynesianism, to an arbitrary redistribution of incomes via the uncompromising use of the graduated income tax. Yet (and this is the strangest paradox of his book) he thinks Roosevelt was a great man for the simple reason that, as a leader of 155 million people in a war against the planned society of Hitler's *dritte Reich,* Roosevelt ignored every blueprint that was placed before him. Roosevelt was the great pragmatist, the great improviser—and he played every tune, from "Chopsticks" up to the Fifth Symphony, strictly by ear. His method was to get the Planners into Washington, where he would set them off against each other and knock their heads together. When their scalps and noses were sufficiently covered with bumps and black-and-blue marks, Roosevelt would appeal over their bruised heads to the country. Washington, as the cliché of those years had it, was a madhouse, and utterly incapable of transmitting any clear line to the nation as a whole. Yet, while the madmen were playing Napoleon in Washington, the people out in the country went to work, rolled out a staggering number of tanks, guns and planes, and quite capably won the war.

Of course, there were good men in Washington, but they were philosophical policymakers and inspiriting leaders in the old sense, not Planners in the modern meaning of that word. Janeway has a keen eye for a phony and a great admiration for an able and effective man. He is contemptuous of Edward Stettinius and Donald Nelson, he considers that William Knudsen (a great mechanic) was miscast as a policy man, he has an ambivalent attitude toward Bernard Baruch (whom he calls a "gabby old sage"), he sets Felix

Frankfurter down as a power-lover who masqueraded as an aloof intellectual, and he patently prefers Walter Reuther as a wartime labor leader to Sidney Hillman. On the other hand, he is lavish with his praise for Jim Forrestal (who ran the Navy Department while Frank Knox was getting the headlines); for Leon Henderson (who never managed really to control prices but who buoyed everybody up); for Ferdinand Eberstadt (who saw, with Baruch, that priorities in the use of scarce materials are at the heart of large-scale war); for Henry Kaiser (as a shipbuilder who instinctively grasped "Roosevelt's rule that energy was more efficient than efficiency"); and for Bill Douglas (who never did get in on the war, thanks to the Machiavellian connivings and opposition of Harry Hopkins).

Reading the roster of Mr. Janeway's heroes, one is forced to the conclusion that *The Struggle for Survival* proves a very definite case against his own theories of successful wartime economic organization. For Janeway admires the smart operator, the man who can ignore the blueprint and slash viciously through the red tape. He praises Assistant Secretary of War Louis Johnson for bypassing Secretary of War Woodring, he cheers the understrappers who pulled several fast ones on Jesse Jones of the RFC. In Janeway's definition of efficiency, chains and hierarchies of command are made to be broken, and organization charts are something for the wastebasket, or at most to hang on the wall.

The real thesis of Janeway's book is that we won the war by making it a grab-bag for 155 million Americans. Wages, despite lip service to the principle of "equality of sacrifice," constantly rose. The farmer got rich. The Stork Club went on the traveler's expense account; the U. S. Treasury paid the Big Shot's liquor bill. Easy amortization policies enabled more than one company to come out of the war with wholly new and efficient plants. Very Important Personages saw the world at government expense, and actually had time for stop-offs in Florida or at Waikiki. With incentive blooming all over the place, the nation really managed to produce. The Office of Price Administration did set prices, but they were prices that took the market into account—and where they didn't, the black marketeer saw to it that people had enough steak and hamburger to provide the energy for a full day's work. If morals supposedly suffered because of the black market, that was merely proof that the very idea of price-fixing is the biggest immorality of them all.

Janeway calls one of his chapters "The Administration of Anarchy," and that was exactly what it was. By allowing people to make their own decisions once the government contracts had been let, we got the "spontaneous cooperation of a free people" that is Woodrow Wilson's definition of democracy. It is true that we had a big cushion of fat in 1940—fat in the form of fifteen million unemployed or semi-employed people, fat in the form of unused factory capacity, fat in the very grain and texture of the American soil. It is also true that next time we may not have so much fat to consume (the labor market is tight in 1951). But fat or no fat, it is not in the books that "controls," strictly applied, can release energy. The excise tax, slapped in varying proportions on all manufacturers that a government needs to discourage, would be a more efficient way of channeling wartime energy.

As one opposed to price controls, statism and government planning, I am inclined to think Mr. Janeway makes a good case for his hero, Franklin D. Roosevelt. But it is a short-term case. Roosevelt (to his credit) was no capital-*P* Planner, but (to his discredit) he was a shortsighted man when it came to the long-term results of policy. His offhand improvisations of the New Deal period (which consisted of spending other people's money) cheered a nation up, but they also set in motion a long-term process that must weaken the individual as the self-reliant entity a man should be. Pragmatism is all very well as an operating procedure provided one's values are good, but Roosevelt had no clear values (or, if he did, they were too anti-Emersonian for my taste). Moreover, Roosevelt never did manage to see that the war against Hitler and Japan was a war within a war, and that a greater totalitarian power would be set free to make a shambles of Eastern Europe and Asia on the very day after our victory.

Janeway realizes this about Roosevelt, but it doesn't turn him against his hero. He seems to think that the challenge of one war is about all that one human being can rise to in a single lifetime. He may be right about this. But if he is right, it remains more than ever true that the people who were wrong about Russia, along with Roosevelt, are the very people who should not be entrusted with the present crisis. They have fought their war, and they are psychologically incapacitated for fighting the next.

26
Academic Politics

January 28, 1952

Just the other day in the back columns of the *Freeman*, Gerald Warner Brace was arguing that the British novel has for a generation "lost touch with mankind and has indulged itself in ironic complacence and somewhat sterile brain stuff." Mr. Brace is almost 100 percent correct in his judgment, but there is at least one English novelist who is an exception to his devastating generalization. The exception is C. P. Snow, author of *The Masters*. Mr. Snow, who has been a Cambridge don, a physicist-director of the English Electric Company, a Civil Service commissioner, a wartime government servant and a university executive, has something of the same ability at making intellectual tradition come alive in ultra-modern personae that Gerald Brace exhibited in *The Garrettson Chronicle*. If his theory of the novel seems defective when compared with Brace's, he is still a finished craftsman, a first-rate dramatist, and a man with a lively sense of the incredible variety of human personality.

What Snow brings out in *The Masters* is the impact, in a college election, that academic conniving and faction can have on the character of a group of presumably mature and responsible men. As *The Masters* opens, the head of a nameless Cambridge University college lies stricken with inoperable cancer. The Master, Vernon Royce, still has about a year to live, but the fellows of the college split immediately into two bitter factions over the choice of a successor. Academic politics, like any species of office politics, can be just as murderous and time-consuming as a quarrel for the perquisites and the spoil of a presidency or prime ministership, and Snow makes the most of a bitterly dramatic situation. As he demonstrates, the love of power does strange things to human beings, and there are not many whom it ennobles. No doubt there are some people in the world who want power for genuinely impersonal reasons, but I have met with very few of them; as the years go by I am more and more impressed with a theory advanced by Alex Comfort and Herbert Read that the craving to hold political office has its roots in pathology far more often than in genuine idealism. Certainly it is pathology that moves C. P. Snow's character, Dr. Paul Jago, to seek the mastership of the college still presided over by the dying Vernon Royce. As for the impassive Redvers Thomas Arbuthnot Crawford, the scientist who is Paul Jago's rival for the office, who can say what it is that moves him? Crawford has an objective habit of mind, but things lie buried in his character that Snow merely hints at. And certainly Crawford is supported by the embittered Nightingale for reasons that belong in a psychiatrist's case notebook even more than they belong in a novel.

Dr. Jago has imagination and sympathetic understanding of human beings, but his basic feeling of insecurity makes it necessary for him to seek the commendation and endorsement of those around him. It is for this reason that he feels impelled to electioneer for himself. His wife, a neurotic woman, has even more need for outside recognition than her husband. Jago is supported by Arthur Brown, the born political manipulator, because Brown wants a man in office through whom he can achieve his own rather commendable and decent ends. Simply because he is so adept at arranging things, Brown creates the illusion over a long period that Jago will be a seven-to-six victor over Crawford when Vernon Royce dies. But the heady flush of almost certain victory brings things out in Jago's character that finally cause the defection of Brown's friend Chrystal. As we take leave of Mr. Snow's little group of dons, the impassive Crawford has just been installed in office. The wounds that are the legacy of ten months of attempted persuasion and counter-persuasion, of hitting below the belt and between the eyes, will throb throughout the college courts and even at high table for a long time. But eventually the dons will close ranks and the ancient enmities and loyalties will change, yielding place to new. Unlovely though the mechanisms of democratic politics are, they provide a better method of ensuring a give-and-take plasticity in human institutions than the arbitrary decrees of totalitarians.

Snow's novel is an exciting fable for our time. If democratic politics depend on appeal to the fundamentally pathological in man, it is nevertheless better that the pathological should be indulged rather than suppressed. One of Snow's characters, the ancient Gay, casts his vote out of a vast frivolity. Another, the venerable Eustace Pilbrow, makes his choice on a complete irrelevancy. Two others, the supple Roy Calvert and the contemplative Lewis Eliot, vote for the more imaginative man because they admire their own considerable virtues of imaginative projection. The waverers waver in their choice because their own characters are in conflict; others stand fast because of a fear of being thought indecisive. Practically no vote is the result of wholly disinterested thought or conviction. No matter, says Snow in effect; the important point is that men are better off when they are faced with the consequences of voluntary choice, even though they may lack the ability to bring fundamental intelligence to bear on the act of choice. The only alternative to the admittedly ugly and often silly reality of democratic faction and intrigue is the still uglier and even more idiotic reality of tyrannical force.

C. P. Snow is a born dramatist. His propensity for sticking to the dramatic unities, however, underlines a somewhat glaring defect in his theory of the novel. What *The Masters* is about is an election, and Snow thinks it incumbent upon him to stick like a limpet to his subject. The consequence of this is that we learn almost nothing about his dons as teachers or as scholars, or as nonpolitical human beings. Moreover, we see nothing of the students—who, after all, are the fundamental *raison d'être* for the college in the first place. In other words, Snow's preoccupation with the political issue of the election forces him to exclude perhaps three-fourths or five-sixths of human life from his pages. Although there are some sidelights on college money-raising, the real values of the academic life do not emerge until Snow gets around to an appendix to his novel called "Reflections on the College Past." These pages are rich with atmosphere, and they deal with professors not as politicians, but as scholars and teachers and gentlemen. The echo of students' feet resounds through the pages of the appendix as it does not resound through the main story.

I have called C. P. Snow's novel a fable for our time. By inadvertence, however, it becomes a double fable. By design it makes out a wonderful case for the politics of democratic choice. By inadvertence it proves that politics should be the least part of a normal human being's range of preoccupation and interest. Men cannot be creative, inventive, curious, amusing and loving if they are faced every day with the necessity of thinking about the consequences of political power. It is for that reason that Thomas Jefferson's maxim—"that government is best which governs least"—retains its truth for all time.

27
A Veiled Irony in Academe

September 8, 1952

The occupational badge of the modern American college professor is a veiled, oblique irony: the breed in general no longer cultivates the explicit commentary of a Charles Townsend Copeland, the enthusiasm of a William Lyon Phelps, the *ex cathedra* tones of a William Graham Sumner. This latter-day habit of speech and mind is half superior, half defensive; the accent is that of a caste which feels it must cope with the world of money, politics and power without sacrificing the theory—or maybe one should say the illusion—that it is responsible only to canons established by itself. The irony is significant of a tension that arises in part from an uneasy conscience, for it is certainly arguable that nobody in this world can be responsible to himself alone when somebody else is kicking up the endowment and paying the bills. But from whatever source the tension rises, it is a subject for drama; and good dramatic art is what Gerald Warner Brace has made of it in his novel of life in a New England college community, *The Spire.*

Like all good novelists, Mr. Brace uses the questions of philosophy as keys to character, not as mere opportunity for ideological harangue. *The Spire* is primarily a story of how a rather self-contained Vermonter, Henry Gaunt, picks up his life again after his first wife dies in the midst of presenting him with a son. Thus it has a broadly universal appeal and reference. But Henry Gaunt happens to be an English professor; he happens to have an appointment to the faculty of the western Massachusetts hill town college of Wyndham, and he happens to become dean in the course of his year at Wyndham. Brace builds his story out of the particulars of life in a college community in the Bill Buckley era, and these particulars twist and shape the course of Henry Gaunt's love affair with Liz Houghton in a way that is peculiar to the local circumstances of Wyndham.

So sure is Brace's technique that one can scarcely unravel the various strands that go to make up his story. A thorough understanding of several worlds is present in *The Spire*, and the several worlds overlap and intermingle with all the heterogeneity of life in the real world. Brace, a New Englander ever since his early transplanting from New York State, knows his Yankees, with their habits of conveying much in little speech. He knows the ways of a decadent Puritanism, too. It was precisely a decadent Puritanism that caused old Mrs. Dudley, the self-elected arbiter of morals in Wyndham, to hound Liz Houghton when that generous, ardent girl involved herself in a love affair that resulted in an illegitimate child. Liz was clapped into an institution for a period, and it has left its mark on her. All this happened long before Henry Gaunt came to Wyndham; in the meanwhile Liz has struggled back to become secretary to David Gidney, the college president. But Mrs. Dudley, who remembers that Liz's father, old George Houghton, was fired from the mathematics faculty because of hysterical complaints that he had pawed some children, has sworn that no Houghton has a claim to complete rehabilitation in the college community.

The irony of this is all the more pronounced in that Mrs. Dudley's most illustrious ancestor, Thomas Gale, had been a somewhat disreputable poet, a Gothic cross between Emily Dickinson and Herman Melville. Thomas Gale would have appreciated Liz Houghton, a gallant child who wears her rue with a difference, as William Lyon Phelps once said of Hester Prynne. After the early repulse to her emotional generosity, Liz has clenched her jaws and dug in for a lifetime siege. She has willed herself to accept responsibility for her eccentric father, who has shut himself up in his room to make an interminable series of experiments with clocks; and for her brother, a brilliant young man who holds himself in tight repression. (Liz's sister has left the nest, and is important to the story only as a *deus ex machina* property that is necessary to a final twist of the plot.) With her family on her hands,

Liz has shut out all ideas of marriage and children. She will carry through her self-imposed tragedy to the end.

Henry Gaunt, however, perceives Liz's true inwardness; he knows even before he becomes dean that she is to be the second Mrs. Gaunt. This means that Henry must buck the entire community of Wyndham. Marriage with a latter-day Hester Prynne is no absolute bar to academic preferment in the modern world, but it is a substantial hurdle in the community of Wyndham.

The love affair of Henry Gaunt and Liz Houghton takes a full academic year to mature. It comes to its fruition amid a muted fight between President Gidney and his trustees over the resignation of Dean Markham and the "retirement" of a "dear old dodo" (Gidney's characterization) from the economics department. Meanwhile there are several other conflicts going on—for example, one in the English department that is expressed by the surly reaction of Greg Flanders, the pretentious Kafka-cum-Freud aesthete, to a suggestion that an authority on Dickens, Dumas and O. Henry be added to the Wyndham faculty. Because of such contention over the curriculum and the type of professor deemed modern by President Gidney, Henry Gaunt's desire to marry Liz is more bothersome than it might have been in, say, 1934 or 1944. Gidney, who is subconsciously jealous of Gaunt, doesn't want to take on any more fights at the moment, so Henry and Liz depart at the end of the academic year.

The Buckley-provoked quarrel over who is to be responsible for the orientation of a curriculum is what makes *The Spire* a contemporary document. Judged solely by what appears in the novel, it would be difficult to know just where Gerald Brace, who teaches English at Boston University, stands on the Buckley issue. As a dramatist he uses it to differentiate and motivate some of his characters, and that is all. Brace's dedication—"to my colleagues, who live, love, labor freely, nor discuss a brother's fight to freedom"—would lead one to believe that the author is anti-Buckley. But when one reflects upon the savage irony that underlies Brace's treatment of Greg Flanders, one is not so sure: certainly the alumni and the trustees have as much right to a voice on matters of the curriculum as have the like of Greg Flanders. Gidney himself as much as tells Henry Gaunt that everybody connected with

Wyndham must be considered when decisions of policy are being made, which is a fair way of putting it.

But just as Jane Austen's novels succeed with only the barest references to the circumambient Napoleonic wars, so Brace's *The Spire* succeeds with only an oblique commentary on the rights or wrongs of Buckleyism. Brace's social opinions do not dictate the course of the drama that finally forces Liz Houghton out of her willfully imposed role of sacrificial lamb. There is a world beyond Wyndham, and Henry Gaunt and Liz choose finally to dare it as husband and wife. Their story is tricky and brilliant as Brace works it out. The flavor of his byplay is unmistakable: Brace knows how to describe a New England village, with its chalk-white houses, or the menacing November sky over a Vermont hill farm, or the curt, quiet beauty of an unused country church. Mr. Brace knows northern New England life in all its phases and localities. He is a first-rate regionalist who happens to be a first-rate novelist, and one hopes his book will have the success it deserves.

28
Belaboring Laissez Faire

February 11, 1952

If I had undertaken, twenty years ago, to write a book about William Graham Sumner, the sociology professor; Stephen J. Field, the jurist; and Andrew Carnegie, the charitable tycoon, it would no doubt have been similar to Robert Green McCloskey's *American Conservatism in the Age of Enterprise.* But something has happened to me in the past two decades. Arthur Schlesinger, Jr. may attribute my change of mind to "fear," but in all sincerity I do not think that mere visceral shock accounts for my shift in orientation. I have simply lived to see at least four major brands of statism tried out. I have seen Leninist and Stalinist statism murder its millions in Soviet Russia. I have watched Hitlerian statism kill Jews by the hundreds of thousands in central Europe. I have been a witness (sometimes on the spot) to the destruction of vitality and initiative forced by socialist statism in Britain. And I have lived through eighteen years of New Deal and Fair Deal governments that have cut the value of every insurance policy in America at least in half. That is what has happened to me, and I wonder therefore at the insulation of Harvard University, where Robert Green McCloskey fills a chair as assistant professor of government.

Professor McCloskey uses Sumner, Field and Carnegie as three excuses for belaboring industrial "laissez faire." He seems to think that Sumner, Field and Carnegie somehow robbed the phrases of the English common law and the American Bill of Rights of their "humane" content. Supposedly they exalted "property rights" at the expense of "human rights." They were all for protecting "free enterprise"; but as the nineteenth century wore on they cared less and less for the exercise of a free conscience and free speech. In

McCloskey's estimation Sumner forgot morality and ethics to promote a "dubious scientism." Field, as a Supreme Court justice, degenerated into an apologist for corporate wealth. And Carnegie let his acquisitive instincts override his humane impulses. Thus Professor McCloskey in this conventional display of the New Academic Orthodoxy.

McCloskey makes out the sketchiest of cases for his point of view. He is addicted to the Big Cliché. Let me document his superficiality in regard to William Graham Sumner, whom I happen to know something about. He argues that Sumner was, in economics, a man of untested preconceptions. According to McCloskey, Sumner's mind was "closed in youth to the entry of new basic ideas, new tastes, the opinions of others." His conceptions of capital, labor, money and trade were "formed" by Harriet Martineau's *Illustrations,* which he read at the age of thirteen in a Hartford library. His ideas about "labor agitators" he supposedly got from his father, a mechanic who quit Lancashire in 1836, the year of a memorable spinners' strike, and emigrated to America.

Now of course Sumner learned something from his father and from Harriet Martineau. They were the "radicals" of their day. But Professor McCloskey is utterly silly when he goes on to argue that Sumner never put his early mentors to the test of experience or sought the lessons of history. In truth, Sumner projected his studies of industrial organization back through the Renaissance to the days of the Roman Empire. He chewed and worried at the fascinating subject of Rome's moral decline, which seemed to him to go hand in hand with the proliferation of Roman trade controls and the increase in taxation. He posed Harriet Martineau's Cobdenism against the background of eighteenth-century mercantilism. And he came to mature conclusions that had nothing to do with "preconceptions."

Those conclusions were profoundly antipathetic to the actuating beliefs of the plutocrats of Sumner's time. Big business in his day fought for the protective tariff. But the protective tariff, to Sumner, was a "job" or a "steal" which aroused his moral passion. He attacked the "nuisance" of the Willimantic Linen Company, which used its tariff-protected price schedule to pay 95 percent dividends to its stockholders. In the campaign of 1884 he was acrimoniously contemptuous of James G. Blaine, the Republican candidate for president, because "all the rings and jobbers in the United States" seemed to be rallying to Blaine's support. He was against the "funny money" proposals of greenbackers and free silverites, not because he cared for bondholders, but because he cared for the "forgotten man" of the industrious lower middle class. "The reason why I defend the millions of the millionaire," he wrote, "is not that I love the millionaire, but that I love my own wife and children, and that I know no way in which to get the defense of society for my hundreds, except to give my help, as a member of society, to protect his millions." Or, as Benjamin Stolberg put it at a later date, "You cannot devalue the dollar of John D. Rockefeller without also devaluing the dollar of John Doe."

It is perfectly true, as Professor McCloskey says, that Sumner had little use for antitrust legislation. But Sumner's defense of large aggregations of capital cannot be equated with any defense of artificially maintained monopoly. He believed in striking at artificial monopolies by eradicating their causes, not by policing their results. His words on the use of a patent system to maintain monopoly sound almost like certain passages from the works of Thurman Arnold or Supreme Court Justice William O. Douglas. "It is obviously most absurd," Sumner wrote, "to establish a protective system and a patent system and then to denounce patentees and protected interests for availing themselves of the advantages which have been granted them." Finally, Sumner denounced in his most impassioned terms the idea of "manifest destiny," which was projecting the United States into such useless and unnecessary ventures as the Spanish–American War. As he put it, his patriotism was of the kind "which is outraged by the notion that the United States never was a great nation until in a petty three months' campaign it knocked to pieces a poor, decrepit, bankrupt old state like Spain." He continued: "To hold such an opinion as that is to abandon all American standards, to put shame and scorn on all that our ancestors tried to build up here, and to go over to the standards of which Spain is a representative."

So spoke Sumner, the "old American." But Professor McCloskey will not permit his subject the honor of remaining an "old American." He insists on Sumner's "aridity" and lack of humanity;

he insists that this defender of old republican virtues became a man whose values were purely "material." Material? Was it a "materialist" who said, "I'm not afraid to die, in fact I have always had a certain curiosity about death"? Was it a "materialist" who went through novel after novel in ten or twelve languages? Was it a "materialist" who, late in life, read the whole body of Greek tragedy? Was it a "materialist" who, on a picnic with a group of young women at Lake Saltonstall near New Haven, amused himself and the others on a rainy afternoon by enacting the part of Shakespeare's Juliet from memory over a cart tail in an empty barn? Was it a "materialist" who served for twenty-odd years on the Connecticut State Board of Education, riding about the state in a buckboard and sleeping in cold spare rooms to see that the public schools were properly maintained? If these were the acts of a "materialist," then, to turn the Christian Science dogma around, all is material, even the ultimate mystery that can bring a sequoia tree out of a tiny seed, or a thinking, purposeful man out of what begins as a mere blob of protoplasm.

What Professor McCloskey does not realize is that Sumner—who did occasionally say confusing and contradictory things about "natural rights" (things that contradict the whole drift of his work)—was actually "all of a piece" in his attitude toward the rights of the free citizen. The free citizen must have the property right because the right to individual ownership is fundamental to the maintenance of human dignity and spiritual freedom in society. Without the property right, the fulcrum by which one maintains civil rights disappears. The curse of socialism, as Professor Jewkes has so well explained in his *Ordeal by Planning,* is that by depriving men of a base in private property it robs them of their ability to maintain themselves against the incorrigible materialism of officialdom. "Social Darwinism," which is a sin that McCloskey imputes to capitalism and to Sumner, rages at its virulent worst in states that have called the property right into question. When the property right is weakened, everyone is increasingly at the mercy of the bureaucracy, and the competition for special privilege becomes too murderous to be borne.

The trouble with McCloskey is that he has only a modern bookman's acquaintance with the tradition and the society that shaped the thinking of Sumner. Raised in Yankee Connecticut, Sumner lived out his life in a community where all of the traditional American rights and freedoms went together. His mature years were spent in New Haven, and if Professor McCloskey wants to know what manner of place old New Haven was, let him read Carleton Beals's fascinating *Our Yankee Heritage.* Because old New Haven was spiritually free, men poured their energy voluntarily into all sorts of curious ventures. The Millerites prayed in the public streets, and Edward Beecher and Thomas Sanford devised a way to dip phosphorous matches by machinery. Yale College turned out Congregational ministers and Eli Whitney invented the system of mass production of interchangeable parts. Josiah Willard Gibbs laid the abstract basis in mathematics for modern physics and Amasa Goodyear invented the steel-tine pitchfork before his son Charles grew up to vulcanize India rubber. Capitalist James Hillhouse planted elm trees at his own expense along the New Haven streets, and Simeon Jocelyn took time out from his clockmaking to invent the first pruning shears. Samuel Morse, son of New Haven's famous geographer Jedidiah Morse, invented the telegraph and Benjamin Silliman established the first university laboratory. The first telephone exchange was opened up in New Haven and the first hinged buckle was made there. Scant wonder that Sumner, living in such a fertile society, looked upon the doctrine of laissez faire and found it good. It added to his well-being and it didn't keep him from enjoying church music.

I had just a taste of Sumner's world during the first ten years of my life (I was eleven years old in New Haven when World War I broke out); the memory of it has helped make me a "reactionary." I plead guilty to wishing to "turn the clock back"—to the year 1913. Arthur Schlesinger, Jr., who accuses me of "fear," is too young to remember that spiritually free day, but if he won't take my word for its beneficence, let him ask his friend Elmer Davis about it. Elmer once wrote a piece called "Good Old 1913," and Elmer never produced a truer title.

29
The Forgotten Man Speaks

February 26, 1951

A nation begins to decline when it neglects its own classics. But no trend is necessarily permanent, and classics can come back. Take the case of William Graham Sumner's *What Social Classes Owe to Each Other*, for example. Published originally in 1883, this little classic of individualism was long unavailable to the general reader. Some three years ago it was reprinted by Pamphleteers, Inc., of Los Angeles. According to my West Coast spies, it has been selling very well.

What Social Classes Owe to Each Other has had the strangest of histories. It was written at a time when the fallacies of welfare-state thinking were just beginning to take hold in America. A professor of economics at Yale in the early 1880s, Sumner sensed the oncoming socialistic deluge when it was the merest trickle. He could hardly know in 1883 that Edward Bellamy was already meditating in Boston on the notions of the utopian socialists, and getting ready to write his *Looking Backward: 2000–1887*, a book which does its best to suffuse the idea of the regimented slave state with a romantic glow. He could hardly have been aware that out in Chicago young Henry Demarest Lloyd was predicting (in the *Chicago Tribune*, of all places) that "the unnatural principles of the competitive economy of John Stuart Mill will be as obsolete as the rules of war by which Caesar slaughtered the fair-haired men, women and children of Germania." Nor could he have known that in Indiana, socialist Eugene V. Debs was taking his first flier in politics, as city clerk of Terre Haute. Yet Sumner felt in his bones that the world of his youth was about to shift on its axis. Faith in individualism was weakening; Sumner knew it from reading the accounts of speeches in the papers. The willingness of the Gilded Age plutocracy to accept government favors in the form of tariffs also impressed him as a sign of decadence; no free society, as he well knew, could be built on hypocrisy.

A profound student of veering social currents, Sumner set his face uncompromisingly against the rising welfare-state principles of the New Day. The record of history told him that the welfare state inevitably becomes the illfare state. In *What Social Classes Owe to Each Other* Sumner tried to underscore the lesson of history by bringing simple arithmetic to bear on the welfarists' proposition. The state, as Sumner said, is all-of-us organized to protect the rights of each-of-us. But when some-of-us try by political manipulation to live off others-of-us, rights necessarily go out the window. In Sumner's estimation the type and formula of most welfare-, or illfare-, state schemes come down to this: A and B put their heads together to decide what C shall be made to do for D. The vice of such scheming is that C is never consulted in the matter; he is simply clubbed by the police power of the state into diverting a part of his earnings to someone he has never seen. C is very likely a most responsible citizen; he is generally the type of person who supports himself uncomplainingly, sees to it that his children are educated, and contributes to the voluntary charities of his neighborhood. If C has any surplus over what it takes to live and provide for his children and his locality, he generally saves it and invests it, thereby adding to the capital equipment by which the nations's standard of living is maintained and raised.

Sumner called C the Forgotten Man. The phrase was doubly prophetic, for by a most ironical sequel Franklin D. Roosevelt picked it up in the 1930s and applied it, not to Sumner's C, but to Sumner's D. This simple act of misappropriation, which made C more forgotten than ever, did much to get the welfare-state notions of the New Deal accepted by a troubled nation. There's nothing like a golden voice uttering a good phrase, misapplied or not, to win votes.

If the attempted rehabilitation of D at the expense of C really served to help D, there might be a case for taking a portion of the product of C's energy by state fiat. But it is written in the arithmetic books of the seventh grade that D is hurt, not helped, when A and B scheme to mulct C of the fruits of his toil. Now it cannot be that Americans have actually forgotten their seventh grade arithmetic; they have merely ceased to apply it to their thinking on social matters. Any child ought to be able to see that if C has, let us say, $3,000, it will buy just $3,000 worth of goods and no more. Let us say that A and B take $1,000 of C's money to spend on D. Some of the $1,000 must be used to support the sterile machinery of state collection, bookkeeping, and redistribution. But after the politicians and their officeholding dependents have taken their cut of the $1,000, D gets some of the money. In the natural course of events he uses it—to consume. What is left to C of the original $3,000 also goes largely into consumption; there simply isn't enough left of the total to enable C to save anything out for investment. So under welfare politics there is no addition from C's $3,000 to the capital stock of the nation. Thus, because of the schemings of A and B allegedly in behalf of D, the industrial system does not expand. The upshot of this is that D is prevented from getting a job. He remains at the mercy of A and B, who continue to take it out on C.

Since A and B are of the predatory type of do-gooder who insists on being unselfish with other people's money, they are not likely to get around to taking a refresher course in seventh grade arithmetic. But if D has any pride at all, he must some day begin to apply what he has learned in the seventh grade to his own social plight. Does he want forever to remain a ward of A and B, getting a continually decreasing portion of consumer goods as the population grows and presses against the limits of a static industrial system? Wouldn't it be far better for him to throw in his lot with C in an effort to expand the capital plant and so create a productive niche for himself in society?

The reason D has not been able to see that his welfare depends on making a common front with C is that A and B have learned to delude him with inflationary tricks. A and B are always pointing out that the "gross national product" is up by so many billions of dollars over the product of ten years ago. What they do not bother to tell D is that the value of the dollar has been debauched and that it is no longer a good measuring stick for anything. It is true enough that the gross national product of the United States has continued to increase. Despite the scheming of A and B, the Forgotten Man has been able to squeeze out some money for investment even after he has paid most of his savings out to support D. But by all the logic of arithmetic the United States would be far richer today in capital equipment if Franklin Roosevelt had made the correct identification of William Graham Sumner's Forgotten Man. If C had been left unmulcted there would be more butter for everybody—and more guns for our allies.

Sumner is usually thought of as a heartless logician, a basically uncharitable man. *What Social Classes Owe to Each Other* is, however, almost biblical in its understanding of the "law of sympathy." At the very best, says Sumner, one of us fails in one way and another of us in another, "if we do not fail altogether." It will not do to condone failure abstractly, but if a man happens to be pinned to earth by a falling tree, it is scarcely appropriate to his immediate predicament to deliver him a lecture on carelessness. True, the man may have been careless; but a lecture won't get the tree off his leg. Amid the chances and perils of life, says Sumner, men owe to other men their aid and sympathy. But aid and sympathy must operate in the field of private and personal relationships under the regulation of reason and conscience. If men trust to the state to supply "reason and conscience," they so deaden themselves that the "law of sympathy" ceases to operate anywhere. Men who shrug off their personal obligations become hard and unfeeling, and it is small wonder then that they are entirely willing to go along with hard and unfeeling politics. It is when he decides to "let the state do it" that the humanitarian ends up by condoning the use of the guillotine for the "betterment" of man.

So far as I am aware, *What Social Classes Owe to Each Other* is not used as a text in any college in the country. If it is reprinted often enough, however, the time will come when it will make its way back to the campus. Students are curious even when they are deluded and misled, and when books are available, students will find their way to them.

30
Natural Law

April 23, 1951

Both the Declaration of Independence and the American Constitution have their origins in the natural law philosophy of the eighteenth century. This philosophy presupposes that the phenomena of nature—and of man, as part of the natural order—can be described in orderly terms, in principles, in *generalities*. The business of the scientist is to seek for the generality that explains the fall of the apple and the motions of the planets; the business of the constitution-maker is to determine and proclaim the political generalities that are best calculated to guarantee the individual "rights" that are deducible from the nature of man.

In all of this I have never been able to see anything "mystical" or "absolutistic." Yet I am constantly being assailed by friends who accuse me of "selling out" to obscurantism, or to Saint Thomas Aquinas, or to a "brooding Omnipresence in the sky," when I say I believe in a natural law for human beings in society, and in the natural rights that may be deduced from the workings of natural law. These friends would not argue that it is possible to jump off a thousand-foot precipice and arrive at the bottom without dashing oneself to pieces on the rocks. Yet they can and do argue, for example, that human freedom is possible in a society in which the state owns or controls the means of livelihood. What they fail to see in the latter instance is the *physical* connection between human freedom and the "right" to possess one's own physical base—that is, property owned privately, or in voluntary mutual association. There are laws governing this physical connection just as there are laws to explain the fall of the apple. And the penalty exacted if a human society ignores the laws governing the natural right to property is just as inexorable as the penalty exacted by jumping off a cliff or by overindulgence in alcohol. The man who jumps off a cliff will be injured or killed, the man who drinks too much will develop delirium tremens—and the society that allows its politicians to seize the economic machine from private individuals will get purges, slave camps, starvation and totalitarian war. Thus the workings of natural law.

The makers of the American state either knew all about the idea of natural law or breathed it in along with the air of their times. Today, however, most of us have forgotten the origins of our Constitution, with its theory of checks and balances, its distinction between individual and states' rights and federal powers, and its individualistic "absolutes" as laid down in the Bill of Rights. All the more reason, then, for proclaiming the contemporary worth of two recent books, *The Key to Peace* by Clarence Manion and *The Way to Security* by Henry C. Link. These books are quite dissimilar in substance, in tone, in purpose, and in vocabulary. Yet they are both based on natural-law thinking, and the God that they exalt is a God that any good eighteenth-century philosopher would recognize as "Nature's God," even though Manion is a Roman Catholic and Link is a Congregationalist.

Clarence Manion is dean of Notre Dame University's College of Law and a founder of the Natural Law Institute. His book is an excellent presentation of the spiritual origins of the American Constitution and the American system of free individual opportunity. It was Peter Drucker, I believe, who first pointed to the fact that the American Revolution was, in reality, a conservative counterrevolution against King George III's revolutionary despotism. The American colonists were fighting for ancient English rights, which were a legacy of Christian natural-law doctrines. When our constitution-makers assembled at Philadelphia, they took with them an old, deeply rooted Christian theory of the nature of man. The result was an American state founded on respect for the individual and his natural rights. It was the first great state to be founded consciously on the individual.

A few years later the generation of the French Revolution had an opportunity to imitate the Americans in this matter of building a state on the theory of natural law and the reserved "inalienable" rights of the person. Unfortunately, the French got themselves boggled in Rousseau's theory of the supremacy of the *general* will over individual rights. When this general will, as interpreted by Robespierre, Napoleon and Joseph Fouché, had had its way a lot of people had disappeared from the surface of the earth. The natural law of a republic, or a democracy, founded on a fundamental disregard for the individual's inalienable rights, had worked itself out through the inevitable cycle of terror, bloodshed, dictatorship, war and collapse.

Dean Manion is an excellent pamphleteer; he is simple, clear, and graphic; he sticks to bold strokes. Moreover, although a Roman Catholic himself, he has done his best to state his propositions in terms that can be easily grasped by Catholics and Protestants alike. Following Jefferson, he argues that government is, even at best, a necessary evil. This claim seems to have involved him in an argument with Roman Catholics who insist that the state should be considered in the light of a positive good. According to Wilfrid Parsons, for example, there is a difference between the "*coercive* state" (which Dean Manion rightly holds to be an evil, even though necessary) and the "*directive* state" (or the state that is set up to guide everyone, even the saints, to the common good). Well, let us admit that there might be a difference between the idea of the coercive state and the idea of the directive state. (The distinction would be fine-spun, at best.) But a directive state implies a theocracy and a state church, and it was the specific intention of our Founding Fathers that there should be no state church in America. In the light of the stated opinions of the American constitution-makers, it is hard for a non-Catholic to see how Dean Manion could have explained the making of the American system in a manner that would be entirely satisfactory to those who believe in a theocratic organization of society. Wilfrid Parsons argues that Dean Manion's philosophy must end in anarchy and the consequent destruction of liberty. But Manion specifically states that "personal rights must be exercised consistently with the equal rights of others." It is by protecting the rights of each and every individual citizen that the state prevents anarchy, preserves liberty—and promotes the general welfare in the only way it can be promoted without subverting the principles of a free society.

Henry Link is not primarily concerned with high constitutional matters in *The Way to Security.* A practicing psychologist, Dr. Link is writing for individuals whose problems arise out of the everyday give and take of life, not out of philosophical embroilment in high politics. Nevertheless, the political climate of opinion plays a large background role in Dr. Link's thinking about the personal relationships of his clients. It is the dominant opinion of our time that security is to be had only through state guarantees: through social-security payments, minimum-wage legislation, politically directed union-management bargaining, and so forth and so on. This accent on security *as a gift from the outside* is breeding a race that is rapidly becoming deficient in inner resourcefulness. Dr. Link has observed the connection between the spread of our dominant modern political theory and the growth of personal insecurity at a thousand and one points. So his useful little book becomes, in the final analysis, a book on politics. It may seem a little far-fetched to allege a direct correspondence between the rise of the welfare state and the growth of the sleeping-pill habit. But Americans never bought three billion sleeping pills a year in the days when they relied on their own efforts to gain them their own social security.

Dr. Link believes that the insights of the good psychologist must often prove the case for the insights of the Scriptures, and vice versa. When he first began pointing out the indubitable fact that human wisdom existed long before the birth of Sigmund Freud, Dr. Link was something of a maverick among psychologists. Now the more pretentious of his professional brethren (see the recent works of Erich Fromm) are catching up with him. We doubt that the academic panjandrums will give credit where credit is due, but Dr. Link can take high personal satisfaction in having been the prophet of a salutary trend.

31
The Welfare Hydra

May 21, 1951

The other day a friend of mine, president of a small Vermont college, chose to twit me about the policies of the *Freeman*. "You say you are for freedom, for libertarian economics," he said, "but the articles you print seem to be in favor of freedom for the big fellows. Why don't you do something for small business?"

The answer is that the *Freeman* fights the battle for small business every fortnight. It does this by opposing the growth of the welfare state. If my friend doesn't believe there is any necessary connection between the decline of small business and the growth of state welfarism (or, for that matter, between the shrinkage of college endowment funds and the steep increase in progressive taxation), I would counsel him to read Jules Abels's *The Welfare State: A Mortgage on America's Future*. For here, in almost mathematical demonstration, is the proof that state welfarism wins its illusory victories by transforming an expanding economy into an expending economy. It dries up the sources of growth, stealing from the future for the sake of the present. And at some point in its hectic development it even begins to eat up the capital plant that exists already: under welfare-state taxation and inflation, businessmen find it increasingly difficult to set aside proper reserves for depreciation.

Abels takes it as axiomatic that the only way to raise the standard of living in a nation is to increase the capital invested per wage earner employed. It follows from this that true welfare (as opposed to tax-supported state welfare) is a function of the investment process. But the welfare state, as it increases the scope of its politically motivated charities, leaves less and less money for investment.

Before the Korean War the American labor force was growing at a rate of between six hundred thousand and a million a year. Since it takes $10,000 of investment capital to make a job for a new worker, this means that the American economy needs at least $6 billion in new risk capital every twelve months. But this is only part of the story, for industry has constantly to replace obsolescent machinery, and the depreciation allowances of the past cannot come anywhere near paying the bills for renewal of equipment in the highly inflated present. Again, if the productivity of industry goes up by 2 percent each year, this means that presently employed workers inevitably tend to become victims of technological unemployment. To reemploy these "released" workers means more new jobs at $10,000 investment per worker.

With these facts in mind it is easy to grasp the relevance of Abels's slogan: "Expand or die!" But who is to do the expanding? Can new enterprisers, the small businessmen who are the hallowed heroes of American tradition, get the capital to create new jobs? As long as welfare-state taxation methods persist, the answer is no.

Abels explains it all in a sprightly chapter called "The Man Who Made the Better Widget." He introduces us to Hugo Jones, a bright fellow who has invented and patented a better widget than those produced by Super-Widget and Mighty-Widget. Jones needs $50,000 capital to launch the Jones Widget. He goes to his local bank, but since he has no security to offer, the bank turns him down. He then turns to Cousin Ernest, who is an official in an investment banking firm. But investment firms don't take issues for small items that cannot count on hitting the popular imagination. So Jones has no other choice than to scout around among individuals. His good friend Brown, who is living in retirement on a large savings fund, won't take a chance on the widget; he insists on sticking to blue-chip stocks that bring both high earnings and liquidity. Friend Bell, who boasts an income of $50,000 a year, is no better than Brown. Says Bell to Jones: "If I put up $25,000, half your capital, I ought to get $2,500. But let's see what happens after Mr. Whiskers takes his cut. First, you pay a 25 percent corporation tax on the $5,000 profit. That drops my share down to $1,875. Then I have to pay a personal income tax in the 75 percent bracket.

That leaves me only $468. *So I haven't gotten a return of 10 percent; I've gotten a return of 1.9 percent.* You'll have to agree that the Jones Widget looks to me like mighty small pickings."

A pertinacious fellow, Jones goes on to solicit aid from his friend Howard. But Howard doesn't want to risk a capital loss of $25,000 when the government limits capital-loss deductions to $1,000 a year for five years. As for Kline, another of Jones's moneyed friends, he prefers to put his capital into tax-free municipal bonds, which he buys on margin.

Jones finally gets the money to start his widget business when his Aunt Letitia dies, leaving him $50,000 after taxes. But the welfare state isn't through with him. It taxes his company profits, it taxes his personal income, it raises his labor costs, it inflates the price of his raw materials, and it taxes his "inventory profits" at a time when he needs those very profits merely to renew his inventory. In the end Jones is forced to sell out to his big competitor, Super-Widget. As Abels says, "mergeritis" is the big disease of the welfare state. And a result of mergeritis is, of course, to encourage monopoly.

My Vermont college president friend is a bright fellow and ought to be able to see that the whole drift of the Fair Deal is to choke American industry at its growing points. He ought also to be able to see that American education will have more and more difficulty in raising endowment money as welfare-state taxation grows. The result of Fair Deal policies is to compel both business and education to turn to government for funds. But government has no substance apart from what it can get from its citizens, either by taxing them or by stealing from them through inflating the currency.

Mr. Abels ends his book on the welfare state by reminding us sarcastically of the fate of Rome in the time of Diocletian, when there were "more recipients of government largesse than there were taxpayers." As Abels says, "The orgy of [Roman] spending consumed the capital of the commonwealth. All business fell under the control of monopolies owned directly or indirectly by the Emperor and milked dry of their profits so that opportunities for expansion were stifled. Poverty keeping step with increasingly reckless government spending marked the decline of the greatest empire of all time."

Unless people like my Vermont college president friend can see what is being done to us under the shibboleths of "liberalism," the day of our own Diocletian is not far distant. Can books like Mr. Abels's *The Welfare State* reverse the swift-running current? I would like to believe it, but my fingers are crossed. The Word seems a feeble weapon these days.

32
What Did Ike Believe?

February 25, 1952

In his *Eisenhower: The Man and the Symbol* John Gunther conclusively proves that Ike is to be liked. We learn a great deal about the particularities of Ike's likable exterior personality from the Gunther method of reporting, which establishes Dwight David Eisenhower as an excellent bridge player, a good amateur cook, a golfer of parts, a painter who ranks a little below Winston Churchill, and a reader whose tastes run to violently gaudy pulp Westerns. We also learn a good deal about Ike's Abilene, Kansas childhood, though this comes secondhand, by way of other books about Ike. The high points of Ike's own *Crusade in Europe* are also well presented by Gunther. But as to Ike's *ideas*, which might make him less likable to certain people if they were known, Gunther proves a very unsatisfactory cicerone. John Gunther may have no difficulty getting inside whole continents, but he has not really got "inside" Ike at all.

Since Mr. Gunther has the equipment to be a first-rate reporter, should one ascribe his failure to a period that does not reward journalists for digging behind official facades? (I know the only time I ever got a real news beat—which was on the contents of the 1944 George Marshall letter to Thomas Dewey warning him to keep the truth about Pearl Harbor out of the political campaign—I was looked upon as a sort of moral leper for some months thereafter.) Whatever the answer to this question of the lack of reward for digging, it remains true that Gunther just hasn't dug hard enough, or talked with enough people, or probed his subject for revealing attitudes on specific matters. Maybe he couldn't have done any better under the peculiar circumstances of the looming political campaign: Eisenhower hasn't wanted to talk in advance of a sure sign from the firmament (or maybe Mr. Gallup), and his friends and even his enemies may wish to remain under wraps until after the New Hampshire primaries. But the fact that John Gunther may have been hampered by circumstances does not help answer the questions that still must be asked of Eisenhower before the Republican convention next June.

Gunther does indeed tell us something about Ike's views on both foreign and domestic matters. But the views on foreign policy, as outlined here, are rudimentary and far from profound. As for Ike's domestic philosophy (it is generally "conservative" in its drift), the statements quoted by Gunther lack the sort of amplitude and seasoning that would enable a reader to know how the man might behave in certain situations. Gunther refers to speeches in which Eisenhower has attacked the idea of federal aid to education, or decried the search for an "illusory" security at the expense of initiative and self-reliance, or warned against the "danger" that may arise from "too great a concentration of finance." It is good to know where Eisenhower stands on some of these things, even good to know that he may be a sort of Kansas populist in finance, but, as Gunther himself says, "probably his chief defect, both in general and as a presidential candidate, is lack of definition."

Gunther quotes Eisenhower as exclaiming: "If only a man can have courage enough to take the leadership of the middle." But the "middle," in our time, is anywhere the collectivists and welfare statists choose by their words and activity to place it. The technique of controlling the whereabouts of the "middle" is as easy as it is infallible. If a leftist wants, say, two billion dollars for a given project, he can establish his figure as the middle figure by the simple expedient of asking for four billion. The sort of thinking that Eisenhower has presumably done about "leadership of the middle" merely provokes the Left to double its demands in quest of a "compromise" that will give it precisely what it wants.

Gunther notes, in Eisenhower, the seeming "lack" of a "fixed body of coherent philosophical belief." But if he truly feels that "lack of definition" and "lack of depth" are Eisenhower's chief defects as a presidential candidate, why didn't he press his subject into efforts at definition? A truly first-rate reporter of the old school—an Alva Johnston, for example—would have hacked away at this until he had either elicited something or proved to his own satisfaction that there was little to be had. In the latter event it would not necessarily be established that no "definition" to Eisenhower exists. A man can hold detailed beliefs and still keep mum for his own reasons. But the reporter who can't get answers to searching and, yes, impertinent questions from a public figure at least should know that he must get out the gumshoes and go to work collecting and cross-checking the statements of friends and enemies of that figure. The trouble with Gunther is that he hasn't given the gumshoes a try. He has evidently disdained talking with Ike's presumed enemies, probably on the theory that it would contaminate him to be seen in company of anyone who might conceivably turn up in a "MacArthur–McCormick–McCarthy axis." (Incidentally, the almost universal assumption that a journalist should mingle only with a Socially Approved Set is a measure of what has happened to journalism in our shallow and benighted era.)

"Liberal" preconceptions make it impossible for Gunther to think about the facing-east-facing-west geopolitical position of Russia with the cold precision of an F. A. Voigt or a Sir Halford Mackinder. John Gunther thus is certainly not the man to discover for us whether Eisenhower really believes the world is round. Stalin's own writings on Asia and the colonial question are pretty good reason for thinking that the Bolsheviks are "Asia Firsters." This does not mean that Europe should not be alertly defended; the Russians could after all become "Europe Firsters" overnight. Nor does it mean that Eisenhower is wrong about the urgency of creating a European army. But it does mean that Eisenhower should be questioned—and questioned relentlessly—about his feelings relative to the Marshall–Acheson policy in the Far East. To their credit both Dewey and Stassen have shown their awareness that Russia can fight at will on any front it chooses, and that undue concentration on Europe might lose us Asia, or vice versa. But as to Eisenhower's world perspective, we are still in the dark. Perhaps even less is known about the broader aspects of his foreign policy than about his domestic ideas.

Mr. Gunther's failure to tackle the most important questions about his subject is all the more glaring when one considers his pages about Eisenhower as president of Columbia University. Gunther shows a fine awareness of what various factions thought of Eisenhower on Morningside Heights. He shows no comparable awareness of what larger factions in the outer world think of Eisenhower as a soldier and statesman-to-be. He tells us that Eisenhower has his doubts about the wisdom of the Yalta and Potsdam decisions. But whether Eisenhower thinks the pressure of fifth-column infiltration played any part in softening us up for Yalta is a subject Gunther does not explore. No doubt he would consider it "McCarthyism" even to mention the matter.

33
Gurus' Days Are Numbered

March 24, 1952

Every time I come into New York City (which is on the average of three days a week) I feel myself entering an unreal atmosphere. New York is the capital of the "intellectuals." Lacking the wit or the common sense of any good small-town grain dealer or plumber, these intellectuals believe in the strangest things. They still think a political rally can be improved if it is left to the devices of Broadway characters. They still believe in the malevolence of a verbal hippogriff called "McCarthyism." They still think that anticommunism is not a local political issue (which means they have never listened to a Polish–American on the subject of Yalta, or to an Irish Catholic on the topic of Marxist materialism). They still think that people like to pay taxes, and that businessmen will take chances for peanuts. They still think that the way to redeem a man's character is to feed him without requiring any payment in work, or that the way to get enthusiastic cooperation out of an individual is to compel him to do your bidding by invoking the club of the omnipotent state.

In short, the intellectuals don't need to import any gurus from Tibet or Shangri-la, for each one carries a guru around in his own head. However, the days of the guru are, happily, numbered. What the intellectuals don't know is that an avalanche is about to hit them. Any good philosophical-weather prophet should know what portends when the *Saturday Evening Post* can increase its newsstand sales some 400,000 in a single week by the publication of Whittaker Chambers's "I Was the Witness." The insulated academics of the land (who take their cues from the guru-logic of Park Avenue) may deride the criticisms of a William F. Buckley

Jr.; but five years from now Buckley will have had a very ponderable impact on virtually every economics faculty this side of Cambridge, Massachusetts. As every guru knows, Bob Taft can't win votes, but every time Bob Taft paddles the bottom of a Tex McCrary in public, a dozen hitherto unconvinced taxicab drivers and Scarsdale matrons go over to his camp. It's naughty in guru town to think ill of Owen (*toujours de l'audace*) Lattimore, but when a Maryland Republican says he doesn't like Lattimorism, he suddenly finds himself elevated to the U. S. Senate or to the governor's chair in the border-state capital of Annapolis. To use the immortal language of Harry Serwer, the American people have at last begun to wake to the fact that when a state welfarist comes to your rescue, he invariably gives you a sliver from a slice off your own hide. If the awakening goes far enough and fast enough, there will be another major political overturn next November.

All of which brings me to Raymond Moley, who has just written a first-rate political and economic guide for the awakening American. It is called *How to Keep Our Liberty: A Program for Political Action.* Moley is the man who bet right on Franklin D. Roosevelt's "availability" in 1932, but who bet wrong on the Rooseveltian character. I would differ with Moley about the soundness of what he calls the First New Deal (which was built, after all, on the fascistic or corporative-state gimmick of the NRA), but he has certainly worked his way through to an all-encompassing philosophy of liberty. He knows that liberty depends on a free-enterprise system operating under a dispensation that diffuses the political power and fosters the well-being of the "middle interests" of society. He also knows that it is disastrous to base any political or economic program on what just ain't so, which sets him apart from other characters who write books in guru-town.

Moley makes no fetish of antistatism. He believes that government must do such things as take censuses, build streets, maintain traffic lights, issue stamps, eradicate yellow fever, conserve the forests, provide playgrounds, and register security issues. He believes that monopolies should be restrained. He believes that government—preferably, the several states—should come to the aid of the helpless and the unfortunate. But Moley is antistatist enough to believe that government should not inject its will into matters that are within the realm of business judgment. Regulation, as he puts it, should have as its objective the preservation of free competition. Beyond that, the regulator should not use his power to further his own notions of what the nature of economic institutions should be. The state should not use the tax power to change the nature of economic relationships, or to channel the flow of investment, or to distribute the national income. Taxation should be for the exclusive purpose of raising revenue—and the revenue should not be spent on doing things which people, by use of the principles of voluntary association and mutual underwriting, can do for themselves.

Mr. Moley's book is heartening for the simple reason that it is not built on negations. The author does not despair of the American people, nor does he think the trend toward socialism is "inevitable." He has discovered that a substantial majority of American family units have annual incomes ranging from $2,000 to $5,000 a year. Ownership of our industrial plant has been moving from the hands of the rich and well-to-do to those in the lower-income ranges. Farmers, despite the Brannan claque, are still tied into the "middle interests." Moreover, it is distinctly not true that a "third of the nation" is ill-housed or ill-clothed. Moley's most surprising statistic shows that 50 percent of the people in the lowest income group—"under $1,000"—own their own home. The fallacy that the "under $1,000" group is in dire need derives, he observes, from failure to recognize that many people in this category are retired and living on self-made means of security.

The fact that the American people are fairly well-to-do is, of course, no argument against adding to the sum total of their welfare. But the welfare state does not and cannot do anything for people that they couldn't do better for themselves. Every time the state undertakes to do anything it inevitably transforms potential producers into sterile bureaucrats. (State administration consumes vital energy and produces no goods.) Moreover, the heavy costs of welfare involve a progressive inflation and/or rates of taxation that prevent capital formation and hence strangle industries before they are born.

Moley shows us how we can have social security within the limits of solvency. He has ideas about bringing voluntary medical cooperatives within reach of all the people. He tells us how taxation can be reformed and how the states can recover sources of tax income that are now being channeled into Washington. He has theories about interstate compacts for handling such problems as flood and irrigation control and the use of water power. He has a program for getting the farmer off the city man's back and for keeping him prosperous at the same time. And, finally, he has a viable program for local political action, complete with ideas for tapping potential leadership. He has learned much from watching the Taft–Ferguson senatorial election in Ohio in 1950 and from his studies of the operations of the Texas Regulars and of various successful citizens' movements in New Orleans and elsewhere.

Mr. Moley's book is about crucial matters in a crucial election year. It is also a book about principles that are as old as John Locke, Edmund Burke, Thomas Jefferson, and James Madison. It won't sell as well as Whittaker Chambers's story, but it is part of the same movement that is about to rescue us from domination by the state-worshiping "intellectuals" and restore decentralized rule by the intelligent man.

34
American Innocence

April 7, 1952

A famous magazine tycoon and publisher, when confronted with the perplexing and exasperating existence of Communist Party mole-tracks in his own organization, once remarked in my presence that he was congenitally incapable of understanding either the psychology or the ramifications of conspiracy. He added, ruefully, that this probably disqualified him as a student of world history in the thirties and the forties. Although he was manifestly indulging in hyperbole (since his awareness is considerably more pronounced than his willingness to act on *all* his insights), his confession sprang spontaneously from that most lovable strain in the American character, the strain of forthright innocence. Long ago Henry James made this innocence a dominant theme of his novels. Henry Adams, who knew both Old and New Worlds, understood the American's innocence; and today the American Communists make wide-scale use of it, either simulating it themselves or exploiting its existence in others to create and manipulate "cover" for their own nefarious doings.

One specific form of this dominating American innocence is the inability, particularly pronounced in university circles, to understand that a man with a college degree and/or a crew haircut could ever have become a Communist spy or courier or infiltrating "sleeper." I still meet with university faculty people who express complete bewilderment over the Hiss case. Even the reasonably worldly editors of the *New York Times* have difficulty ingesting the idea that Communist sympathizers and operators, wearing Brooks Brothers shirts, could have penetrated such institutions as the Carnegie Foundation or the Institute of Pacific Relations.

Yet it should be obvious, on reflection, that Marxism-Leninism is an intellectual construction requiring for its grasp a virtual Ph.D. grounding in the ramifications of Hegelian philosophy as applied to the history of the industrial revolution. Who, if not an intellectual, could be capable of becoming a high-level Communist spy and infiltrator?

Since Americans can hardly bring themselves to think ill of any of their better educated fellow-citizens, maybe they could be induced to cut their historical eyeteeth by reading the story of a Communist spy ring that operated far across the sea, in China and Japan. The story is told in forceful, if somewhat circuitous, fashion in Maj. Gen. Charles A. Willoughby's *Shanghai Conspiracy: The Sorge Spy Ring*, which comes to us with a preface by Douglas MacArthur. General Willoughby's narrative involves German, Yugoslav and Japanese intellectuals—and where is the American who needs feel demeaned as long as the evidence of a hissing sound comes in German or Japanese? True, the American journalist Agnes Smedley had palpable connections with the Sorge group, but she was, after all, the daughter of an unskilled Colorado laborer. She never finished grade school, much less the Harvard Law School, so it will be easier for the American reader to think of her as conspiratorial material.

The man whose personality dominates General Willoughby's book is Richard Sorge, a German Communist who paraded as a newspaper correspondent and a Nazi Party member in Tokyo in 1941. This Herr Sorge, although German on his father's side, ought to be reverenced in Moscow as the savior of the Soviet Union. From the Soviet point of view he deserves canonization even more than Marshal Stalin. The successful defense of Russia against Hitler in 1941 turned on two of Sorge's tips from Tokyo to the Red Army's "Fourth Bureau" in Moscow. The first tip was the intelligence, picked up by Sorge in the German embassy in May 1941, that the Reichswehr would hurl from 170 to 190 divisions against the Russians on June 20. (Actually, the German attack came on June 22.) The second tip was the information, gleaned from various sources including the "braintrust" of Prince Fumimaro Konoye, that toward the end of the year the Japanese would strike at Indochina and the East Indies, not at Soviet Siberia. This tip enabled Stalin to move his Siberian forces to the western front in time to save Moscow from capture in December, 1941. If it hadn't been for Sorge, Moscow would certainly have fallen and the Soviet government probably would not have been able to continue the war with any effective battle order once its north-south railroad network had been cut at the heart.

The one thing that stands out from General Willoughby's account is that it takes a very superior intellect to make a good infiltrator or spy. Sorge, as a boy, had all the "advantages." His grandfather, Adolf Sorge, had been the secretary of Karl Marx's First International, but his father, an engineer, had amassed some wealth in the Caucasus and elsewhere and had climbed into the ranks of the well-to-do German bourgeoisie. As a boy in Berlin, Richard Sorge studied Goethe, Dante and Kant, and he developed an avid interest in the history of the French Revolution, the Napoleonic wars, and the Bismarck period in Germany. He fought as a mere child in World War I, serving on both fronts. Wounded a couple of times, he went back to school, to the University of Berlin. There he encountered Hegel—and, of course, Engels and Marx. He became an active Communist during the disorientation that followed the war. Eventually he went to Moscow, rising high in the Comintern. He shifted to Red Army Intelligence in order to carry out his Far Eastern assignments.

It will hardly do to toss Sorge off as "scum," or as a "traitorous rat." For he was one of a very important breed, the breed of earnest young intellectuals who developed a philosophy of the "higher good" in the 1920s. In America the breed included Whittaker Chambers, a Columbia University student. In England, it included such people as John Strachey. I myself knew scores of the breed in New York in the 1930s. Not that the ones I knew necessarily became active spies; the point is, they paid emotional and intellectual homage, not to the United States of America, but to a world movement whose capital was in the Kremlin. Their allegiance sprang from a misapplied effort to be good, not evil, and Sorge was like them in his own motivation.

So much for Richard Sorge, the man of brains and gentle upbringing who betrayed his German "homeland" to the Soviets for reasons that seemed honorable to him. Sorge worked in Shanghai in the thirties, and there, through the American Agnes Smedley, he met a Japanese intellectual named Ozaki. Ozaki was a profound student of China. A journalist like Sorge, he had been educated at the Law School of Tokyo Imperial University. The measure of Ozaki's intelligence can be found in his accurate prediction in early 1942 that Japan would lose the war and that China would become a "transitional" Communist state. Ozaki believed in the Communist cause with his whole heart, but his belief did not keep him from maintaining long years of "cover" as a journalist, or from penetrating Prince Konoye's "braintrust" as a "bright young man."

Sorge and Ozaki used many people in China and Japan to advance their espionage purposes. They used Agnes Smedley; they used the British journalist Guenther Stein. Both Ozaki and Stein, incidentally, had connections with the Institute of Pacific Relations, now under congressional investigation for its influence on the Far Eastern policy of the United States.

The pattern of how a Soviet spy ring grows and operates comes clear in General Willoughby's book. It is a pattern that should be pondered by all those Americans who have refused to believe that the Communist conspiracy might include many from the Hamiltonian category of the rich, the well-born, and the able. What General Willoughby has demonstrated is that the "white shoe" intellectual is the *sine qua non* of Communist success; without the allegiance of the campus aristocrat, communism would die for lack of voice, ears and eyes.

The Ingenious American

35
From Huffman's Pasture

August 13, 1951

If anyone really wants to know what has made America tick, let him read *Miracle at Kitty Hawk: The Letters of Wilbur and Orville Wright,* edited by Fred C. Kelly. Strung together with commentary by Kelly, these letters are eloquent reminders that the way to get creative results out of human beings is to leave them alone. The airplane could hardly have come into being in an economy or a nation that was even so much as 15 percent "planned": a mere year or two spent in compulsory universal military training, for example, would have so disrupted the intimate and intricate collaboration of the Wright brothers that they never would have discovered the principles that underlie successful human flight. Let General Marshall, Eleanor Roosevelt and other proponents of compulsory peacetime "national service" take note.

The Wright brothers had virtually nothing by way of promising substance when they started thinking about gliding through the air. They had no "capital" beyond their small Dayton, Ohio bicycle shop, which provided them with a barely sufficient living. They had no formal education beyond high school; indeed, Wilbur never bothered to pick up his high school diploma. What they did have was uncoerced possession of their own time and energy, plus an environment that enabled them to follow where their curiosity led them. The pragmatic results of such freedom may have made wars more extensive and more horrible than they might otherwise have been. But who can read these letters of the Wright brothers and doubt that it is laissez faire, not state planning, that has permitted America to keep ahead of coerced societies both in the arts of peace and in the creation and elaboration of complex and winning instruments of war?

The double portrait that emerges from Kelly's collection of Wright letters is most remarkable. Neither brother could have invented the airplane singly. Orville Wright had a little edge on Wilbur in the importance of suggestions offered. It was Orville who first thought of the basic principle of presenting the right and left wings of the plane at different angles to the wind for lateral balance. But it was Wilbur who first hit upon the practical device of warping the wings. The one brother invariably picked up where the other left off. Wilbur, in the early years, seems to have been the better businessman of the two. But after Wilbur's death from typhoid in his mid-forties, Orville proved to be just as shrewd in practical affairs as his older brother had been; it seems that he had merely deferred to Wilbur in the matter of business judgment because of a kid brother's natural reluctance to put himself forward. In any case, nobody ever rooked either of the Wright brothers out of anything no matter which one was taking charge of things. They dealt successfully with governments, with patent offices, with military men, with litigious patent infringers and with all manner of leeches and scoundrels. If it is the normal fate of the inventor to be mulcted of his product, the Wright brothers were certainly exceptions to the rule.

The Wrights carried their understanding about proper energy relationships into spheres that normally baffle those of a purely mechanical turn of mind. At one point their good friend Octave Chanute, himself a profound student of gliding, offered to help bear the expense of the Wright brothers' experiments. But the Wrights refused to accept the money "because," as Wilbur put it, "we would be led to neglect our regular business too much if the expense of experimenting did not exercise a salutary effect on the time devoted to [the experiments]." "Creative" individuals who insist that society has a duty to support them while they are busy creating will probably be nonplused by the Wright brothers' attitude. For here were a couple of creators who didn't need the help of government grants and who stood ready to pay their own way. The Wright brothers did get aid in carrying out their experiments; a Dayton bank president named Mr. Huffman let them use his pasture for practice flights. But that was all the tangible outside help the Wrights received. The total cost of their first successful power plane, the one that flew at Kitty Hawk in 1903, was less than $1,000, which the Wrights took out of their own bicycle shop business.

As is usually the case with something drastically new, human beings everywhere were slow to grasp the significance of what the Wright brothers did when they put the first power plane into the air. The city editor of the hometown *Dayton Journal* didn't think a flight of less than one minute worth recording. But the Board of Ordnance and Fortification of the U.S. Army exhibited the real obtuseness. As late as October 19, 1905, this board was answering letters from the Wright brothers which proved the inability of an army captain to read simple English. To stir even rudimentary curiosity about their product in Washington, the Wrights had to carry on a long series of dickers with European governments. Finally it began to penetrate the bureaucratic mind that the plane might be a useful instrument for war purposes. Bureaucrats cannot afford to make mistakes with the taxpayers' money, so it is not to be argued that the U.S. Army should have rushed to take the Wright invention without ample investigation of its potentialities. On the other hand, it should never be asserted by anybody that invention itself should be put under the control of governments. State control is an absolutely foolproof way of stopping primary scientific innovation in its tracks.

Miracle at Kitty Hawk deserves the widest possible reading. But one could wish that Fred C. Kelly, the editor, had seen fit to point the antistatist moral of the tale. One could also wish that someone, sometime, would make a philosophical study of what constituted the society of Dayton, Ohio, in 1903. In a short span of time this town in the American midlands produced the world's first plane, the automobile self-starter, and a number of other innovations and inventions. There was something in the atmosphere of the place that released human energy and called forth human ingenuity. What was it? If social "scientists" were really scientific (which they are not), they would get busy and find out.

36
Once There Was Henry Ford

April 21, 1952

The curious thing about education, formally considered, is that it makes so little allowance for curiosity. One prepares for education by signing up for certain courses and reading the prescribed books. One continues it by taking recommendations from the *Zeitgeist,* or spirit of the times. In obedience to the spirit of my own times, I dutifully read through a vast literature prescribing various forms of Sidney Webbicalism, Veblenism, Marxism and interventionism as the cure for all our ills. As a glandular optimist I never liked the idea of socialism, for it seemed rooted in a pessimistic theory that man was not capable of the sustained practice of freedom. But everyone around me in the early thirties kept saying that socialism was both inevitable and necessary. With bread lines lengthening all over the world, the anvil chorus was hard to refute.

The point about education, however, is that curiosity keeps breaking through. It is sparked by the chance encounter, which can be more powerful and formative than the whole weight of numbers and tradition and the social pressure of the times. One of my own chance encounters was a novel by Garet Garrett called *The Driver.* At this date I don't remember too much about it as a novel aside from the fact that it was a dramatization of the life of old E. H. Harriman of the Union Pacific. But the opening pages of *The Driver,* which described the experiences of a young reporter in the great depression of the 1890s, kept haunting me all through the Franklin Rooseveltian years. What Garet Garrett had to say about the economic recovery of 1895 and 1896 seemed to make hash of everything the New Dealers claimed. What the New Dealers—or, as Bernard Baruch used to call them, the New Stealers—had done was to institutionalize the depression, making it necessary to jolt the economy periodically by wider and wider diffusions of public spending channeled into forms presided over by the wasted manpower of a burgeoning bureaucracy. The America described in Garrett's novel was saved in the nineties from this sterile fate by the horse sense of a people who knew that a rich land must recover quickly once its debt structure was brought into a workable relationship with its capacity to produce.

The years have done something to Garet Garrett, making him a pessimist about the future. In a brilliant pamphlet titled *Ex America* he sees us going the way of all statist empires. We are pumping out our substance into nothingness. Rome has started to haunt his mind, and with the next spin of war, inflation or depression he foresees that we will bind ourselves to creative impotence by imposing our own Edict of Diocletian. Tyranny and decay are just over the horizon.

I have nothing in my own armament with which to refute Garet Garrett's theory of Roman decay beyond that same glandular optimism that originally made me receptive to the message of *The Driver*. Looked at rationally, Garrett is right: the spirit which he once hymned so eloquently in novels like *The Driver* and in books of prophecy like *The American Omen* has been broken beyond redemption. There is no immediately visible way back to the doctrine of natural rights, the economics of free choice. In a nation that is committed to supporting a passive, sullen world there can never be a surcease from grinding taxes, militarism and inflationary budgets. And in a country where thirty cents out of every dollar that a customer pays for an automobile goes for accumulated taxes on the materials and services that go into manufacture and sales, there will never again be a cheap car. Model T is gone, and its successors must support Washington.

The spirit of man dies hard, however, and it is impossible for Garet Garrett to welter in pessimism. Rome may haunt him, but when he goes to his desk in the morning he must needs create images of the American Omen that will live again in some future, whether far or near. He has just created a magnificent image in a book called *The Wild Wheel.* This is the story of Henry Ford and what Ford did to overthrow the last vestiges of the hold that European economics had on the mind of the American. It is also the story of how a rocket burned out and the stick fell. The wheel is no longer wild, and the European mind has again prevailed in the America that once broke free.

Henry Ford was that sublime American figure, the mechanic who saw all things fresh because he worked from a complete innocence. Before his time a thousand economists had preached the idea that if wages rose profits must decline, since both wages and profits apparently came out of a fixed sum. All the great European economists, both of the Right and of the Left, had believed this. Before Henry Ford's time an American economist, Francis Amasa Walker, had done something in theory to refute the idea that wages and profits were in mortal conflict. But nobody of consequence believed Walker until 1914, when Henry Ford announced a minimum wage of five dollars a day for all his employees down to the floorsweepers. Five dollars a day was more than double the prevailing wage scale in 1914, and everybody predicted that Ford would go broke. But the energy which the Ford idea released in the shop proved that both John Stuart Mill and Karl Marx were wrong about the "iron law of wages" and the linked theory that profits had to be squeezed out of the worker's hide. By paying his men more, and by adapting the old mass-production-of-interchangeable-parts theory of Eli Whitney to the moving belt line, Henry Ford increased the productivity of both labor and capital to the point where there was a magnificent "take" for everybody, whether worker, stockholder or consumer.

America boomed on Fordism; it even had energy to spare for that cultivation of antique hunting which Ford himself carried to its crest in the restoration of the Wayside Inn and the assembly of staged pieces in Greenfield Village. And then America turned to doubt again. The American labor movement deserted the free theories of Samuel Gompers in favor of the old-fashioned Scottish economics of Philip Murray and the statist German economics of Walter Reuther. The American capitalist, frightened to death by the tax take of a Europeanized American government, quite understandably fell back into the habit of thinking that seed-corn capital must come out of the worker's hide since the state seemed bent on leaving no other sources available.

Garet Garrett has a wonderful eye for the foibles, the idiosyncrasies, the hobbies of Henry Ford and his bosom friend, Thomas A. Edison. He pictures these "heroes of the same mythology" as emotional children who made power their toy. "As they set it free in a muscle-weary world, the roar and heat and light of it filled them with innocent glee." These innocent children were more mature than most, however, when it came to seeing effect in the light of cause, and vice versa. The story I like best among all the wonderful stories in *The Wild Wheel* concerns the destruction of the Ford statistical department. Ford had a saying that statistics never manufactured a car. One day he walked into a room at the plant and saw innumerable people bent over books, punching business machines, and drawing ruled lines on paper. He went out forthwith to see Sorensen, his production manager, who had asked for more space. Ford pointed to the statistical department room and said, "You can have that space if you will go and take it." Whereupon Sorensen called two men to come in a hurry with crowbars, armed himself with a blunt instrument, and the three of them proceeded to wreck the statistical department: typewriters, computing machines, everything. It is not recorded that the Ford Company lost a single sales dollar as a result of this depredation, which gives one pause when one contemplates the mountains of aimless paperwork that are deemed necessary in business today. True, paperwork must be done and preserved in anticipation of the tax collector, but it is not recorded that the Department of Internal Revenue ever made an automobile, either.

Garet Garrett wastes little time haranguing the American people to return to the world of Henry Ford. Apparently he thinks they got what was coming to degenerate stock. He hates the world of the collectivists and the statists, but he puts the primary blame for the death of laissez faire on its own supposed votaries. Laissez faire, he says, "was betrayed by its friends, not for thirty pieces of silver but for debased paper money that would be legal tender for debt. Then it was stoned to death by the multitude and buried with hymns for the easier life. The obsequies were performed by the government. . . ."

So the pessimist in Garrett has the last word in this book about an exhilaratingly optimistic day. But don't fool yourself about Garet Garrett: he will never succumb personally to his own pessimism. If Caesar does take over in the United States, Garrett will denounce him unreservedly and go to the scaffold with a sardonic smile on his lips and a light as of two contemptuous imps in his mocking eyes.

37
Frank Chodorov
A Man for Our Time

May 5, 1952

Along about 1935, in response to the so-called challenge of communism, America was blanketed by a literature of crypto-collectivism. There were neo-technocrats and "planners" by the score; the Keynesians and "middle-way" journalists were out like nightcrawlers after a vesper shower. If numbers and the sort of thing that passes for intellectual journalism in this country were ever definitive, the cultural climate of our nation would have been altered beyond recall in those years. But one of the grand lessons of history is that you cannot break the continuity of a culture or a tradition unless you are prepared to liquidate *all* those who have known the *douceur de la vie* of the Old Regime.

Lenin said it long ago: To make collectivism stick in a land that has known the blessings of individualism, you must catch a whole generation in the cradle and forcibly deprive it of tutors who have learned the bourgeois alphabet at their mothers' knees. In a land of republican law this is impossible; no matter how clever or omnipresent the collectivist propaganda may be, a few culture carriers of the old tradition will escape. They may be reduced to publishing broadsheets instead of books; they may be compelled to conduct their straggling classes in dingy rooms in old brownstone fronts. Certainly they will have a hard time getting posts on a university faculty. But they will be still hanging around—and still talking—when the tinsel begins to wear off the latest Five-Year Plan or government-sponsored Greenbelt colonization scheme. Their books and pamphlets, ready for the chance encounter that sparks all revolutions or "reactions," will fan the revival of the old tradition that periodically displaces the callow presumptions of the "new."

A recent preoccupation with my own intellectual autobiography has led me to reflect on the culture carriers who brought me back to what I had originally soaked up unconsciously in the individualistic New England of my childhood. One of these carriers was Albert Jay Nock, whose *Our Enemy the State* hit me between the eyes when I read it in the thirties. Another potent carrier was Franz Oppenheimer, whose concept of the state-as-racket (see his epochal book *The State*) was too formidably grounded in history to permit of any easy denial. Still another carrier was Garet Garrett, the only economist I know who can make a single image or metaphor do the work of a whole page of statistics. Then there were Henry George, the Single Taxer; and Thoreau, whose doctrine of civil disobedience implied a fealty to a higher—or a natural—law; and Isabel Paterson, the doughty and perennially embattled woman who wrote *The God of the Machine.* Finally, there was a man who sometimes spoke in parables and who always had a special brand of quiet humor, Frank Chodorov, whose lifetime of broadsheet writing and pamphleteering has been brilliantly raided by Devin A. Garrity of the Devin-Adair Co. to make a forthcoming book, *One Is a Crowd.*

Frank Chodorov is sixty-five years old, which means that he has been around. But he has the intellectual resilience that one would associate with a man in his twenties or thirties—if the young of 1952 did not seem so frightened, so recessive, so pinched and so antique. The formal biography of Chodorov says that he once lectured at the Henry George School of Social Science; that he revived and edited the *Freeman* with Albert Jay Nock from 1938 to 1941 (the *Freeman* is a magazine that is always coming up out of its own ashes, like the phoenix); that after one of the intermittent deaths of the *Freeman* he published, wrote, and edited his own four-page monthly broadsheet called *Analysis*; that he is currently engaged in editing *Human Events* with Frank Hanighen in Washington, D.C.

A craftsman from the ground up, Frank Chodorov has always made his own words pirouette with the grace and fluidity of a

Pavlova. Beyond this he is one of the few editors alive who can make individual stylists of others merely by suggesting a shift in emphasis here, an excision there, a bit of structural alteration in the middle. To talk over the luncheon table with Frank about the problems of writing and editing is a liberal journalistic education. But this is only the least important part of the education that one can absorb from him when he is expanding in his own ruefully humorous way.

Listening to Chodorov, you won't get any meaningless gabble about "Right" and "Left," or "progressive" and "reactionary," or liberalism as a philosophy of the "middle of the road." He deals in far more fundamental distinctions. There is, for example, the Chodorovian distinction between social power and political power. Social power develops from the creation of wealth by individuals working alone or in voluntary concert. Political power, on the other hand, grows by the forcible appropriation of the individual's social power. Chodorov sees history as an eternal struggle between social-power and political-power philosophies. When social power is in the ascendant, men are inclined to be inventive, creative, resourceful, curious, tolerant, loving and good-humored. The standard of well-being rises in such times—*vide* the histories of Republican Rome, of the Hanseatic cities, of the Italian Renaissance, of nineteenth-century Britain, and of modern America. But when political power is waxing, men begin to burn books, to suppress thought and to imprison and kill their dissident brothers. Taxation, which is the important barometer of the political power, robs the individual of the fruits of his energy, and the standard of life declines as men secretly rebel against extending themselves in labor that brings them diminishing returns.

According to the Chodorov rationale, *all* the great political movements of modern times are slave philosophies. For, no matter whether they speak in the name of communism, socialism, fascism, New Dealism or the welfare (sometimes called the positive) state, the modern political philosophers are all alike in advocating the forcible seizure of bigger and bigger proportions of the individual's energy. It matters not a whit whether the coercion is done with a club or by a tax agent—the coercion of labor is there; and such coercion is a definition of slavery. Nor does it matter that the energy-product of one individual is spent by the government on another: such spending makes beneficiaries into wards, and wards are slaves too.

Chodorov is a mystic, but only in the sense that all men of insight are mystics. His mystical assumption is that men are born as individuals possessing inalienable rights. This philosophy of natural rights under the Natural Law of the Universe cannot be "proved." But neither can the opposite philosophy—that society has rights—be proved. You can say it is demonstrable that a state, as the police agent of society, has power. But if there is no such thing as natural individual rights, protected by a correlative superstructure of justice organized to maintain those rights, then the individual has no valid subjective reason for obeying state power. True, the state can arrest the individual and compel his temporary obedience. But it cannot compel his inner loyalty; nor can it keep men from cheating, or from the quiet withdrawal of energy. The rebellious individual can always find ways of flouting state power—which makes it dubious that society (or the collectivity of men organized to compel individual men) has rights in any meaningful sense of the word. A collectivity cannot have anything that its constitutive elements refuse to give up.

Since the human animal must make either one mystical assumption or another about rights, Chodorov chooses the assumption that accords with the desire of his nature, which is to protect itself against the lawlessness of arbitrary power. He is mystical in the same way that James Madison and Thomas Jefferson and the rest of the Founding Fathers were mystical; and he is religious enough to believe in nature's God, which is to say that he believes in natural law.

The utilitarian argument is that natural law does not apply in the field of ethics, since it is not demonstrable that a thief will always be caught and punished, or a murderer apprehended, or a polygamist forced to relinquish his extra wives. But if there is no natural law of ethics, then any system of ethics is as valid as the next—and the choice of fascism or cannibalism is no "worse" than the choice of freedom as defined by John Locke. Chodorov's answer to the utilitarians is that men are diminished and blighted under certain ethical systems, whereas they flourish under other systems. And it is demonstrably the nature of man to prefer life to death, or to the slow agony of death-in-life that goes with slave systems.

Mr. Chodorov never labors his principles in either his writing or his speaking. Nor does he indulge in debater's tricks. He prefers a good parable to formal argument, and he is at his best when he is raiding the Old Testament to make a modern point. His essay "Joseph, Secretary of Agriculture," which is a simple recapitulation, with Chodorovian "asides," of the Old Testament story of Joseph and the Ever Normal Granary, tells us all we want to know about Henry Wallace and the Brannan Plan. This essay is first-rate entertainment. But it is also good instruction; like all good teachers, Chodorov knows that instruction is always improved when it comes in the form of entertainment. What he offers in his essays as entertainment is, of course, worth ten of the ordinary political science courses that one gets in our modern schools. It is a measure of our educational delinquency that nobody has ever seen fit to endow Mr. Chodorov with a university chair. But his successors will have chairs once Frank Chodorov has completed his mission in life, which is to swing the newest generations into line against the idiocies of a collectivist epoch that is now coming to an end in foolish disaster and blood.

38
Herbert Hoover's Voluntarism

May 19, 1952

"Smear Hoover!" Thus decreed Charlie Michelson, the Democratic Goebbels in 1930, and thus it has been ever since. But history, as has often been said, is written by the survivors, and Herbert Hoover has survived to write several installments of his autobiography. The second installment, *The Memoirs of Herbert Hoover: The Cabinet and the Presidency 1920–1933* does not contain the name of Michelson in the index, which indicates an almost incredible forbearance and gentleness of spirit. Nevertheless, the book is a sufficient answer to Michelson. When the third volume of the Hoover autobiography, the one dealing specifically with the depression and its aftermath, finally appears, one hopes that the gentle Hoover will take on a far more savage guise. There is such a thing as carrying Quakerism too far, and Charlie Michelson should not be cheated of his due place in history.

This second volume of Mr. Hoover's narrative is mainly devoted to the policies and activities which he initiated as secretary of commerce from 1921 to 1928 and their prolongation under his presidency from 1929 to 1933. The record paints a portrait of a man who is astoundingly different from the Hoover of popular legend. It also recalls the much maligned decade of the 1920s as a period of sound and sober development and progress. Hoover, as secretary of commerce, used the principle of voluntarism, whereas his successors have relied on coercion, and the record shows that true voluntarism is sufficient to even the most devastating crises. Under the regime of Hoover's voluntarism, the business community of the United States abandoned more "reactionary" practices than have ever been abandoned in a comparable period of time before or since. Even the suffering and dislocation that follow in the wake of great natural catastrophe vanished at the organized touch of voluntarism when Hoover raised some $26 million from private sources to rehabilitate the Mississippi flood victims of 1927. There was a day when self-help was ingrained in the American character, and the nation was considerably the better for it. This is something that will not fully dawn on our children until they are called upon to deal with the ultimate consequences of the opposite philosophy—consequences that have a social face in galloping corruption and a financial face in the staggering growth of unproductive dead-horse debt.

Since Hoover is generally accounted a "reactionary" in this day of meaningless epithets, it is piquant to read the running story of his encounters with American business over a twelve-year period. When he took office in 1921 as secretary of commerce, we still had the twelve-hour working day and the eighty-four-hour week in steel. As Hoover said, it was "barbaric." The barbarism was defended by Charles M. Schwab and Judge Elbert H. Gary of the steel industry as something that was economically necessary. With the help of other industrialists such as Charles R. Hook, Hoover took his fight to the public. By stirring up his friends in the engineering societies and by enlisting the aid of President Harding, Hoover eventually proved to Gary and Schwab that the twelve-hour day was not only barbaric but also distinctly uneconomic. When Hoover first went to Washington as secretary of commerce nearly 75 percent of American industry insisted on a work week of fifty-four or more hours. When he left the White House twelve years later only 13.5 percent worked fifty-four hours or more. This transformation had been wrought by public opinion without the passage of a single law (except in the case of the railways).

Hoover's encounter with the steel men was followed by a conflict with certain railway executives. Assigned by President Harding to negotiate the railway strike of 1922, Hoover found he had two different types of railroad president to deal with. The ones who had their offices in New York City held out against him to the last; others, such as Daniel Willard of the Baltimore and Ohio and a number of western presidents, came up with conciliatory suggestions. An almost populist echo comes into Hoover's words when he speaks of "New York promoter-bankers" who "manipulated the voting control of many of the railway, industrial, and distributing corporations. . . . Their social instinct belonged to an early Egyptian period."

Far from being the reactionary that twenty years of virulent New Deal–Fair Deal propaganda has painted him, Hoover was "liberal" to the point where he could, by stretching it a bit, almost be called the father of the welfare state. Such things as the Farm Board, the RFC and federal control of errant rivers such as the Colorado, the Mississippi and the Tennessee were Hoover patents before they became FDR's. But it would be sheer slander actually to insist on Hoover's responsibility for Roosevelt–Truman welfare statism. For Hoover drew the line against coercive federal participation in decisions involving business judgment. He did not believe in the "yardstick" public corporation. He supported federal aid to the states in building big dams, but he insisted that it was no business of government to engage in the sale of electric power to the retail market. He was willing to help California build a big bridge across San Francisco Bay, but he made certain that the RFC loan for the bridge should be repaid with interest out of tolls.

Both as secretary of commerce and as president, Hoover was willing to use the powers of government to help improve the general environment in which business had to operate. He believed in deepening and linking our inland waterways. He believed in federal aid to coastal communities for the improvement or rehabilitation of fisheries, and he believed in the mobilization of tax resources to control rivers and to put our water to work. But the demarcation of the Hoover philosophy of federal aid becomes more or less clear when one reflects upon the fact that nobody can very well establish a legal claim to private ownership of an ocean or a big river. It is a far cry from building Boulder Dam across the public Colorado River to seizing and operating the scores of units of the privately owned steel industry.

Although most of Hoover's book is given over to the discussion of matters of public policy, there are quiet and flavorsome interludes that belong to general history. The story of President Harding's trip to Alaska (Hoover was a member of the party) offers some invaluable sidelights for the historian or biographer of "normalcy." The account of the development of the radio industry adds an essential bit to the story of the twenties. Hoover's humor is gentle, but it is unmistakably genuine; and when he tells about evangelist Aimee Semple McPherson's attempt to roam all over the waveband in broadcasting her sermons, the reader's smile comes without prompting. There is also much unforced humor in Hoover's interludes bearing on social life in Washington during the Harding and Coolidge days. As for Calvin Coolidge himself, Hoover ticks him off in such remarks as "Mr. Coolidge was cold to this development because of its great cost," or "Mr. Coolidge . . . suggested that I take a cruiser—'it would not cost so much' [as a battleship]."

Mr. Hoover does not speak as a political science theoretician in his memoirs. But the philosophy of voluntarism so pervades this book that it might very well be made standard reading in political science courses that presume to teach basic theory. Certainly some generalizer of political science ought to levy on Hoover's record to prove a series of related points. For the good of the Republic, Herbert Hoover's wisdom is needed in the schools. It would go far toward countering the modern trend that tends to confuse all "civics" with the debilitating idea of coercive collective action.

39
Ruled by Terror

March 10, 1952

We sent a book a few weeks ago to Whittaker Chambers for review. It was the story of a European Communist who had been dragged through the great Moscow purge trials of the mid-thirties and had somehow lived to tell the tale. "I can't review this," Chambers said. "The poor fellow has suffered horribly, but he hasn't learned anything from his experiences. He's still a socialist."

The full implication of Mr. Chambers's attitude should be readily apparent to those who have read the first two installments in the *Saturday Evening Post* of his own story of the Hiss case. Unlike most ex-Communists, Whittaker Chambers is not merely a witness *against* the malignant view of life that is behind Marxism. He is a witness *for* the fundamentally religious view of life that regards the human being as a sacred entity. The human being must not be involuntarily subjected to experiments decreed by politicians or even by a democratic majority. Chambers's story, which is that of a brave man who has had a religious conversion, or an illumination, or an experience that has disclosed to him the operations of natural law (it doesn't really matter what you call it), will certainly mark a turning point in the literary treatment of the problem of communism. But it will have failed of its mark if it does not substantially help to produce a regeneration of the beliefs that underlie the whole structure of Western society.

Chambers's experience proves that one man who is willing to stand his ground on truth can defeat a million. But the truth must involve a complete repudiation of socialism, which is the spirit that denies in the name of a materialist hierarchy. The creative (or, if you like, the divine) in man must have scope: the way must be free for spontaneity to carry individuals where they would voluntarily go, either as individuals or as voluntary adherents to a group. The notion that man's future can be planned collectively, with the state serving as the compulsory planning agent, seals the creative and the spontaneous founts that lie deep in human nature. It closes the future to the benefits of inventiveness, of energy, of elegance, of amusing diversion, of adventure, of expression, and of success in any one of the seven arts and the manifold theoretical sciences. It is not only that a Henry Ford would have no chance under socialism. A Shakespeare, a Josiah Willard Gibbs or a Max Planck would be equally impossible. And a Jesus of Nazareth would be strangled at his first suggestion that Caesar is not God.

Whittaker Chambers is right when he implies that our anti-Communist literature, so ubiquitous at the moment, is all too often the product of those who think that socialism might have been better if Lenin had lived, or if Trotsky had defeated Stalin. (Such people still think the British Labour party can pull the job off.) But every so often an anti-Communist or an anti-totalitarian writer catches a glimpse of what Chambers is talking about.

Robert Ardrey, in an excellent novel called *The Brotherhood of Fear,* stands as a witness *for* something as well as *against.* Ardrey's book got very little attention from the routineers of our literary marketplace, but that should not keep it from making its way. A superbly imaginative tale, *The Brotherhood of Fear* highlights all that is real about human nature without ever once succumbing to the trappings of "realism." It is set in the middle of the sea in a mythical part of the world, although an obviously Mediterranean climate bathes the island dependency of Ardrey's mythical totalitarian state. By isolating his characters, and by joining the symbolic to the "real" in them, Ardrey gains prodigious dramatic impact. As an Erich Maria Remarque character says in *Spark of Life,* "Feeling does not grow stronger through numbers. It can never count beyond one. One—but that's enough if one feels it." This truth is exemplified by Ardrey, who deals with his characters one and two at a time.

The Brotherhood of Fear makes the point that in a planned state everyone is ruled by terror of the one above him. The individual fears the member of the Secret Police who is set to watch him, but the member of the Secret Police is also caught up in a chain of fear that permeates totalitarian society from bottom to top. The hunter must either catch his prey or become the prey of others. This means that every man in totalitarian society must be infallible—or else. It is usually "or else."

Certainly it is "or else" in Mr. Ardrey's fable. Konnr, who is the perfect policeman because he lacks the ability to question directives, has the trail-sniffing expertise of a bloodhound, the tenacity of a limpet, and the singleness of view of a horse in double-size blinders. He pursues his quarry, Willy Bryo, to the great port of D__, only to discover that Willy has escaped by freighter to sea. Since disgrace (and the labor camp or worse) must await him if he fails to bring Willy back to land, Konnr puts out in a fishing vessel, the *Maria Voltin,* and overhauls Willy. But a storm overwhelms the *Voltin,* and Konnr and Willy are cast upon the beach of an island inhabited by shepherds. Willy escapes into the interior before Konnr recovers consciousness. *The Brotherhood of Fear* becomes the story of what happens to human quarry and huntsman under the disturbing influence of a pastoral society that still maintains a latent belief in God, in freedom, in the inviolability of the family, and in the wisdom imparted by a visiting Englishman who long ago taught the Elder of the island to read Shakespeare and the Old and New Testaments.

It would be unfair to divulge the outcome of *The Brotherhood of Fear.* But, in a much different way, it makes all the points about human nature that Whittaker Chambers is making in his *Saturday Evening Post* series. In one phase of the argument the matter comes down to this: Can a human being be fully human if he must depend for life on the order of his identification papers? When Konnr, the policeman, loses his papers, it is "the approximate loss of identity itself." Long ago, in *The Death Ship,* B. Traven, that mysterious novelist of Mexico, made a similar observation about a sailor who had lost his passport. For Americans, the lesson should be heeded before it is too late. Won't someone please start a movement to tear up all documents that tend to reduce the human being to the status of a number on a card?

Erich Remarque is a witness for the religious view of the individual in his story of a Nazi concentration camp, *Spark of Life*. But this novel, although it has its moments of tremendous power, falls into the error of trying to make the reader feel for thousands, not one or two. True, Remarque always comes back to individuals; he tries not to count beyond one in his specific paragraphs and page-length vignettes. But the overall canvas is too broad, and the plotting of *Spark of Life*, which ignores the vistas of the pre-Hitlerian past and the post-Hitlerian future, makes it impossible for the author to plumb the specific character of Prisoner 509, or Bucher, or Lebenthal, or Lewinsky. These men have suppressed their memories and curtailed their dreams. They live for the moment, and into the momentary future. That is what a concentration camp does to one, and Remarque does not spare reiteration in making the point. But when humanity must diminish itself in order to live, the novelist becomes diminished too. That is another horror to be chalked up against the totalitarian disease of our benighted century.

40
The Far Eastern Line

August 25, 1952

If Dwight Eisenhower is elected president in November, our next secretary of state will almost certainly be Thomas E. Dewey. For it was the Dewey–Brownell organization that put Ike across at Chicago, and gratitude for such an important service must assuredly be measured in something far more important than a mere ambassadorship or attorney general's portfolio. Dewey can have what he wants, even unto the fiefdom of Foggy Bottom, the claims of Paul Hoffman and John Foster Dulles notwithstanding.

Because he can have what he wants, more than ordinary interest attaches to Tom Dewey's recent book, *Journey to the Far Pacific.* If Dewey were not a public figure, this account of a two-month sojourn in the nations of the free Pacific would pass as a pleasant, informative travel diary. But since it is also the work of a prospective secretary of state (and in any case an influential voice should Ike win), it must be combed for its clues to high policy to come.

The really interesting thing about the book is that it is the work of an eastern, "internationalist" Republican who also happens to be a MacArthurite as regards the Far East. On page 143 Tom Dewey sums up the feeling engendered by his stay in Formosa: "Despite all the arguments, one thing is clear: Free China and its Formosa stronghold are essential to Pacific defense. The solid line of our Pacific defense structure runs from Alaska down through Japan, Okinawa, Formosa, and the Philippines. Without Formosa, the whole chain of defense would be cracked wide open; with it, the free world holds a mighty position which both serves the free peoples of the Pacific and keeps the threat of war thousands of miles from American shores." That sounds almost like a paraphrase of MacArthur addressing the Veterans of Foreign Wars. True, Tom Dewey has said some unsatisfactory things about the standoff in Korea. He is not an uncritical admirer of Chiang Kai-shek, and he doubts that Chiang's army is good for much more than a holding operation on Formosa; and he had a stormy tea-time session trying to defend the Japanese treaty against the typhoon attacks of the generalissimo. But the broad outlines and even the details of Tom Dewey's Asia policy add up to a distinct repudiation of Achesonism.

Indeed, so specific is Governor Dewey on the subject of Truman's and Acheson's mistakes in Asia that one hopes Eisenhower will base more than one campaign speech on the substance of page 136 of *Journey to the Far Pacific.* Says the governor: "Perhaps one of America's greatest diplomatic blunders was the language of President Truman's order in December 1945, when he sent General Marshall to China. This order made it clear to the world that Chiang Kai-shek had been directed by the American government to settle with the Communists under pain of withdrawal of all American aid. To the Communists the president's order meant that all they had to do was stall for time. . . ." Tom Dewey follows this criticism of our basic Chinese policy with some acerb remarks on the State Department's 1949 White Paper, which "hit Formosa like an atom bomb."

What struck Tom Dewey most forcibly in his Pacific peregrinations was the fact that the Chinese are not limited to China. In Singapore, for example, there are eight hundred thousand Chinese out of a total population of one million. Chinese businessmen keep shops in Saigon; they run the business of Malaya; they are important in the economy of Manila; they operate tea and rubber plantations and tin mines in Indonesia. Most of these out-of-China Chinese are Chiang Kai-shek partisans. But this does not mean that they are last-ditchers. Indeed, Tom Dewey's visits to Manila, Saigon, Singapore, Djakarta and way stations convinced him that if Formosa falls to Mao Tse-tung, the Chinese community of Southeast Asia will lose heart and go over to the cause of Red China as a matter of *sauve qui peut.* This would mean the collapse of a good half-dozen economies and defense systems. Tom Dewey is for a Pacific Area Defense Pact that will include all the nations of Southeast Asia. But the key to any successful defense pact is the continued integrity of Nationalist Formosa; without the presence of Chiang's troops on that island the whole cause of freedom in Asia would vanish.

When I lived in Washington, in Georgetown, I frequently saw Felix Frankfurter and Dean Acheson swinging down Dumbarton Avenue on their morning walk to the doors of the State Department. What they talked about is a guess, but I know from my own talks with him that Justice Frankfurter is a European-minded, specifically a British-minded, man. He has no discernible feeling for the Orient. In this matter Acheson is Frankfurter's disciple. The British aren't concerned about holding Formosa, for they have written off India and tend to think of Africa as their bastion against the Orient. (The fact that this way of looking at things consigns Australia and New Zealand to the wolves does not bother Britain's Bevanites.) But the United States is a two-front power, and Africa is important to only one of its fronts. We have no more business following the British line in the Far East than we have in following the Pied Piper. War is a matter of positions, and a two-front power cannot defend its position by adopting the foreign policy of a one-front power.

To see the truth about one's position on the globe entails one of two things: either one must have an instinct for the map, or one must have traveled with one's eyes and ears open. Acheson has no instinct for the map, and he is both blind and deaf as a traveler. Tom Dewey may or may not be able to read maps, but he has certainly kept his antennae adjusted while voyaging. On his recent journey to the Far Pacific he saw and smelled Asia—the teeming millions, the effluvium of fields soaked in "night soil," the peasants who put all their money into pigs as a hedge against the ever-continuing monetary inflations. He sensed the pressures of population; he learned about the importance of "face" as the key to controlling and directing these pressures. And as he looked down upon Japan, Korea, Okinawa, the Philippines, Hong Kong and Indochina from the air, watching coastlines and mountain ranges and valleys unroll below him, he got a good notion of the geography of the lands subjected to the pressures of Asia's millions. The experience should prove invaluable to him if he becomes

Eisenhower's secretary of state. Certainly, on the evidence of his book, Tom Dewey is no "Europe-Firster."

The fact that Tom Dewey has learned a lot about the realities of geography and populations, however, does not necessarily mean that he has yet digested the realities of campaigning against Fair Deal politicos. To mean anything at all to our future, *Journey to the Far Pacific* must be translated quickly into some devastating campaign speeches. Ike Eisenhower must be persuaded to say the things that Dewey says about the Acheson–Truman Far Eastern mistakes. If Ike fails to be a Deweyite—and a MacArthurite—in this area, Tom Dewey's sensible views about the Far East will never have a chance to prevail in the environs of Foggy Bottom.

Whittaker Chambers and
A Generation on Trial

41
Alistair Cooke's Exterior View of Whittaker Chambers

October 2, 1950

A Generation on Trial: U.S.A. vs. Alger Hiss, by Alistair Cooke

Seeds of Treason: The True Story of the Hiss-Chambers Tragedy, by Ralph de Toledano and Victor Lasky

Alistair Cooke's book on the Hiss–Chambers case is nicely done to a formula, that of the patronizing social anthropologist who takes the "exterior view" of the queer customs of the natives. Not that Mr. Cooke is an anthropologist; he is merely the English-born chief American correspondent of the *Manchester Guardian,* with a background of specialization at Yale in the American language. But the main effort of his book, as it must strike a U.S.–born reviewer who is satisfied that the American jury system is as safe an instrument of justice as can be devised in a fallible world, is to cast doubt on the benighted legal norms and customs of a people who might be conceded the equals in general culture of the Trobriand Islanders or the Arapesh of Melanesia.

This is not to say that Cooke's running account of the two Hiss–Chambers trials lacks merit. The author, who has been a movie critic and a writer on the theater, has an extremely cultivated sense of the dramatic, and he makes the most of the histrionic poses of Alger Hiss's first counsel, Lloyd Paul Stryker, and of the slower, but infinitely more subtle and tenacious, methods of Thomas F. Murphy, the government prosecutor. The reader who can come to Cooke's book with the "exterior view" will undoubtedly go away with a rewarding feeling that he has read the best whodunit since Dorothy Sayers stopped clanging the bell clappers in *The Nine Tailors*.

Unfortunately for my own literary pleasure, I knew Whittaker Chambers, chief witness against Hiss for the prosecution, for ten years as a journalistic colleague at Time, Inc. I knew him as an honest, far-sighted, courageous and almost uncannily prophetic magazine writer and editor, and as a most tender and devoted husband and father. What appalls me about Cooke's method is his relative lack of curiosity as to the manner of man Whit Chambers is and was. He doesn't precisely say that Chambers rushed in the summer of 1948 to inform the House Committee on Un-American Activities that Alger Hiss was a spy, but he leaves the unwary reader with that impression. The fact of the matter, however, is quite different.

Whit Chambers did go to the government in 1939, when the Nazi–Soviet pact sent a chill through the bones of this ex-Soviet agent and courier, by then thoroughly repentant. He did warn Adolf Berle of the State Department that certain strategically placed Soviet sympathizers were drawing their checks from the U.S. government and were in a position to mess up policy. But during all the years of Chambers's service on *Time* magazine, his chief pride was that, unlike other "ex's" who had quit the half-world of the Communist underground, he refused categorically to make his living by dishing up the usual fare of the literary informer. As an editor of *Time*, he took a deep satisfaction in writing about such things as Rebecca West's love for her Buckinghamshire acres and herd of cattle, or Reinhold Niebuhr's complex theological distinctions, or Theodor Mommsen's historical insight into the decay of ancient Rome. When *Life* decided to run a long series on the development of European culture, Whit Chambers took the job with alacrity. One of his disillusionments as a journalist came when a *Life* editor decided to give more weight to the R. H. Tawney economic interpretation of the Protestant Reformation than Whit Chambers, the ex-Marxist, thought was justified.

When he first got word that he was to be subpoenaed to testify before the House committee, Whit Chambers got into something of a blue funk. Or at least it was as close to a blue funk as an ex-Bolshevik could experience. A *New York Sun* reporter had dragged out the old story of the Chambers–Isaac Don Levine visit to Berle in Washington in 1939. Chambers tried to get the story killed in late editions of the *Sun* but did not succeed. When people in the *Time* office urged that he had nothing to worry about, he looked down the hallway toward the desk of his managing editor, Tom Matthews, and said, "Have you ever heard the word 'informer'? People don't like informers." Later on in the day he remarked with a philosophical sigh: "Oh, well. I always feared I'd have to cross this bridge sometime, and now it's here."

Cooke could have discovered something of Chambers's reaction to the summons if he had done a little legwork. But the projected form of his book precluded any such investigation. Having decided to stick to the court record for the sake of "objectivity," Cooke arbitrarily cut himself off from a true exercise of the reporter's function, which is to pursue the facts even where the lawyer cannot go. He did not go to the bottom of the question of the credibility of Chambers as a witness. For that matter, he did nothing to get behind what he calls the "fine bone" of the countenance of Alger Hiss. He was apparently predisposed to accept Hiss's word for a lot of things until the evidence of the typewritten documents shook him. But if he had really wanted to give Hiss the benefit of every doubt, he should have interviewed a score of people who knew Hiss as a U.S. Department of Agriculture employee, as a counsel for the Nye committee, and so on.

Mr. Cooke's lack of reportorial enterprise comes out most startlingly in his handling of the testimony of Malcolm Cowley, who swore that Chambers had told him over the luncheon table in 1940 that Francis Sayre, Woodrow Wilson's son-in-law and Hiss's old chief, was the head of a Communist apparatus in the State Department. Cowley, who is a man of precise, if sometimes misguided, opinions, may have heard it that way. But the fact of the matter is that Malcolm Cowley is hard of hearing in one ear, and sometimes gets things a little wrong when he misses a key word. Chambers probably told him that someone in Francis Sayre's office was head of a Communist apparatus. I would not for a moment impugn Cowley's honesty, for I once knew him fairly well, and knew him, too, as a truthful man. But deafness does not always make a person an accurate diarist.

The Cooke book on the Hiss–Chambers case is the product of loving care. Every sentence bears the evidence of a craftsman who delights in fine intaglio work. It is, as I have suggested, very good reading. In contrast, reporters Ralph de Toledano and Victor Lasky were accused of turning out a "quickie" when they published *Seeds of Treason* last spring. True, the Toledano–Lasky work was hot off the griddle. But both Toledano and Lasky had a background knowledge of the Communist conspiracy that stood them in good stead, and, unlike Alistair Cooke, they were not afraid of wearing out shoe leather and ringing doorbells. Their quickie still tells a lot more about the Hiss–Chambers case than Cooke's loving re-creation of the two trials that first acquainted thousands of Americans with the fact that dalliance with communism, even to the point of treason, was "in the mode" in the thirties among the intellectuals.

I don't advise against a reading of Cooke's book, but it should certainly be balanced by either a subsequent or a preliminary reading of the Toledano–Lasky work. And those who are disposed to deference toward the "exterior view" of the social anthropologist might well reflect that field observation can never take the place of real reflection based on a mixture of hard investigation and long immersion in a culture. Alistair Cooke apparently did not know the literary and intellectual communism of the thirties from close contact with it. His book reflects his newness to the pastures in which he has chosen to graze.

42
The Chambers Memoirs

June 2, 1952

Whittaker Chambers's teeming eight-hundred-page *Witness* is one of those fecundly great books that cannot be adequately handled in even the most comprehensive of reviews. Dealing with it is like dealing with the whole of life.

This book, which has been advertised as the inside story of the Hiss case, is only incidentally the story of a famous trial. As Chambers says in the eloquent and tenderly moving letter to his children which opens the narrative, this book is about a spy case. All the paraphernalia of a Communist underground apparatus, both human and inanimate, shuffle through it—agents, commissars, couriers, informers, stolen documents, microfilmed secrets. But these are, in the last analysis, just paraphernalia. The real essence of the book is that it is symbolic of all our lives, or at least symbolic of the life of every living mother's son who has been touched with the grace that enables him to see the great and overwhelming evil of our time and to fight against it. Not many of us have been spies, not many of us have ever joined the Communist Party, either openly or secretly. But that has not been because of our superior virtue. In truth, most of us who came off the college campuses of America in the twenties and the thirties succumbed to the evil of collectivist thinking in little, comfortable ways. We were the Fabians. We were the lukewarm. Whittaker Chambers, who believed in being a living witness to his faith (whatever it happened to be at the moment), was never lukewarm. Nevertheless, in his journey to the end of the night and back again, Chambers described at high-voltage intensity the arc of experience that has been universal to a generation. That is what makes *Witness* (which is five times the length of the version that ran with such spectacular success in the *Saturday Evening Post*) the transcendently important work of literature that it is.

Witness is many stories. It is the story of a young man who grew up in a doomed household (it wasn't a home, for the tension in it was loveless) in the suburban reaches of Long Island. It is the story of a boy who reacted against the lingering *fin de siècle* atmosphere of the twenties by joining the Communist Party. It is the story of what happens when a Columbia University education cannot account for the aftermath of a great war that leaves a whole continent in a shambles. It is the story of how a basically religious and mystical nature must erringly seek for a materialist substitute when the flame of the great historic faith of the West—Christianity—burns low. It is the story of how a young idealist can paradoxically be dragooned by his better impulses into doing dirty underground work for an apparatus organized for treason. It is the story of a moral awakening—the awakening that came, in one guise or another, to scores of young men and women who measured the pretensions of Marxism against the realities of the murder of the Kronstadt sailors, the purge trials, the liquidation of the Ukrainian kulaks, the barbarian cynicism of the Nazi–Soviet pact. It is the story of what happens when an ex-Communist faces the historical necessity of becoming an informer. It is the story of a family seeking the stability and the assurance of life on a Maryland farm (some of its loveliest pages are devoted to the rhythm of the seasons and the pull of the soil). It is the story of how one man did much to save a great journalistic enterprise (Time, Inc.) from making the mistakes of judgment that have made other journalistic enterprises (the *New York Herald Tribune,* for example) the dupes of the enigmatic Joseph Barneses of this world. Finally, it is the story of a religious illumination that caused Whittaker Chambers, even in the most weary moments of the two Hiss trials, to stand up as a witness not only *against* the Communist conspiracy but also *for* his fighting Quaker faith.

To deal adequately with so many overlapping and interpenetrating stories would involve a comprehensive discussion of everything from psychoanalysis to theology, and from soil chemistry to Dostoevski. Since no reviewer can command the space for such comprehensive treatment, even assuming he is up to it, let me begin by grasping *Witness* by a small, personal handle. I first met Whittaker Chambers in 1939, either just before or just after he had told his story of Communist penetration of the U.S. State Department to Adolf Berle. I had heard that he had been a Communist, but knew nothing beyond the fact that he had once worked for the *Daily Worker* and the *New Masses*. In 1939 a few of us in the Time, Inc., unit of the Newspaper Guild were mystified by a queer phenomenon: the manipulation of a whole host of well-meaning "liberals" by what amounted to a mere handful of obvious Communist Party stooges (or at least they were obvious stooges to those of us who had some knowledge of Marxism). The anti-Communist unit in the Guild was organized by a young Roman Catholic named Larry Delaney, who had a latent talent for politics. But none of us—Delaney, John Davenport (now the editor of *Barron's* magazine), James Agee, Calvin Fixx, Robert Cantwell, to name a few—had good prophetic insight into the Communist techniques of subverting meetings. When Whittaker Chambers joined our group for a short period he provided the necessary prophetic insight. In his somber, slow-spoken, ironical way he would outline what might be expected from the Communist caucus. Invariably he proved to be right.

It was the making of a number of us in an intellectual and journalistic way, for Chambers's knowledge of how to diagnose, and deal with, the future in a microcosm also enabled us in subsequent years to deal with the future on the stage of world history. None of us who knew Whit Chambers in those days ever went wrong on expectations of what might be looked for from our Russian "ally" both during and after the war. None of us went wrong on what would happen at Yalta, or in China, or in Poland, or in Germany. None of us went wrong on the workings of internal U.S. politics under the prod of the Communist conspiracy and infiltration, of which Chambers had himself been a part. And all of us, since 1939, have been able to take the disappointments and the setbacks attendant upon an often hopeless minority fight in a philosophical spirit. For Whit Chambers taught us that in the linked fight *against* the Communist conspiracy and *for* the preservation of the historic continuity of the West, we are not to expect any easy victory. Whether we win or lose, it is enough, as Chambers says, to act as a witness for our faith. If history is to go against the concept of the West, then it is history that is wrong, not we. And one does not cooperate in a crime merely because the criminals seem to be winning.

Having known Whittaker Chambers in the days of the Time, Inc., Newspaper Guild fight of 1939 and 1940, I have had the queer sensation ever since of living in a world of blind men. Chambers tells something of the fight against the blind men as it was waged on the level of Time, Inc., office politics. The whole push of the majority in the *Time, Life,* and *Fortune* offices was toward a complaisance in the face of Russian political successes and of New Deal connivance at those successes. Those were the days when Theodore White, the *Time* Chungking correspondent, was actively indoctrinating everybody from the *New York Times*'s Brooks Atkinson on down against the Kuomintang. Those were the days when *Time*'s war correspondents—Jack Beldon, Charlie Wertenbaker, Bill Walton, John Hersey, Dick Lauterbach—carried the spirit of Stalingrad to the insufferable point of patronizing the contributions of the West to Russian power. Whit Chambers stood actively against these mistaken people, and to his eternal credit publisher Henry Luce stood with him insofar as he was able to do it and still get out his papers. (It would have been hard indeed in those days to find enough technically competent anti-Communist journalists to staff a small fortnightly or weekly of opinion, let alone *Time, Life,* and *Fortune.* Moreover, Henry Luce is temperamentally incapable of understanding the ramifications of conspiracy, even though he is sound in his understanding of basic philosophical principles.)

In the country of the blind, the one-eyed man (as H. G. Wells long ago demonstrated) is certainly *not* the king. That is why Whittaker Chambers's vindication in the Hiss case must on the face of it seem to be a miracle. He himself has set his vindication down to the grace of God working through prosecutor Tom Murphy and through the native common sense of a number of jurors who just never had bothered to read the intellectuals who have dominated our newspapers and book publishing concerns for the past two decades.

Since the truncated *Saturday Evening Post* version of *Witness* rocketed the newsstand circulation of that journal by hundreds of thousands, it is possible that the blind are at last learning to see. The proof of the awakening must await, however, the reception of *Witness* as a book. I have spent some sardonic moments trying to visualize the reviews of *Witness* that will appear in the *New York Times*, the *New York Herald Tribune*, and the *Saturday Review of Literature*. Just who on their staffs is capable of reviewing it? Who has the knowledge and the insight to do it? We shall see.

Even the most recalcitrant reviewer, however, can hardly fail to be shaken by the massed weight of Whittaker Chambers's evidence that there *was* a Communist apparatus, or series of apparatuses, working in Washington from 1933 to 1941. Chambers names names—Harold Ware, Lee Pressman, John Abt, Nathan Witt, Alger Hiss, Charles Kramer, Vincent Reno. He tells of the fellow-traveling aid accorded the Communists by Harry Dexter White, assistant to Secretary of the Treasury Henry Morgenthau. In the case of Alger Hiss, there are the penciled notes, the common memories of what went on in the Hiss household, the records of the sale of Hiss's car for use by a Communist organizer, the State Department documents copied on the Hiss typewriter, the corroborative testimony of Hede Massing and Nat Weyl.

At the moment a movement is afoot which seeks to prove that Whit Chambers somehow fabricated a typewriter that was a duplicate of the one owned by the Hisses, on which he might have copied State Department documents. This strikes me as the laugh of the year, if not the century. It would have cost either thousands of dollars or a lifetime's investment in acquiring mechanical skill to forge a duplicate typewriter. Having seen Whittaker Chambers working with his hands, I know he is no typewriter technician. And having watched him over the years scrabbling to pay off mortgages and to buy farm machinery, I know he has never been able to hire the requisite skills to make a duplicate of a child's Corona, let alone a substantial Woodstock. This means that if a typewriter could be made and *was* made, either the Republicans or the FBI made it. Well, *you* prove that one.

Anyway, even on the cock-eyed assumption that Chambers did copy those State Department documents himself, how on earth did he obtain them in the first place if not through Alger Hiss? And if someone else gave them to Chambers, what possible motive would there have been for naming the wrong man? If Chambers *didn't* meet Alger Hiss in the Washington Communist underground of the thirties, when did he meet him? The sections of *Witness* devoted to Whittaker Chambers's underground days conclusively prove that Communist underground couriers have no time either to cultivate or to frame people who are completely outside the orbit of their party-dictated attention.

For the immediate present, the important thing about *Witness* is its absolutely certain demonstration that Communists have been able to penetrate to high position in the federal government. And if two rings—the Chambers ring and the Elizabeth Bentley apparatus—have been able to steal secrets and to affect high policy, it is hardly common sense to assume no other rings are possible. Indeed, such things as the loss of China and our inability to solve the German problem or to wind up the Korean War would seem to demonstrate that such rings are not only possible but highly probable.

Whittaker Chambers has staked much on warning the American people about the nature and workings of the Communist underground. But his primary purpose in writing *Witness* is religious. He wants to move people not only to reject communism but to accept and rejoice in the Christian God. As a reticent New Englander who has an instinctive aversion to talking about private problems of the soul (I don't boast of this aversion, I just make note of it), I am hardly the right person to make a public judgment of Chambers's theology. All I can say is that he uses his own vocabulary and symbolism for what seems to me to be an approach to universal truth. Whittaker Chambers feels the presence of God where I feel the need for a certain view of the free man possessed of free will and an innate moral sense. But I also feel that my felt need for freedom and Chambers's felt need for God are mystical approaches to the same divine reality that exists beyond the veil imposed by the limitations of a mere five senses. Let us put it this way: Whit Chambers feels that Christianity is right, while I feel that the *insights* of Christianity are right. On the practical plane that seems to me a distinction without a difference.

There is so much in *Witness* that I haven't been able to touch upon in this review that I feel very apologetic. I would like to talk about Mr. Chambers as a social historian of the New York of the twenties and early thirties. I would like to talk about his theories of farming. I would like to talk about his relations with his father, his brother, and his mother. I would like to talk about his children, Ellen and John, whom I knew briefly as wonderfully modest yet spontaneous kids when I used to visit at the Chambers Maryland farm during the days when I worked in Washington. I would like to talk about Whit and Esther Chambers as parents. I would like to go into the Chambers theory of the Popular Front mind. I would like to discuss Chambers's theory of the economic nature of the modern crisis (he still seems to have a lingering respect for Marxism as economic prophecy, and I would like to combat him vigorously on that). I would like to write a whole essay on the perversity of the so-called "best people," who cannot get it through their skulls that Chambers believes in saving the American heritage. (The stupidly malicious behavior of these people during the Hiss case has done more to make me doubt the soundness of American educational institutions than any number of arguments about progressive education.) But there isn't room for any of this here. It will have to wait for another time.

Meanwhile, let it suffice that Whittaker Chambers has written a book that is unique in American literature. *The Education of Henry Adams* was great in one way; *Witness* is just as great in another. The two books are utterly different, yet they are alike in the fact that they exist on the same plane of greatness. Both of them will be read for years to come by those who wish to understand the evolution of the American spirit in its effort to make sense out of the human adventure.

43
Female Exemplars

June 16, 1952

The women! Vivien Kellems, the Connecticut industrialist who has just written a galvanic personal anti-tax manifesto, *Toil, Taxes and Trouble,* insists that they reach their conclusions by intuitive processes, not by the "logical" sequences that are supposedly the exclusive technique of the masculine thinker. Well, I just don't believe Vivien. The most logical people I know in the contemporary writing world happen to be five women: indeed, their sharp, unblinkered analyses of our modern chaos of values have so much in common that these women might be said to constitute a distinct movement in modern letters. Two of the women are novelists: Ayn Rand, author of *The Fountainhead,* and Taylor Caldwell, whose tumultuously exciting *The Devil's Advocate* has just been published amid the almost total silence of those who know how to kill by indirection. The other women are Isabel Paterson, author of *The God of the Machine;* Rose Wilder Lane, a fiction writer who is also a brilliant pamphleteer; and Vivien Kellems herself.

It is not to be supposed that the five women who constitute this movement for individualism, freedom and sanity necessarily approve of each other; individualists seldom do. Mrs. Paterson, who has never been a collectivist of any sort, would probably sniff contemptuously at Rose Wilder Lane, who spent some youthful years in dalliance with socialism. Risking being caught in their crossfire, however, I, a mere intuitive male, insist upon their essential intellectual and moral kinship. Moreover, I am inclined to think that their presence on the scene is so fortunate that it makes personal differences of little moment. The only thing that bothers me about the whole situation as it affects these women is that men, the dopes, don't know how to listen to them and use the lessons they offer.

Take the case of Isabel Paterson, for example. Her *The God of the Machine* was a brilliantly original and sound exposition of the moral, intellectual, theological and psychological justifications for the linked phenomena of free capitalism and the representative, strictly limited government of our forefathers. Since she has written a basic book on the American system, you would think the so-called capitalist press would continue to feature her. Yet the "Republican" *New York Herald Tribune* supinely retired her. And none of the free-enterprise journalistic entities—the *Wall Street Journal, Barron's, Human Events,* to name a few—has sought her out. She is intransigent and therefore "difficult," so there may be reasons for this: editors, like other people, like to exist in comfort. But the good editor, the *really* good editor, has no right to consider his own comfort: he should be prepared to suffer to get the good stuff.

To continue, let's take the case of Rose Wilder Lane. She can write like a breeze, she can make abstruse things come alive, and she knows American history far more thoroughly than any baker's dozen of academic historians. Her early experiences of socialism have sharpened her appreciation of capitalistic freedom. But, for one reason or another, she lives up near Danbury, Connecticut, in communion with her honey bees. Someone ought to put her to work. (I've tried, on occasion, but it is a reflection either on my powers of persuasion or on my choice of suggested topics that I haven't been able to succeed.)

Vivien Kellems, being a competent industrialist (the president of the Kellems Company of Stonington, Connecticut) as well as a writer, would probably not allow herself to be affronted or maneuvered into silence. A scratch-and-claw-'em exponent of the "savage poetry" that is at once the glory and the necessary hardship of the free business world, she would hardly pay her enemies the compliment of allowing them to shut her up. Her book, which comes to us with an introduction by Rupert Hughes, is a fighting recapitulation of her attempts to get the federal government to indict her and her cablegrip manufacturing company for refusing to collect the withholding tax from her employees for the U.S. Treasury.

Being a creature of refreshingly direct logic, Miss Kellems knows that the withholding tax law is in direct contravention of the federal Constitution. How so? It's really simple, my dear Watson: the Constitution expressly forbids involuntary servitude, and when the officers of a corporation are compelled, without compensation, to collect U.S. tax money from their employees, they are being reduced to slave status.

Taylor Caldwell's novel, *The Devil's Advocate*, is a gripping melodrama of the totalitarian future that awaits us if people like Vivien Kellems fail in the various libertarian crusades. Her story is set in the years 1969 and 1970, and it takes off from a Scottish legend about the lawyer who sought to discredit the devil by defending him with such an excess of zeal that the people would be able to see through the tragic farce. In Miss Caldwell's own version of the frightful Orwellian future, the America of the super–Fair Deal (rebaptized as The Democracy) will be saved, not by a rebellion from below, but by an organization of devil's advocates who can be counted upon to worm their way into powerful places in the totalitarian state apparatus. In *The Devil's Advocate* a band of these devoted souls takes the totalitarian dictator's words at face value: they insist that everybody, even including the farmers and the administrators of big state enterprises, live according to the slogans of "work, suffer, sacrifice." By goading everybody, from bureaucrat to common laborer, the Minute Men concealed in the government finally provoke the government's overthrow.

Miss Caldwell has written a fable for our times that may seem wildly improbable. But don't be too sure that it is improbable. Anyway, improbable or not, the story is a humdinging thriller. If anyone is dumb enough to miss its profound, yet simply stated, truths, he or she can still read it with excited admiration for its quality as a tale of adventure.

We hope Taylor Caldwell has another best seller on her hands. We hope Vivien Kellems can enroll all of America's women in her Liberty Belles. It is our masculine intuition that the logic of women will yet save us from the consequences of the cretinism that seems to have assailed the male population of America when it began trifling with the governmental architechtonics of Hamilton, Madison, and Jefferson back around 1908 or 1912.

44
Godfrey Blunden—A Rarity

June 30, 1952

Godfrey Blunden is an Australian newspaperman who covered the Stalingrad and Kharkov fronts in Russia in 1943. He is also a rarity—a perceptive novelist. He is one of the few creative artists in the Anglo-Saxon world who has really managed to come to an understanding of the totalitarian mind. His *A Room on the Route* was a terrifying story of Moscow in wartime; his *The Time of the Assassins* is an even more terrifying account of what happens when the soul of a people—this time it is the population of the Russian Ukraine—is offered a choice, not between good and evil, or even between relative gradations of kindness or brutality or hardship, but simply between two sets of totalitarian masters, the Nazi S.S. and the Communist NKVD.

The historical lesson of *The Time of the Assassins*—that a people will ordinarily end up by giving voting preference to the home-bred tyrant—is almost incidental to the acrid irony that limns a world in which the only reward for making moral distinctions is swift obliteration. Blunden begins his story at a time when the Germans still had a chance to win the Ukrainians to their side. Kharkov (spelled Kharkhiv in this book in the Ukrainian style) had been captured, and the Wehrmacht was not yet irretrievably committed to making its great mistake of diffusing and watering its strength by attempting to probe for the illimitable—that is, the great reaches of Russia-in-Asia. Hating their Communist masters, the Ukrainian peasantry could have been had in 1942 and 1943 by Dr. Karandash and other separatist Ukrainian exiles who had returned home in the wake of the Nazi armies. But the Nazis were totalitarians, and no totalitarian can ever offer a true cultural and spiritual autonomy to a people. Professor Shevchenko, the professor who had kept the memory of Ukrainian traditions alive through a generation of bolshevism, listens to Karandash in Blunden's story, but he really knows the bitter truth, that "the time for republics is over."

The Ukrainian peasantry began to learn this truth when the Nazi S.S. began its indiscriminate killing, looting, burning and enslaving. Having seized the NKVD files, the Nazis were able to wipe out most of the Ukrainian Communists who had dossiers. But with the lack of sympathetic imagination that totalitarianism breeds, the Germans were soon seizing anybody and everybody for labor service, for impressed military service, or (in the case of women) for duty in the soldiers' brothels. In addition to all this, the peasants did not get title to the land; the Nazis could not take time out to restore the property right in the middle of total warfare.

Blunden, in a series of flashing episodic vignettes that remind one of the earlier Dos Passos, shows how the moral and individualistic view of life tried to merge in the Ukraine in 1942 and 1943, and how it was universally blighted and extinguished by the "assassins" on both sides of the Nazi–Soviet war. Maryusa, the teacher, might seek to protect her children as children; Olympia, the healthy peasant girl, might attempt to win her way to freedom by a pro tempore exercise of the courtesan's ancient wiles; Professor Shevchenko might obtain release by telling Ukrainian fables to kids who were hungry for something besides the party line. But in a world dominated by the clash of totalitarians none of this could bear any real fruit. The price of survival in the Ukraine in 1942 and 1943 was the ability to settle all questions by use of the naked will. Fomin, the child of murdered small-time Communist functionaries, had such a will. So too did little Sophia, who wanted to see all Communists murdered.

Godfrey Blunden has the novelist's eye for the individual's predicament. He also has an historian's ability to grasp and depict the clash of great forces. He doesn't quite succeed in marrying his fiction and his history, for amid the roll and thunder leading up to Stalingrad the individual episodes of *The Time of the Assassins* tend to shrivel and get lost. *The Time of the Assassins* is bifocal, not unified, writing, and the reader is forced to extraordinary feats of agility in shifting his sights instantaneously from one type of lens to another. But Blunden's philosophical grasp is broad, and his book is most rewarding if it is approached as an exercise in sheer philosophical understanding.

It so happened that I learned of the death of John Dewey, the instrumentalist philosopher, when I was in the middle of reading Blunden on the use of the lie as a pragmatic instrument. This set up a curious train of reflection. "When you are on the side of truth, when you *possess* truth," says one of Blunden's characters; "the lie is a tactic." Since John Dewey never lied or supported liars, this must mean one of two things: either he had an absolutist (that is, a nonpragmatic) regard for the inviolability of truth, or he was not possessed by any truth to the point of being willing to lie in its service. By extension of this reflection, doesn't it become apparent that the only people who can be trusted not to use instrumentalism to make a shambles of the world are those without philosophical purpose?

Maybe it is lucky that we Americans, who are all too prone to be easy pragmatists, have not had any real convictions in the past two or three generations. If we had had a national purpose or purposes at a time when instrumentalism was taking over in our educational institutions, we might have become as murderous and as lying a set of monsters as the Nazis and the Communists. By the same token, it behooves us to return to an absolutistic view of morality—that is, that it is universally and unexceptionably sinful to lie, steal, and murder—now that we are becoming purposive about the necessity of saving the Western world in the fight against communism.

45
The Rise of Leonard Read

July 14, 1952

If you happen to be one of the fortunate 28,712 people who are on the mailing list of the Foundation for Economic Education, Inc., you know all about the vital pamphlets and releases proclaiming liberty that issue periodically from its editorial sanctum at Irvington-on-Hudson. The Foundation is by any count a remarkable institution. It was founded six years ago by Leonard E. Read, formerly the manager of the Los Angeles Chamber of Commerce and executive vice president of the National Industrial Conference Board. Read is a curious mixture of American go-getter, Tolstoyan Christian, Herbert Spencer libertarian, and dedicated medieval monk. Every strand of his personality is entwined in his Foundation, which, in Emersonian terms, is simply the lengthened shadow of the man. The Foundation, which has a most capable staff of economists and libertarian thinkers, lives on voluntary contributions, which it never solicits. Read holds to the Emersonian belief that a good mousetrap advertises itself by its own goodness—and the world of folk who wish to see all totalitarians, statists, welfare staters and believers in political compulsion at the bottom of the ocean (figuratively speaking, of course) has been beating a path to his door.

Recently the Foundation published *Essays on Liberty.* Consisting of the cream of the Foundation's releases to date, this book is the definitive answer to the captive intellectuals of the New Deal–Fair Deal in America and to the various issues of Fabian essays which have, over the course of three or four generations, rotted out the entire social fabric of Great Britain. In this book we have such notable things as Dean Russell's discovery that the first leftists in the French Revolutionary National Constituent Assembly in 1789 were libertarians who were pledged to free their economy from government-guaranteed special privileges of guilds, unions, and associations whose members were banded together to interfere with the workings of the free market. These first leftists, as Russell succinctly tells the story, held a slim majority in their parliament for two years. They did a remarkable job of confounding authoritarians. Then they were bowled over by the Jacobins, the terroristic Leninists of their day. The tragedy that flowed from Robespierre's and Marat's despicable statist counterrevolution has bedeviled the world ever since. Not only did it pervert the whole vocabulary of freedom; it also established the theory of the totalitarian "general will," which permits any majority, "transient" or not, to ride roughshod over the God-given natural rights of the minority. In the guise of killing royal totalitarianism it popularized the totalitarianism of 51 percent of the population. The supposedly individualistic peoples of western Europe have been kowtowing to this totalitarian conception since that evil day when the first head spurted blood under the guillotine that was set up in the name of liberty, equality and fraternity.

In America, as Betty Knowles Hunt and other contributors to Leonard Read's book make plain, the complex of ideas flowing from the Robespierrean counterrevolution never managed to become domesticated until after 1933. In Europe they had rent control and a concomitant shortage of houses, as Bertrand de Jouvenal shows in an excellent paper in this book, but in America a people free of rent control could rebuild the entire city of San Francisco after an earthquake in what amounts to the twinkling of a gnat's eye. In England, as Sir Ernest Benn says in an essay called "Rights for Robots," the Webbs and the other Fabians robbed the people of their Christian heritage of individual responsibility (which nurtures the divine, or the creative, spark), but in America (see W. M. Curtiss's amusing "Athletes, Taxes, Inflation") a Babe Ruth who climbed out of an orphanage to hit sixty home runs in a single year could reap the full reward for a highly individualized skill. The period of Babe Ruth's development and ascendancy preceded, of course, the reign of Franklin I. After 1933 came the deluge, which is measured accurately by the cosmic water meters operated by Maxwell Anderson, C. L. Dickenson, Russel Clincy, W. M. Curtiss, F. A. Harper and other contributors to Mr. Read's volume.

Not that these people deal in personalities: Mr. Read's genius is for collecting writers whose self-imposed duty is to explain the principles (or the perversions of principles) that underlie the antics and the convolutions of the various saints and devils who have been struggling for the control of our destiny. The approach in *Essays on Liberty* is not that of daily, weekly, or fortnightly journalism, which must inevitably deal to some extent in the personalities that make or mar principles. Read's idea is to plant seeds that will mature in the fullness of time; he doesn't aspire to compete in immediacy with the editors of papers and magazines. Nevertheless, Leonard Read is a journalist on a high level: he knows how to ask the relevant journalistic questions, and he knows that principles (or their lack) are at the bottom of elections, wars, and legislative and administrative acts. The thing that distinguishes Leonard Read from most of our journalists is that he seeks to assess personalities by their basic philosophies.

Long ago, as a young Chamber of Commerce man in the San Francisco region, Read was a Light Brigade soldier who simply executed the commands from on high. In those days the national Chamber of Commerce, under Henry Harriman, was promoting what amounted to trade association fascism. (It was the Harriman thinking that created the Blue-Eagled NRA, that ill-starred adventure in price-, wage- and production-fixing that had us all salaaming to Hugh [Iron Pants] Johnson in the days of the first New Deal.) A crusader then as now, Read went down from San Francisco to Los Angeles in 1932 to lecture W. C. Mullendore of the Southern California Edison Company on the virtues of NRA-ism. The trip south was his Road to Damascus, for in the space of an hour the persuasive Mullendore tore apart all of Read's thinking. The new Saul-become-Paul emerged from the Mullendore presence a changed man, a firm believer in freedom and voluntarism in all their phases, social, political and economic. The session with Mullendore was a pedagogical revelation to the young Read. It started him thinking about techniques and means of bringing collectivists of one stripe or another to a full realization of the slave state implications of their position. As Read thinks back on it, the Foundation for Economic Education—and *Essays on Liberty*—were really born in Mullendore's office that day.

Like most men of individualistic distinction, Read is not a mere product of our more conventional educational institutions. He learned the rough way. In World War I he was dumped from the torpedoed *Tuscania* into the Irish Sea. Saved from a watery grave, he knocked about England in war camps as a rigger in America's pioneer air force, learning the truth that you can't fake or fudge a problem in mechanics. He came home to take on Chamber of Commerce jobs in Palo Alto and San Francisco. During his years with the Los Angeles Chamber of Commerce he had a wonderful time fighting the myriad versions of collectivist lunacy that flourished on the Pacific Coast in the wake of Ham-and-Eggism, Townsendism, and Upton Sinclair's attempt to hornswoggle the voters with his EPIC (End Poverty in California) platform. With Mullendore and others he started the Freeman Pamphleteers, a group which gaily revived such forgotten individualistic worthies as Bastiat and William Graham Sumner.

Meanwhile, as a hobby, Read was exploring the fascinations of good food, and making himself into a *cordon bleu* cook. He can look at a complicated recipe in a cookbook and taste the thing accurately in his mind. Since he can also smell a believer in state compulsion fifty or even a hundred miles away, Read is a fit candidate for some of Professor Rhine's future investigations into extrasensory perception. He is a canny and extremely perceptive man with a vested interest in other people's variations, and if his assembled *Essays on Liberty* were to be made even an elective part of our school curriculum, America might have a new birth of freedom virtually overnight.

46
Me-tooism and the Independent Voter

July 28, 1952

As I write there is a vast tumult in Chicago, where a host of New Dealish cuckoos are vying with the more legitimate birds for control of the orthodox Republican nest. The stress is heavily on the Menckenian side of politics, but if there is one safe generalization that can be made this July it is that the people who will vote on candidates and platforms next autumn are not in a harlequin mood. Indeed, it is entirely possible that voters may be ready to ponder such serious campaign literature as James L. Wick's *How NOT to Run for President: A Handbook for Republicans* and Harley L. Lutz's *A Platform for the American Way.*

The Wick book is presented as an elongated pamphlet, but for all its unpretentious cover it contains the soundest analysis of Republican defeats of 1940, 1944 and 1948 that has been printed to date. Taking the bull by the corns (to quote Jimmy Durante) on the very first page, Wick refutes the idea that there is a great bloc of strong-minded "independent voters" who characteristically wait until November before making their decision about the candidates. According to Wick's researches, 80 or 90 percent of all persons of above-average political intelligence know which party will get their vote before the presidential candidates have been nominated. The ones who remain uncommitted until late in the campaign tend to be of two types. Either they belong to the group of passive followers who are weak and indecisive by nature or they are people who are subjected to terrible inner conflicts.

In either case, it takes unequivocal leadership, not "me-too" or "let's-have-unity" tactics, to catch the last-minute voter.

Both Wendell Willkie (in 1940) and Thomas Dewey (in 1944 and 1948) misread the nature of the electorate. Willkie went into the Republican convention of 1940 as a fighting symbol of opposition to the New Deal. As the spokesman for free enterprise in general and the Commonwealth and Southern utility empire in particular, Willkie had had the temerity to take on the Tennessee Valley Authority. The pet of the sainted George Norris, the TVA was merely the most sacred of all the New Deal cows. It was seemingly tempting fate to touch the TVA, yet Willkie had a resurgent business community behind him, and he might have won in November if he had continued to take his true line, which was that of bold opposition to Franklin Roosevelt's statist philosophy.

Wha' hoppen? As everybody ought to know by now, the symbol of anti-Rooseveltism went out to Elwood, Indiana, to make an acceptance speech filled with "me-too" psychology. Instead of appealing to the natural leaders of the Republican Party, the men who might have persuaded the weak and the indecisive in November, Willkie figuratively doffed his cap to "Champ" Roosevelt on every possible occasion. Moreover, he learned nothing from his defeat, for in his campaign for a renomination in 1944 he persisted in courting the approval of New York's Park Avenue intellectuals. I wrote an article for *Life* magazine in March 1944 arguing that Willkie needed the votes of some Republican regulars in the primaries, not the votes of Dorothy Thompson and Samuel Grafton (who were Democrats anyway), but it had no effect on Mr. Willkie, who was above listening to advice from presumed whippersnappers.

Simply because Willkie persisted in stupidity beyond the call of duty, Dewey won the Republican nomination in 1944. He did this by sticking to the pros, letting Willkie have the amateurs. Then he, too, threw away the election by turning his attention to the nonexistent "independent vote." And he played the same fatal record all over again in 1948. Truman, a pro in politics if there ever was one, made some fighting speeches guaranteed to catch the weak and indecisive in the last-minute rush, and the Democrats were in for four more years when, by all the odds, they should have lost. The whole free world was moving to the "right" in 1948, and America would have moved in that direction too if Dewey had taken a firm antistatist line.

No matter who the Republican nominee is this time, he must take his stand on a traditional form of Americanism if he is to win. Harley L. Lutz, the well-known Princeton economist, has presented a first-rate Americanist platform for any Republican candidate in his *A Platform for the American Way.* Dr. Lutz begins soundly by proclaiming the right to own as the basic human right. This, as Isabel Paterson says, is a matter of mechanics: if a person lacks the right to own land, he must appeal to the state for permission to occupy the ground he stands on; and if he lacks the right to own tools he must turn to a political agent for the very things that are needed to bring food to his mouth. The right to free speech is dependent on the right to own paper, printing presses, and such; the right to worship is dependent on the right to own a church in community with other like-minded people.

Dr. Lutz's book goes into technicalities about taxation, social security, and other "difficult" subjects. But it is a clearly written document, and the main points are made in sharp little paragraphs set in small type throughout the book. A confirmed antistatist, Dr. Lutz wants no paltering: he is for getting the federal government out of the fields of lending, giving, and competing with private industry and banking. Neither the Republican nor the Democratic platform will tally to any marked degree with Dr. Lutz's own platform, for politicians are a temporizing breed even at best. But you can judge the comparative virtues of the platforms that are written at Chicago by putting them alongside Dr. Lutz's book and seeing which one approaches it as a limit.

Ben Hecht once wrote a story about stone-eating termites. A crazy notion, but not too crazy, for the fact of the matter is that we all eat stuff that originated in stone, as Jacquetta Hawkes shows in *A Land.* In the beginning everything was stone; humus and chlorophyll are merely added starters.

Miss Hawkes is paleontologist, archaeologist and poet. *A Land* is the story of the rocks of Britain and what these rocks, crumbled into soil or quarried and shaped into building materials, have done to form the culture, even the bone and marrow, of the British people. A book of scientific precision, yet it has much of the excitement of Jack London's *Before Adam.*

47
Joseph McCarthy
The Sandlot Debater

August 11, 1952

Joseph R. McCarthy has written a book called *McCarthyism: The Fight for America.* I found myself momentarily puzzled by the title, for there isn't a thing that corresponds to the popular notion of "McCarthyism" in a hundred-odd pages of closely packed text. What we find here is not rant, or wild charges, but sober citations from books, magazines, and newspapers, and the incontrovertible evidence presented at congressional hearings. Strictly on the evidence of this book, one would be forced to choose between two conclusions: either Senator McCarthy has been basely slandered by the McLiberals, or he has become a quite responsible scholar overnight.

There is more than the evidence of this book, of course. The truth is that Joe McCarthy has learned more and more about his subject—the influence of communism on the foreign policy, the domestic politics, and the culture of America—as he has gone along. When he first became aware of the workings of infiltrators, spies and fellow-traveling dupes, he was an unsophisticated young politician from the midwest. Being a Leo Durocher–John McGraw sort of fellow, a take-charge guy, he fumed, bit his nails, and rushed out of the dugout to protest before a large crowd that some illegal spitballs and emery balls were being pitched by Lefty Lattimore. True, he hadn't seen Lattimore nick the ball on his spikes. But there were certainly some strange optical hijinks as Lefty's curve dipped over the outside corner of the plate.

Like Durocher and McGraw, McCarthy is not particularly subtle in the heat of debate. He learned to argue on the sandlots, not at Oxford. And right off the bat he made a mistake: he called Owen (*toujours de l'audace*) Lattimore the "top Soviet agent" in the United States. Since Gerhardt Eisler was the number-one Soviet agent in America throughout the historical period in question, this was in obvious contempt of the law of physics that says only one solid object can occupy a given space at a given moment. On the other hand, there might be a quibble to justify McCarthy: maybe the Soviet apparatus allows for plenty of room at the top. (Just under the space occupied by Joe Stalin, of course.)

In any event, McCarthy's loose use of the king's English gave Lattimore the chance to come back at him. And Lattimore did. But events moved on, and Joe McCarthy kept on digging. He read books, he listened to dozens of people. And he began to learn something about the refinements of debate. The result is particularly apparent in his chapter titled "The Evidence on Owen Lattimore." Here McCarthy eschews the pop-off language of the dugout. Instead, he quotes, quotes, quotes, levying upon Lattimore's own writings and upon the evidence presented by thirteen witnesses who have testified under oath to Lattimore's party-lining activities in behalf of the Wave of the Future: Mao Tse-tung-style.

Joe McCarthy follows the same sober question-and-answer method in chapters on Dean Acheson, Philip Jessup, George Marshall, the Tydings committee, and his own speech delivered at Wheeling, West Virginia, where his use of sober arithmetic regarding questionable loyalty cases in the State Department was distorted by an inexcusably careless and vituperative opposition. In clearing up the details about the charges and countercharges involved in the struggle known as McCarthyism, Joe McCarthy gives evidence that he can challenge Ph.D. workers at their own business of clearing all things back to authenticated sources. Furthermore, McCarthy shows signs of learning that the outright Communist "spy" and "agent" may be less important than the Communist culture-carrier or peddler of influence in the McLiberals' fight to transform America into a version of Lower Slobbovia. (How's that for a title: "McLiberalism: The Fight for Lower Slobbovia"?)

Not that the Dick Tracy approach to spies and infiltrators in the State Department isn't necessary as long as Dean Acheson and his gang are moving the levers of power in Foggy Bottom. The infiltrators have been there, and McCarthy has proved it. There remains, however, the larger problem of explaining how Acheson got that way, or Who Sold Our Ruling Class the Bill of Goods? This is something that Joe McCarthy is just tumbling to. Before he can fully understand it, he needs some briefing on the Communist attitude toward what carries influence, which is: words.

Long before Communist Harold Ware, son of Communist "Mother" Bloor, planted his cell in the Department of Agriculture in Washington (the cell from which emerged such characters as Lee Pressman and Alger Hiss), the Communists were busy with Objective Number One, which was the capture of New York, the word capital of the United States. This job was pulled off in the thirties. It was an impalpable capture, and probably at no time did actual Communists ever occupy more than a few big jobs in the book publishing, magazine, and newspaper world. But ever since the Communists first created their League of Professional Groups for Foster and Ford in 1932, they have managed to put their coloration on the American Word.

The League of Professional Groups lasted no longer than most Communist fronts, succumbing in due order to the Trotskyite schism of the mid-thirties. But for every Communist cultural "front" which broke up, five new ones were formed. There were the League of American Writers, the League Against War and Fascism (later the League for Peace and Democracy), the Descendants of the American Revolution, the League of Women Shoppers, et cetera, et cetera. The turnover in Big Name membership was fast and furious, since it took only a little face-to-face experience with the Communists to open the eyes of anyone with a modicum of critical sense. But always the Communists managed to retain the types that liked organization for its own sake. They couldn't hold an Edmund Wilson, a James Rorty, a Sidney Hook or a John Dos Passos, but they did hold the natural politicians of the cultural world. And these they infiltrated into bigger and better posts in publishing, in Hollywood, and in such organizations as the Book and Magazine Guild and the New York Newspaper Guild.

In time, the infiltrees achieved a wide amount of power to give and withhold jobs, to accept and to refuse manuscripts, and to exalt or to sabotage books and articles. In the late thirties and on up to 1945 and 1946, any author who deliberately provoked the Communists could count on a standard smear treatment. I well remember the fate of Ben Stolberg's *Story of the CIO.* The book was an expansion of a series of Scripps–Howard syndicated articles exposing the Communists in certain of the CIO unions. Inasmuch as Phil Murray got around to purging the Communist elements from the CIO a decade later on charges that were essentially the same as those made by Stolberg in the thirties, the truth of the book is hardly to be questioned. Nevertheless, one of the Viking Press's own employees organized an inside-the-office crusade to discredit his own firm's book on the ground that it contained "mistakes." Stooge "petitions" rolled into Viking from all over asking the company to suppress Stolberg's "lies." The campaign was rolling furiously when Harold Guinzberg, the Viking Press president, came home from Europe and put a stop to it. But the damage had been done: Stolberg had been "discredited" in the eyes of a number of duped reviewers.

The extent of Communist influence on American cultural life in the late thirties is perhaps best measured by what has gone down in anti-Communist history as the "letter of the 400 fools." Issued on August 14, 1939, this letter pointed to the "fascist" character of anyone who dared suggest the "fantastic falsehood" that the USSR and the totalitarian states are "basically alike." Vincent Sheean, Irving Fineman, Granville Hicks, Dashiell Hammett, Langston Hughes, Waldo Frank, Arthur Kober, Max Lerner, Frederick Schuman, Kyle Crichton and Robert Coates were among the 400 who put their names to a palpably idiotic document. Nine days later Berlin and Moscow made known the terms of their "pact of friendship," and a number of faces took on a purely physiological tinge of red.

Many of the 400 fools later beat their breasts and proclaimed their own gullibility. But so slickly had the Communist penetration of the "opinion industries" done its job that it is still considered disreputable to make a career of attacking communism. Today there is a small but growing market for the anti-Communist writer—he can get himself published in such organs as the *American Legion Monthly* or the *Freeman.* He can, if he will first piously proclaim that he is neither a McCarthyite nor an anti-McCarthyite, get published in the *New Leader.* But he will still have difficulty getting work from the fashionable old-line press—say, the *New York Times Book Review,* or the *Saturday Review of Literature,* or the slicks. By their oblique control of writing in the thirties and the early forties, the Communists managed to poison the intellectual life of a whole nation—and the poison has lingered on. The Communists created the stereotypes that move college professors, suburban women's club program chairmen, small-town editorial writers, and Washington, D.C. bureaucrats even down to this year of 1952.

This was the really important job that was done on America—the job of poisoning the word. And now the big job is to extract the poison, and to change the stereotypes that move preachers, professors, editors and women's club speakers. In its essence, it is not a job that can be done by congressional investigation, and we sincerely hope that Joe McCarthy will not attempt to take on a Senatorial Battle of the Books, which would involve destruction of the First Amendment to the Constitution. The job is one for journalism, and for journalism alone. But where are the journals and the journalists to do it? Alas, most of our editors are still snoring. They are still devoting most of their dream-walking energies to battling "McCarthyism" and kowtowing to McLiberalism. They still think it is the quintessence of moral courage to denounce McCarthy—even though Richard H. Rovere, who denounces McCarthy periodically, admits that he has found such denunciation "no more taxing or dangerous than drinking my morning coffee."

When will our editors tumble to the truth that McCarthy has merely uncovered the end result, on governmental levels, of the subversion of the word that took place in the thirties? When will they start the laborious business of redefining the American Word? In my more pessimistic moments I doubt that they ever will. But my glandular optimism always reasserts itself, and I have had a long lesson in patient waiting.

48
Setting Russia Up

September 22, 1952

In the early days of the war, whenever the quality of Soviet resistance to Hitler was being discussed in Washington, the names of two American army officers were cited as sources of information. Those who believed that Stalin could stand up against Hitler usually quoted the optimistic statements of Colonel Faymonville. Those who believed the Nazis would demolish the Russian armies based their conclusions on the pessimistic reports of Colonel Ivan Downes Yeaton.

Yeaton knew much about Russia. But he reckoned without two things. One was the effect of great distances and extreme cold on the supply problem of the Nazi armies. The other was the stiffening attitude of the Russian peasants as the Nazis increased their insane barbarities against the civilian population in conquered territory.

It so happened that Harry Hopkins, Roosevelt's intermittent deputy to the court of Stalin and the lord of Lend-Lease, sided with Colonel Faymonville. That was his privilege, and he happened to be right about it. Both General George Marshall and Harry Hopkins considered Russia as the key to the war, and, with Roosevelt concurring, the orders went out to help Stalin in every possible way. Speaking at a Russian Aid Rally at Madison Square Garden, Harry Hopkins cried: "The American people are bound to the people of the Soviet Union in the great alliance of the United Nations. . . . *We are determined that nothing shall stop us from sharing with you all that we have and are* in this conflict, and we look forward to sharing with you the fruits of victory and peace." (My emphasis) After the war was over, Hopkins, according to

James Byrnes, reminded Stalin "of how liberally the United States had construed the [Lend-Lease] law in sending foodstuffs *and other nonmilitary* items to their aid."

There was never any mystery about Harry Hopkins's extreme pro-Russian partisanship; he gloried in it. But when Major George Racey Jordan, a businessman who had served as wartime liaison officer with the Russians at Great Falls, Montana, chose in 1949 to tell via a Fulton Lewis, Jr., broadcast what he knew about the liberality of Harry Hopkins's construing of the Lend-Lease law, the journalistic roof fell in on him. There seemed to be a taboo about stating the obvious. Jordan was accused of blackening and slandering the name of a great patriot. If Senator McCarthy had been anything more than an obscure Wisconsin politico at the time, Racey Jordan would almost assuredly have been damned from coast to coast as a practitioner of that crime of crimes, "McCarthyism."

Why all the heat about Racey Jordan's citations from the diary he had kept during the war years as an "expediter" at Great Falls, the staging base for the Alaska–Siberia air "pipeline" for Lend-Lease? Quite obviously the 1949 hue and cry against the major arose for one reason: the desire of very powerful forces to maintain an "official" history of the war that will admit of no mistakes in judgment by Roosevelt, Marshall and Hopkins. It is noteworthy that in his book, *From Major Jordan's Diaries: The Inside Story of Soviet Lend-Lease—from Washington to Great Falls to Moscow,* done in collaboration with Richard L. Stokes, Racey Jordan makes no "McCarthyite" charges. He sticks to what he knows and remembers, producing from a documentation that was made on the spot when he was on friendly terms with the likable Soviet Colonel Kotikov at Newark, New Jersey, and at Great Falls. If the sum total of Major Jordan's revelations tends to bear out the view that Harry Hopkins made a disastrous miscalculation about Russian postwar intentions, the blame should be placed on Hopkins, not on the major.

What Racey Jordan saw during the war was horrendous from a long-term view. He knew nothing at the time about the atom bomb, nothing about the Manhattan Project, yet from 1942 on he was aware that Colonel Kotikov and the Russians were intent on getting something called "bomb powder" out of the United States. In 1942, through the Lend-Lease pipeline, graphite, aluminum tubes, cadmium metal and thorium, all of them useful in atomic experiments, started moving to Russia. The amounts may have been negligible, as were the amounts of uranium nitrate and uranium oxide of Canadian origin that later moved through the Great Falls pipeline at American expense. But the important thing to note about the shipments of atomic materials to Russia in 1942 and 1943 is that they indicated the Soviets were early and thoroughly aware of virtually everything that was going on in American atomic research laboratories. Moreover, on the basis of Major Jordan's evidence, Harry Hopkins knew that the Russians knew far in advance about the Great Secret, which was officially not divulged to Stalin until Potsdam in 1945.

It was in April, 1943 that Colonel Kotikov, who was at the Great Falls end of the Washington wire, handed the phone over to Major Jordan with the statement: "Big boss, Mr. Hopkins, wants you." Said "Hopkins": "Now, Jordan, there's a shipment of chemicals going through that I want you to expedite. . . . I don't want you to discuss this with anyone, and it is not to go into the records. Don't make a big production of it, but just send it through quietly, in a hurry." Naturally, Major Jordan did not see Hopkins standing at the other end of the line, and it is theoretically possible that he might have been talking to a Soviet agent who was pretending to be the boss of Lend-Lease. But if it was a Soviet agent disguising himself as Harry Hopkins, how come the random question, "Did you get those pilots I sent you?" The probability is that only Harry Hopkins himself would have known enough about those pilots to ask about them.

Quite legitimately, the Great Falls–Alaska–Siberia pipeline carried lots of military material, and hundreds of Bell Airacobras, the small fighting planes which enabled the Russians to turn back the German Messerschmitts. But there were also the "black suitcases" that moved under "diplomatic immunity." Major Jordan opened some of these suitcases. They contained a variety of things, ranging from maps of the Panama Canal to documents relating to the Aberdeen Proving Grounds, and from State Department folders tabbed "From Hiss" to road maps with the locations of American industrial plants ("Westinghouse" and "Blaw-Knox") penciled in. One suitcase contained engineering and scientific treatises, plus a brief note to "Mikoyan" on White House stationery. An excerpt from the note read: ". . . had a hell of a time getting these away from Groves [the commander of the Manhattan Engineer District, later the Manhattan Project]." The initials signed to the note, according to George Racey Jordan, were "H. H."

Major Jordan kept his copies of the Russian lists of Lend-Lease shipments, which carry with them an itemized notation of the dollar value of every category. The grand total for four years came to some $9.6 billion. Major Jordan calls the lists "the greatest mail-order catalogue in history." The significant thing about the $9.6 billion of Lend-Lease aid is that a third of it consisted of material which could not possibly be of use in stampeding the Nazis out of Russia. Under Harry Hopkins's admittedly "liberal" construing of the Lend-Lease law the Soviets received vast quantities of industrial material which they wanted for strictly postwar purposes, including the purpose of abolishing freedom in Europe and Asia. They even got such things as lipsticks, dolls, bank vaults, antique furniture, calendars, false teeth and "one tobacco pipe" worth ten dollars, under the general heading of "defense" necessities. They also got enough telephone wire to circle the globe some fifty times.

Major Jordan admits that he has only his word to offer about the alleged Hopkins note and the Hopkins telephone call. But he has documents to prove virtually everything else. There are the bills of lading to prove uranium shipments. Finally, there is a chapter called "Clouds of Witnesses," wherein other people bring corroboratory evidence to bear on what happened along the various pipelines to wartime Russia. If Major Jordan is telling the demonstrable truth about a thousand and one items, why should there be any reason to suppose him a prevaricator in one instance or two? For my money, his book carries the air of complete authenticity, and I am happy to see that the reputable "old-line" publishing house of Harcourt, Brace has had the courage to bring it out.

The China Story

49
The China Tale of Betrayal

June 4, 1951

Freda Utley's *The China Story* is a great piece of history and a fine model of crusading journalism. My first impulse is to say that it ought to be stuffed down the throats of George Marshall, Dean Acheson and Harry Truman. But aside from the vengeful satisfaction such action might give some long-suffering people, that would hardly help get the United States off the hook in its foreign policy. To save this nation from disaster, some means should be found of trepanning the skulls of Marshall, Acheson and Truman and getting Freda Utley's words inside their heads.

Whittaker Chambers, who knows the Communist conspiracy from the inside out, once remarked that there is only one instance in history in which a nation has succeeded in using the State Department of its number-one enemy to kill off its number-two enemy. He was obviously speaking of Soviet Russia, the United States and Nationalist China. The truth of Chambers's epigrammatic flash is underscored by Freda Utley's patient display of statistics and textual analysis in ten pointed chapters. Her book begins with Yalta, but soon Mrs. Utley is dipping back into the thirties, when the attitudes that gave birth to Yalta first found a habitation in the minds and emotions of scores of young Americans who thought that communism, unlike fascism, had a "progressive" destination.

The story as it affects China began in Hankow, in 1938. The United States military attaché in Hankow in those early days of the Sino–Japanese War was Colonel (later General) Joseph Stilwell. A softhearted and sentimental man despite his "Vinegar Joe" nickname and his gruff exterior, Colonel Stilwell was easily captivated by Agnes Smedley, a gallant and basically idealistic soul who had the blindest sort of admiration for the Chinese Communists. Agnes Smedley not only captivated Joe Stilwell, she also won over practically everybody else around her in the Hankow, or "Wuhan cities," region. Among her conquests were Captain Evans Carlson of the United States Marine Corps, and John Paton Davies, the elegant and sophisticated American consul in Hankow. Together with Davies, Carlson, Smedley and Stilwell in Hankow was journalist Edgar Snow, whose books did such an effective job in presenting the Chinese Communists to book-reading Americans as romantic Jeffersonian agrarians. Later on Snow was to become a favored writer for the *Saturday Evening Post;* he has continued his sophistical dissertations in that medium over the years, although his name has been dropped from the *Post* masthead.

The "Hankow last-ditchers," as Utley calls them, were scattered to the ends of the earth by 1942. But Joe Stilwell, by then a general, was appointed American military representative in China in that year. The appointment brought most of "Joe's Boys" (Victor Lasky's phrase) back into effective action. John Davies became Stilwell's political adviser—and with him Davies brought his protégés, John Stewart Service, Raymond Paul Ludden and John Emmerson. Since Stilwell was chief of staff of Chiang Kai-shek as well as American military representative in China, Joe's Boys had the opportunity of seeing all, knowing all—and influencing all. Their lines of infiltration and persuasion went deep into the State Department in Washington; and, by playing on Stilwell himself, they were able subtly to make their point of view on China prevail with General George Marshall, who was Stilwell's friend, patron and boss. They worked hand in glove with John Carter Vincent, who succeeded Joe Grew as head of the Office of Far Eastern Affairs of the State Department in 1945; and they formed a united ideological front with Lauchlin Currie of the Foreign Economic Administration and with Owen Lattimore, deputy director of OWI in 1942–44.

Utley does not contend that Stilwell, Davies, Service, Ludden, Emmerson, Vincent, Currie and Lattimore were Communists; what she does say is that they followed a plan of agitation and action that was eminently satisfactory to Joe Stalin, Mao Tse-tung, and Chu Teh in their efforts to communize China. It may be important to note that John Davies is today a key member of the Policy Planning Committee of the State Department, in which position he is still able to influence policy affecting all the sensitive agencies of government.

Freda Utley not only tells how Joe's Boys and their journalistic counterparts managed to capture the diplomats and the secretary of state (first Byrnes, then Marshall, then Acheson); she also shows how they made a virtual corner of the book market through taking over practically all the white space devoted to Far Eastern affairs in the important review media of New York City. There was a time in New York's literary history when a General Chennault, a George Creel or a Freda Utley could no more get an unbiased, let alone a favorable, notice in a big New York paper than a zombie could win high place on an Olympic athletic team.

Most of Utley's book is devoted to the fellow-traveler crusade for the American mind as it looked westward to the Pacific and beyond. But she also does magnificent work in exploding certain stereotypes that the fellow-traveler writers and speakers have falsely established as axiomatic with practically everyone from college presidents to golf caddies. There is the stereotype, for example, that Chiang Kai-shek's "corrupt" entourage somehow frittered away from two to four billion dollars' worth of American military and economic aid after V-J Day. Dean Acheson and Senator Tom Connally have both repeated this old chestnut (using the two-billion figure); and it crops up in editorials, articles, speeches and conversation almost everywhere. (The most recent place I read it was in an article by Ralph McGill, the Atlanta editor and journalist.)

What actually happened was that our State Department by one ruse or another kept the military aid to Chiang from arriving until it was way too late. As for the two-billion figure, Utley breaks it down in a way to show that Nationalist China got very little of value, no matter what dollar price is attached to the sum total. Acheson's figure of two billion includes a total of $799 million of "economic" aid and $797 million of "military" aid. That comes to just under $1.6 billion. (The balance is not itemized, but presumably it includes $404 million of United Nations Relief and Rehabilitation Administration aid.) But of what did the "military" aid consist? Some $335 million of it consisted of "services and expenses" connected with repatriating the million or more Japanese soldiers in China and transporting Chinese Nationalist soldiers to accept the surrender of Japanese armies. Even President Truman has said that these "services" cannot properly be regarded as "post-war" Lend-Lease; they should come under the heading of World War II expenses. If the United States had not transferred the Chinese to take surrender of the Japanese, American troops would have had to be used, at considerably greater expense.

Deducting the $335 million represented by the cost of repatriating the Japanese and accepting their surrender, we have a total of some $460 million of postwar military aid to China. But this figure must be trimmed further by disallowing most of the non-military "surplus war stocks" sold to China in 1946, which Acheson misleadingly includes in his total of "military aid." The truth is that out of a total of $100 million worth of so-called surplus war stocks, 40 percent consisted of quartermaster supplies; only a paltry $3 million of the $100 million represented the small arms and ammunition needed to fight the Chinese Red Armies in the field. Subtracting all the surplus war stocks that were useless for fighting, we get a figure of some $363 million of postwar military aid to China.

At least $125 million of this was never brought to bear in time against the Chinese Red Armies for the simple reason that the executive department of the government in Washington persistently dragged its feet. The United States Congress allocated $125 million of munitions under the China Aid Act of April 1948. But where the British had received arms from American arsenals within a few weeks after the evacuation of Dunkirk, the China Aid Act munitions were not delivered until nine months or a year after Congress had spoken. Meanwhile, the Communists had overrun most of China.

During the long, wearisome interval between the passage of the China Aid Act and the actual delivery of the arms, the Truman government diddled and fiddled. At one point, after President Truman had written to Secretary of State Marshall advising him of the procedures to be followed in permitting China to make use of the sums appropriated, Marshall waited more than three weeks before communicating the relevant information to the Chinese

Nationalist ambassador. The Chinese fumed as the State Department sat on its hands, getting nowhere with their pleas for the right to begin purchasing what Joe Stilwell had called "bullets, damn it, just bullets."

Long before the executive sabotage of the China Aid Act, people in the Truman government were busy cutting off military aid to Chiang Kai-shek. During 1946 and part of 1947, General Marshall embargoed the shipment of arms or ammunition to China. The embargo was lifted in July, 1947 when the State Department allowed Chiang's government to purchase 130 million rounds of ammunition—or *enough for three weeks of fighting.* In December, 1947 the Chinese Nationalist troops had enough 7.92-mm. ammunition for only twenty-two days. Dean Acheson has said that Chiang lost no battles because of lack of bullets. Well, you can't lose battles when you haven't enough ammunition to start them in the first place. But you can lose wars, very definitely.

If Joe Stilwell's Boys had not "planned it that way," the Chinese Nationalists might have received a large consignment of war materials right after V-J Day at no additional cost to the American taxpayer. But someone in Washington had put through the order for "Operation Destruction." By the terms of this order (and who, pray tell, issued it?) large quantities of munitions and equipment intended for China were destroyed or thrown into the sea. Smaller-caliber ammunition was blown up; 120,000 tons of larger caliber were dumped into the Indian Ocean. Consignment of 40,000 captured German rifles had actually left a German port for China when Lauchlin Currie, writing on White House stationery, signed an order forbidding the sale of German arms and ammunition to Chiang. Weapons that might have gone to Chiang actually ended up in Russian hands in East Germany.

Too Little, Too Late is the burden of Freda Utley's story of the aid to China that was provably impeded by the American State Department. Because of the facts, Utley cannot find it in her heart to join the strident clamor of the "liberals" against "McCarthyism." She willingly admits that Senator McCarthy may have stretched things a bit when the senator referred to Owen Lattimore as a spy and the "chief architect of our China policy." But her own careful comparison of Lattimore's writings with the twistings of the Communist party line establishes one fact for certain: Lattimore has always tried to make it easy for Mao Tse-tung's Reds in China.

The sum of the whole China Story is that General Marshall, John Davies, John Stewart Service, John Carter Vincent and many another pro-Mao man and "Hankow last-ditcher" lost the United States some four hundred million Oriental allies. Yet this gang remains almost wholly in the employ of the United States government. It has even been whispered that one of Joe Stilwell's Boys, John Emmerson, may step into General MacArthur's shoes in Japan! Moreover, President Truman has served notice that the Stilwell gang will continue to run our foreign policy, at least until 1953. May heaven help us until we can get to the polls in November 1952.

50
James Michener's Paradise

May 7, 1951

James A. Michener is a marked man. He wants to write about what is under his nose, about life in the United States. But ever since his Pulitzer Prize–winning *Tales of the South Pacific* was levied upon by Rodgers and Hammerstein and Josh Logan to make a Broadway musical vehicle for Mary Martin and Ezio Pinza, he has been typed as a literary beachcomber. His public insists that he write about atolls, about the sound of surf on coral rock, and about slim brown Polynesian maids who advertise their easy morals by sticking frangipani flowers in their hair. He can no more escape his literary fate than he can jump out of his skin.

Bowing to the inevitable, Michener recently returned to the scenes of his wartime success. He has insisted, however, on writing a book (*Return to Paradise*) that is something more than a mere collection of moderately romantic tales. Half of *Return to Paradise* is made up of fact-packed essays about the changing life of Polynesia, Melanesia, Australia and New Zealand. The rest of the book consists of stories written to illustrate the themes of the essays.

The stories will bring mild pleasure to any bed-bound reader who likes James Norman Hall or who remembers Jack London's *Jerry of the Islands* with affection. But the best part of *Return to Paradise* is the essay material. The United States Department of State keeps its eyes steadfastly on Europe and tries to forget Asia, but Michener tells us in many a prophetic sentence that Asia is America's fate. It is in Asia that the world is in flux and ferment; it is here that the wars of the future will start. The great value of *Return to Paradise* is that it never forgets the pressure of Asia on the Pacific Islands and hence on the United States. In Tahiti there are the Chinese. They aren't Communist now, but they will become Communist once their consulate has been thoroughly indoctrinated from Peking. In Fiji there are the Indians. They already outnumber the native Fijians, and they are breeding like mad. Australia has no "color" problem, but it is a vast and empty land—and extremely tempting to Asiatics who are starving for lack of rice in China and lack of wheat in India. The Japanese are under control for the moment, and the United States stands ready to protect its national shrine at Guadalcanal. But some day the Japanese freighters will be roving the seas again and calling at Sydney and Rabaul.

Meanwhile, pressing on the nations of Asia and forcing them to look to the Pacific, the Soviet Union complicates everything. In the New Hebrides and the Solomons the natives are waiting for the day of "Mazinga Rule," or "Marching Rule"—pidgin English for "Marxian rule." They confidently expect that "Marxian rule" will bring them free shiploads of refrigerators, meat, jeeps, axes and ice-cream stands. And if the United States doesn't counter the "Marching Rule" expectations by providing some sort of future for the islands, the Soviet Union will have a fertile field for agitation.

James Michener is no economist. But you have to go to books like *Return to Paradise* to learn the facts of economic life. Long before England became a social-service state, the countries of the Antipodes—New Zealand and Australia—had labor governments and welfarist ideas. Michener does not inveigh against the welfare state, but he casually notes:

> A totally inadequate labor force plus a rigid 40-hour week means that New Zealand is underproduced in everything except mutton, butter, and wool. For example, the country has immense deposits of coal, yet coal is often imported from Australia or even the United States. There is abundance of wool, but carpeting is simply not available. There are fine forests, but no lumber; great wealth, but not enough homes.

And of Australia Michener says:

> A glaring result of labor's domination is a critical underproduction of everything. Practically all items that go into building a house are unobtainable through normal channels. Bathtubs, toilets, tiles, telephones, cement, and steel cannot be bought. As a result, the housing shortage is much worse than in America, for even the smallest town is brutally overcrowded.

The answer of Australian labor leaders is that their charges don't want luxuries, they don't want chrome fittings, they don't want nightclubs, they don't want the extra things that might be available if the state would only get off people's backs. The Australian labor leaders even hope to unionize the baby-sitters, and when they have managed to do that, few people will be able to enjoy the long Australian weekends. Australians already have plenty of leisure time, but nobody stands ready to serve anybody else in the enjoyment of that leisure.

Michener is excellent in conveying the atmosphere, the flavor, of social life in the various places he has visited. He makes you feel the super-Anglicanism of New Zealand, the polyglot laziness of Tahiti, the brooding animosity of the Indians on Fiji, the almost insulting independence of the Australians. His novelist's eye and ear are busy even when he is writing his essays. Or perhaps I should say his novelist's eye and ear are busy *especially* when he is writing his essays. For the sad fact is that in only one instance—the short story about the New Zealand girls' behavior in a wartime land bereft of New Zealand men—does Michener make his fiction more telling than his fact. The essays in *Return to Paradise* are concentrated; the fiction—see "Povenaaa's Daughter" and "The Story" for examples—is diffuse. Nevertheless, the essays benefit considerably because Michener is primarily seeking material suitable for fiction. He is interested in sociology only as it affects human drama, and his forays into the sociological essay are more warmly human than anything a mere essayist or a mere sociologist might have turned out.

51
John T. Flynn
The Keenest Journalist

December 31, 1951

Every time I look at John T. Flynn I marvel at what human beings—good human beings—can do. Flynn has been smeared more than any other living American journalist, and he has been called a thousand things that he quite definitely is not. Yet he bobs up smiling and ready to do battle for what he thinks is right. He doesn't care about justice for himself; indeed, he thinks it a waste of time to fight for purely personal vindication. But he cares mightily for justice for others. Altogether he is a marvel of human resilience, good humor, and integrity. I think he underestimated the military power of Hitler after Maurice Gamelin and the other French generals proved to be such hollow shells in 1940, but in spite of this one mistake in judgment, no one has been a more effective campaigner for a libertarian (that is, non-Fascist, non-statist) America in his generation. He is the truly libertarian man, ready to attack big business in an era of Wall Street malfeasance, or the Big State in a time of political misfeasance.

Moreover, as the keenest journalist of our day, Flynn has been uniquely true to his calling—an astonishing fact in a profession that has seen perfidy honored, if not deified. John Flynn kept quiet about many things for patriotic reasons during the war, but in 1945 he was ready and raring to go. If it had not been for his pertinacity, the true story of Pearl Harbor might never have been broken. And if he had not risked blacklisting in editorial sanctums by insisting that Franklin D. Roosevelt was a mortal man with mortal failings, the politicos of the Truman administration, assuming the attributes and continuity of godhood, would probably have succeeded long since in saddling us with a statism even more onerous than that of socialist England.

In the early years of our benighted century the journalists of the muckraking press acted as effective watchdogs on political shenanigans. But when the "liberals" took over in Washington in the name of a nonliberal statism, John Flynn, the libertarian who hated both the fascist National Recovery Administration and the whole system of centralized Bismarckian social security, was just about the only good watchdog left on the horizon. Flynn has picked up allies since the 1930s, but if he had not been around to label the NRA "Chamber of Commerce Fascism," and to attack the Treasury theft of our social-security payments to finance the running expenses of government, the libertarian movement of the 1950s might have been blighted before birth.

This is a long preamble to a review of John T. Flynn's newest book, *While You Slept: Our Tragedy in Asia and Who Made It.* But Flynn has made a blanket indictment of a majority of the American reading public in his title; the proper way of beginning a review of a book called *While You Slept* is to examine the record of the author to test his own credentials proving wakefulness. As a man who has seldom been caught napping, Flynn has a right to his title: while most Americans (including nearly all editors of important review media) were sound asleep, Flynn had his eyes wide open.

John T. Flynn is not an Asia expert. Thank God for that; the Asia "experts" of our generation have proved just about as stupid and obtuse as men can be. But if Flynn is not an Asia "expert," he is a man of morality and common sense. He is moral enough to know that one should not desert an ally in the midst of war, and he has sufficient common sense to realize that it does not constitute a diplomatic victory to lose a vast continent and hundreds of millions of people to one's sworn enemy. Even if Flynn is not an "old China hand," his morality and his common sense make him enough of an Asia expert for me. Owen Lattimore may know all about the tribal customs of Turkestan, but he doesn't know enough to come in when it rains. John T. Flynn does.

While You Slept tells a horrifying story with a brilliant economy of means. The American people know by now that the Communists have succeeded in capturing China. They know it because their sons are dying in Korea, which is next door to Mao Tse-tung's Red paradise. But despite such trail-breaking articles as Irene Kuhn's "Why You Buy Books That Sell Communism," and despite the informed journalism of Freda Utley's *The China Story*, not many people know the story of how the "thought controllers" of Stalinist communism poisoned American public opinion on the subject of China. Flynn tackles that story with all his old-time zestfulness and his unmatched facility at statistical analysis.

The story of our Asian debacle is one of a skillfully executed pincers movement. One of the Communist pincers was provided by the infiltration—or, if you prefer a non-McCarthyan type of delicacy, the "persuasion"—of the upper levels of government, including the Far Eastern Division of our Department of State. Skillfully refusing to fall into the trap of name calling, Flynn labels no living man who is out of jail or unconvicted a traitor; neither does he fling the term *Communist* around lightly. He is not against Dean Acheson and George Marshall because of any alleged duplicity or presumed corruption; he is against them because he thinks their Far Eastern policies were wrong. He is not against Owen Lattimore because Senator McCarthy called Lattimore a "top Soviet agent"; he is against Lattimore because he has read the man's books and finds them full of subtle propaganda for the cause of Mao Tse-tung's China.

Flynn makes it indelibly plain that our State Department was won over in the late stages of World War II to the idea that Mao Tse-tung represented the "wave of the future" in Asia. But it takes two pincers to get a grip on a nation as large and as free as America. The second pincer that the Communists had ready was the infiltration of the media that control the making of public opinion.

How did the Communists do this? They did it not by planting holders of party cards in editorial positions. No, they did it by far more subtle means. They did it by placing their sympathizers in key positions in such organs of "expert" opinion as the Institute of Pacific Relations. Flynn pens a long and sordid story about this institute and how its sponsors were gulled. Having captured at one remove the business of creating "expert" opinion, the Communists (working at two removes) were in a position to control what went into most of the books about Asia. Because of stupidity in the editorial sanctums of the *New York Times Book Review* and the *New York Herald Tribune Books,* a small pro–Mao Tse-tung clique was enabled to make a racket out of the reviewing of books on China. Flynn makes no loose charges here: he takes thirty books on China and analyzes their fate at the hands of the reviewers. Of twenty-three pro-Communist China books, "all of them" says Flynn, "where reviewed, received glowing approval in the literary reviews I have named—that is, the *New York Times,* the *Herald Tribune,* the *Nation,* the *New Republic,* and the *Saturday Review of Literature.* And every one of the anti-Communist books was either roundly condemned or ignored in these same reviews."

Flynn goes on to tell the story of how the Communists, again working at one or two removes through fellow-traveling sympathizers, infected the popular magazines and the motion pictures. He also tells the story of that strange magazine called *Amerasia,* which specialized in stealing top-level secret documents from government files. It had at least one purloined document for every subscriber.

With public opinion softened up, the State Department had a clear field for its China policy—for a time. But in the long run realities must prove stronger than propaganda, and facts must prove more compelling than words. The post-1945 behavior of Soviet Russia was such that the Red-dominated pincers operation on American foreign policy was inevitably doomed to fail. As the ugly realities intruded on the sleepers' dreams, the resonance faded from Dean Acheson's speeches and Owen Lattimore's book reviews. There is nothing like a fact to kill a theory.

There remains, of course, the problem of public trust. Our State Department is no longer working (outwardly, at any rate) at the job of building Stalin's strength in Asia. And decently competent reviews of Far Eastern books have begun to blossom shyly in the *New York Times Book Review* section. The American public is no longer being drugged the way it was drugged in the middle and late 1940s. But public confidence would be vastly enhanced if Dean Acheson would make just one little confession of error, or if Lester Markel, who controls the Sunday publications of the *New York Times,* would say, just once, "I was taken in."

I don't want to seem mean to either Dean Acheson or Lester Markel. I myself was taken in by the Communists in the 1930s. I know from experience that it is not easy to say *mea culpa.* But I can say this: once you have said it you feel a lot better, and you can go to work again with a clear conscience.

52
The Commonsense British

June 18, 1951

For over a decade Arthur Bryant, brilliant English essayist and historian, has been writing books about the ordeals and the triumphs of his country in the period of the French revolutionary upheaval and the Napoleonic cycle of wars. Although he is not as penetrating as the great Italian historian Guglielmo Ferrero on the subject of war and peace in the age of Talleyrand and Metternich, he still makes entirely satisfactory reading. His *The Years of Endurance: 1793–1802*, which appeared in the dark days of 1942, impressed me as far more understanding of the phenomenon of Hitlerism (a variant of Bonapartism) than most of the excited yawpings then appearing in the British or the American press. His *Years of Victory: 1802–1812*, which came later, was entirely relevant to our own period of victory over the Axis.

Now comes the final volume of Bryant's trilogy, *The Age of Elegance: 1812–1822*. True to my expectations, I found it far more informative about our present predicament in a world that unfortunately includes Stalin than anything that can be culled from journals and books which presume to be covering the year 1951. Bryant may be writing about Wellington's 1808–13 campaign in the Spanish peninsula, but his loving re-creation of an ancient story is closer to the day's headlines than a passel of columns, say, by the Alsops when they are in a mood to tailor their commentary to the need of protecting their pipeline to the office of Dean Acheson.

The main thing that stands out from Bryant's pages is the enormous common sense exhibited by the British a century and a half ago. This common sense extended from their dietary habits to their appreciation of literature. An island people whose numbers could not match Napoleonic France, the British of 1800 had a problem on their hands that must seem startlingly familiar to the American reader in 1951. The British of 1800 had the best, indeed, the only, factory system in the world, which meant they could produce for war as well as for peace. But there was always the problem of the right allocation of a limited amount of energy. The British cabinet ministers solved the problem of energy allocation by making the decision that the United States of 1951 must make: they did not attempt to pile a conscript mass army on top of a factory system that requires a free society for its proper articulation. The army that the British raised was qualitatively excellent, but it was deliberately aimed to function at the end of an overseas supply line that naturally required a heavy draft of the national energy on its own.

The national energy of Britain in 1800–1815 had to be stretched in order to cover manufacturing, transport, the protection of the seas, and the strategic and tactical needs of battle per se, so the British statesmen of Napoleonic times made a careful study of the efficient care and feeding of allies. They learned to waste no motions. From the proceeds of a nation's trade and manufacturing they subsidized guerrillas and local armies all around the fringes of the Napoleonic empire. The Russians, the Prussians, the Spanish, the Austrians, the Corsicans, and the Netherlanders were all, at one time or another, in the pay of "perfidious Albion."

Meanwhile, the British made tremendous use of their navy to support troop action everywhere. They put their own limited army, under Wellington, into Portugal and Spain—an army that sometimes ran to fifty thousand men. This army fought a chivvying kind of war until 1812, its prime motive being to keep the Spanish guerrillas in action on Napoleon's southern flank. It was not until the Russians caught Napoleon in his overextended lunge to Moscow in 1812 that the army of Wellington went over to the offensive. It had waited for years for its chance, and it closed in on its prey for all the world like the fox hunters of the English shires that had bred some of its most efficient horsemen.

The British choice of 1800 did not have the benefit of modern public relations support. This was all to the good, inasmuch as the art of cultivating "public relations," when indulged by government, usually ends by perverting the common sense of the electorate. Unconfused by the presumed needs of high-power governmental press agentry, the British ratiocination of 1800 far surpassed any thinking on war and peace that Americans in high places have been able to produce since 1945—or 1935. Like the Americans of 1951, the British of 1800 were in the business of supporting a loose and shifting coalition. But mark this: the British made their subsidies of arms, money and food conditional on fighting performance. There were no Marshall Plans for Prussia, for Austria, for Russia—the Continental powers got money and arms only when they showed an eager willingness to use them to the common end of beating Bonaparte. It was a question of "no fight, no subsidy." The British of 1800 insisted on a "matching" policy.

This seemingly cold-blooded attitude caused many Continental citizens to curse the British. But the England of 1800 didn't necessarily want to be loved; it wanted to prevail in the name of a just peace. A strange blend of humility and complete self-confidence, the average Britisher of 1800–1815 did not care what his allies were saying of him as long as he felt justified in the sight of God. The long-term end of the British was to defeat tyranny abroad without undermining freedom at home. As Bryant puts it, it was a matter of maintaining "cohesion without coercion, wealth without slavery, empire without militarism." This formula naturally provoked envy, irritation, and charges of hypocrisy on the European continent, but the British statesmen of 1800-1815 knew that military coalitions depend on self-interest properly exploited, not on love universally cultivated and applied. As long as the Russians, the Prussians, the Austrians and the Spanish had personal motives for fighting the French, it mattered nothing to an Englishman whether he was loved.

The Age of Elegance draws no parallels; it is simply an objective, fully documented story of how a nation lived and fought and made peace in the years between 1812 and 1822. But the modern reader can hardly get past a paragraph without thinking of Korea, or Formosa, or Germany, or Turkey, or Iran. When Bryant speaks of the Spanish guerrillas in the mountains, the modern reader thinks of anti-Communist guerrilla activity in the hill country of southern China. If we had the common sense of William Pitt and his disciples, we would be subsidizing those guerrillas and establishing aviation "drops" to give them the materials of resistance.

The modern parallel emerges despite everything from Arthur Bryant's treatment of the Congress of Vienna. Then, as now, the Western allies were troubled by the bear-hug "peace" tactics of a Muscovite collaborator. Tsar Alexander, like Stalin, had an inexorable urge to push his "beneficent" control as far to the west as possible. Appalled at the prospect of Russian control of Poland and Russian "cooperation" with Prussia, Castlereagh of England and Metternich of Austria turned at once for help to the Frenchman Talleyrand, emissary of their defeated enemy. They made a deal with France to put restraint on their own wartime ally in the east.

Reading about this quick postwar shift in national alignments in 1815, the reader cannot help thinking of the need for a few modern Talleyrands in Germany and Japan. Would to heaven we knew who they are!

53
Owen Lattimore
Whose Right to Slander?

October 16, 1950

Leafing through Gilbert K. Chesterton's delightfully tonic *George Bernard Shaw*, I was struck by GKC's passage on the Irishman as fighter. "The very logic of the Irishman," said Chesterton, "makes him regard war or revolution as extra-logical, an *ultima ratio* which is beyond reason. When fighting a powerful enemy he no more worries whether all his charges are exact or all his attitudes dignified than a soldier worries whether a cannon-ball is shapely or a plan of campaign picturesque. He is aggressive; he attacks...he tries to hurt his enemies because they are his enemies.... He seems to us wild and unreasonable because he is really much too reasonable to be anything but fierce when he is fighting."

That passage, said I to myself, explains Senator Joseph McCarthy of Wisconsin even more than it explains George Bernard Shaw. But what explains Owen Lattimore, whose *Ordeal by Slander* is soggy with every type of unfair tactic that Lattimore professes to be against? If Lattimore's name were O'Lattimore or McLattimore, I could account for him on a Chestertonian basis. But the name is not O'Lattimore; and for a professed believer in the very non-Hibernian rules of cricket, Lattimore is guilty of a pretty deplorable performance.

Take the matter of slander, for instance. Lattimore rightly objects to being called the "top Soviet agent in the United States" by a man who has offered no proof of the charge. But does the fact that he has been wronged in the heat of battle give Lattimore the right to slander just about everybody who has ever fought Stalin since 1938? Lattimore flails about him, using a most McCarthyan shillelagh on Freda Utley, Louis Budenz, Alfred Kohlberg, Senator Hickenlooper, and anyone else who has doubted the pristine purity of the Institute of Pacific Relations when the Commie maggots were boring from within its hallowed institutional walls. He speaks of the "long record of [Freda Utley's] pro-Nazi writing." He strives to leave the unwary reader with the distinct impression that Louis Budenz just loves to be put under subpoena and questioned about his past in the Communist movement. And in his snide remarks about a mysterious "China lobby," he tries to make it appear that anyone who has doubted the wisdom of handing China to communism on a jade dish is ipso facto a bad American, not to say a treasonable tool of a foreign power.

The truth about Freda Utley is that she was an America Firster along with Chester Bowles and other presumably good patriots in the early days of World War II. That may make her "pro-Nazi" in Owen Lattimore's eyes. All the more curious, then, that Lattimore so bitterly resents being called a "pro-Communist." If Miss Utley's isolationist passages were unwittingly devised to give pleasure to Adolf Hitler, then how much more pleasure must Stalin derive from Lattimore's Chinese line! Applying the same test that he himself applies to Freda Utley's works, Lattimore is a pro-Communist from way back.

The funniest thing about Lattimore's book is his attempt to hide behind the full military regalia of General George Catlett Marshall's reputation. "General Marshall," he writes, "went out to China and, with the quick eye of the magnificent strategic analyst that he is, he understood that he was in a situation in which salvation was impossible and salvage was all that could be hoped for. He therefore endeavored to salvage as much of the situation as he thought was possible. . . ." According to Lattimore, General Marshall set the pitch for U.S. policy toward Chiang Kai-shek in 1946 and 1947 and Lattimore dutifully followed after.

All this made a very touching story when Lattimore explained it last spring to Senator Hickenlooper. But how does it read in the light of General Marshall's recent statement that he went out to China in 1946 to carry out a policy that had already been decreed in Washington? At the very least it makes Lattimore a "me-too" rider on the coattails of a great me-tooer. To anyone who has read Lattimore's books on Asia, which abound in a form of panjandrumry that makes Samuel Johnson look like a coy violet by comparison, the thought of Lattimore kowtowing to a mere general on the subject of oriental policy is definitely rib-tickling.

Lattimore would have his readers believe that *Ordeal by Slander* was written in blood, sweat, and tears. I cannot swear to the blood and sweat, but the tears, if any, are crocodile tears. What a horrible thing, Lattimore says in effect, if only one point of view on China were to be printed in the American press. We must, so he cries out, maintain full freedom of debate. Well, well! And just who has closed out whom in this literary battle over China and the Communists, anyway? Who has had almost untrammeled access to important review media, the Freda Utleys who have been Chiang Kai-shek partisans or the Owen Lattimores (and John Fairbankses and Edgar Snows) who have been making learned, if sometimes cryptic, cases for Mao Tse-tung and the Communists? The "China lobby" which Lattimore scorns may have a nefarious power over, say, the Scripps–Howard press, but it isn't in it with the Mao Tse-tung lobby when it comes to capturing white space in the *New York Herald Tribune* book review section.

Some day in this space I want to present a searching discussion of Owen Lattimore's books on Asia, with a view to determining just how much effect the man has had on U.S. State Department policy. Inasmuch as policy, despite what Lattimore says, is not made in a vacuum, I am certain that Lattimore's writings have done much to paralyze our thinking on the subject of China. But the documentation of any such opinion requires more space and time than I have at my disposal at the moment. All I want to say now is that Owen Lattimore's "quickie," *Ordeal by Slander*, counters one ordeal by subjecting others to similar ordeals. Lattimore has a right to be angry with Senator McCarthy for calling him the "top Soviet spy" without proof, but he has no right to take it out on virtually everybody else in the country who disagrees with him on the way to handle things in Asia.

54
From Crush to Crush

October 30, 1950

The American liberal (professional variety) is like the average bobby-soxer: his life goes from crush to crush. Yesterday the crush was Stalin (or Trotsky); today it is Tito—or India's Pandit Nehru. The search for an adorable political image takes a Jo Davidson or a Louis Adamic from Moscow to Belgrade; it takes a Vincent Sheean or a Louis Fischer from Moscow to India. This yen for kowtowing to strong men, or to supposedly super-spiritual men, in distant lands of drought, disease, penury, and famine is one of the revealing mysteries of our goofy times. I don't know just what it portends in psychoanalytic terms, but it certainly argues a most un-Emersonian lack of self-reliance. They didn't act that way in the age of the lyceum circuit and Walden Pond.

Unlike the bobby-soxer's crush, the political calf love of the professional liberal is a highly dangerous thing. Take the liberal's present-day crush on Jawaharlal Nehru, for example. For weeks now the adoring liberals have been trying to set Nehru up as a god in Asia. We must let Nehru settle the Korean problem. We must let Nehru settle the problem of Red China and the U.N. For Nehru once saw Gandhi plain, and Nehru knows.

Why does he know? It is at this point that the argument gets a little tenuous. Nehru knows because he is the spokesman for that "spiritual" country India; and India, of course, is the obvious leader of "non-Communist Asia." The liberal does not stop to analyze the Indian claim to leadership; he simply asserts it. He assumes that Nehru is the spokesman for a great and powerful nation that knows all about combating the appeal of communism to the Asiatic mind.

Having read a bit in Nehru's autobiography and in his astoundingly catholic *Glimpses of World History,* I am quite ready to admit that the pandit is most remarkable. But I have just finished reading a book called *Interview with India,* by John Frederick Muehl (John Day), and if one-tenth of what Muehl writes is true, then India is not in a condition to assert its leadership in anything. It is a land struggling incompetently for the barest subsistence—and in the southern part of the peninsula it has a Communist problem of its own. Muehl loves India, but unlike the average traveling liberal he has eyes to see, ears to hear—and a highly sensitive nose to smell. His reporting overcomes his sentimentality on almost every page.

Muehl's book is as horrifying as it is excellent. The author made his first trip to India during the war, as an American Field Service man attached to the British Indian Army. He hated the rampant hypocrisy of the British *pukka sahib* from the outset, but he also saw that the curse of India has an ancient lineage, one that antedates Lord Clive by centuries. The faults of India were there when the British came; they are still there now that the British have departed. As *Interview with India* makes plain, they exist at the Indian village level, far below any of the strata the British managed to penetrate.

Muehl's story is cast in the form of a travel diary. By bullock cart and on horseback, by boat and by camel, he made his way from Kathiawar above Bombay to the far south of the Indian subcontinent. He saw the horrors of caste; he watched what the Indian moneylenders and tax collectors did to keep the villagers in eternal subjection. He traveled through salt wastes and through deserted towns that were being consumed by the advancing sand. He hobnobbed with people who were dying of diseases contracted from contaminated water. He talked with drought-distracted farmers who, in an agony of miscomprehension, ripped to pieces a dam built by the government across a river. "Who ever heard of stopping a river?" the farmers sneered.

It is not all darkness in Muehl's book. The remains of an ancient culture lend a man-made grace to certain of his landscapes. And the oppressed who jostle and scrabble for food in his pages confront their lot with a rueful wisdom that is the chief sign and seal of the brotherhood of man. But the innate human urge to dignity has the devil's own time of it in *Interview with India.* There was only one place in Muehl's itinerary where health and *joie de vivre* proved to be the normal accompaniments of daily existence. That was along the Kanara coast far to the south of Bombay. Significantly, the men and women of the Kanara coast are isolated by jungle and mountains from the Indian hinterland. They face the Arabian Sea, they live in the sun and the surf, and they feed their children on a health-giving diet of shark's liver. Along the Kanara coast caste is less important than almost anywhere else in India. Hinduism is lightened for the Kanarese by a sense of humor.

Now, if the American liberal as exemplified, say, by Dr. Eduard Lindeman were to argue that the Kanarese fishermen have a right to offer moral leadership to the rest of Asia, it would make some sense. But I have yet to hear of a Lindeman or a Vincent Sheean discovering a practical saint on the Kanara coast. Far from being bulwarks against communism, the Indians to the north, east and south of Kanara coast could be had by any energetic conqueror from the rugged lands of the temperate zone. The whole Indian peninsula, on Muehl's evidence, is ripe, not for conquest from within, but for the next determined imperial push from without.

All of which brings me back to Nehru. The pandit seems to be obsessed with the idea that any Asiatic nationalism is a good nationalism. What he does not recognize is that Communist nationalisms become internationalisms the very moment that the victory has been won at home. (Tito is no exception; he will turn imperialist in the Balkans the moment he is free to do so.) The Communists preach anything that is useful to them for a specific job; they even pose as capitalists in NEP eras. But the goal of one world (or Wonworld, as my colleague Henry Hazlitt calls it) is always at the back of their minds. And the Wonworld must be Communist.

The reason Pandit Nehru is a danger to Asia, to the West, and to himself is that his foreign policy tends to release Communist energies for pressure all along the line from Iran to Batavia. A year ago I sat in a house in the Georgetown section of Washington talking with an escaped Russian who goes by the name of Bergstrom. "Bergstrom," an authority on inner Asian dialects, had been brought here by the State Department to tell what he knows about Stalin's blueprint for oriental conquest. A former adviser on texts to the Stalin School for Toilers of the East, Bergstrom is full of information about the systematic training of Asiatic revolutionaries. Every year full complements of Chinese, Annamese, Indians, Afghans, Japanese, Arabians and Burmese go to Moscow for indoctrination in Communist "nationalist" tactics and strategy. They return home with Marxism in their heads and at their fingertips. All of which means, of course, that they do not go home to be permanent "nationalists."

As Bergstrom has tried to tell the State Department, the Chinese Communist agents who have been trained at the Stalin school in Moscow are ready to move on into Indochina the moment the Mao Tse-tung regime is consolidated in Peking. Since the Chinese have done business in Southeast Asia for decades, the Chinese Communist agents are prepared to pose as shopkeepers, traders and bankers throughout the southern Asiatic world. And Nehru, by asking for acceptance of Red China in the councils of the powers, is doing all he can to bring these Chinese Communist agents right next door to his own harried and struggling homeland. For the sake of Nehru, for the sake of India, the West must fight India's own voice in world affairs. It is not the mark of friendship to cooperate with an urge to suicide.

Can we tell this to the American liberal who sets Nehru on a pedestal? I doubt it. But when all of Asia has fallen to the Communists, where will the American liberal go for his next crush? It will be hard to find a political tin god among the Bantu tribes of Africa or the Sekani Indians of British Columbia.

Index

Index

Index

Index

Index